TENFOLD

Marilyn Fiegel

Marilyn Fiegel

ISBN 978-1-64569-348-2 (paperback)
ISBN 978-1-64569-350-5 (hardcover)
ISBN 978-1-64569-349-9 (digital)

Christian Faith Publishing, Inc.
832 Park Avenue
Meadville, PA 16335
www.christianfaithpublishing.com

This book is a work of fiction. Names, places, events, locales, businesses, organizations, or characters, other than those clearly in the public domain, are either the product of the author's imagination or are used fictitiously. Any resemblance to actual persons, living or dead, is entirely coincidental.

Printed in the United States of America

Many thanks to Barbara C. Cunningham for her tireless assistance in the publication of *Tenfold*.

CHAPTER 1

It was almost six-thirty in the evening as Jenny Murray was completing the preparation of her employer's dinner. Lionel Hawkins, a Latin teacher at the Chaucer Scole for Ladde on Surrey Street, was already late. With a bag full of books under one arm and a hickory walking stick in his hand, he walked hurriedly across the Waterloo Bridge to his home on Exton Street just beyond.

The oxtail stew was hot and ready to be served to him as soon as he arrived home and hung up his things. He was very fond of the way Jenny prepared oxtail for him.

Jenny sat at the old oak table and waited with Mary, her ten-year-old daughter; a beautiful blue eyed, blonde youngster who always accompanied her mother to work each day. It was a difficult life for them. They had little money except that which Jenny earned as a cook and housekeeper for Mr. Hawkins. She had worked for him ever since her husband, Jeremy Murray, had disappeared without a trace shortly after Mary's birth when Jenny was just seventeen years old. His wages as a street sweeper were meager, and they were hard-pressed to make ends meet when he was home. He was a very selfish man who preferred to spend his money on drink and other women rather than on his own family. On that last day, Jenny packed Jeremy's lunch and saw him off to work at seven o'clock in the morning. He never returned home. Sometimes, Jenny would imagine that he had been robbed and his body disposed of in some back alley. Other times, she wondered if he had run off with another woman, perhaps to a better life. For that, Jenny could not fault him, because together, they had so little. Alone, however, with a young child to raise, it was a difficult cross for Jenny to bear.

Mary sat across from her mother, looking lovingly at her as she rose from her chair, cut some three-day old brown bread, and placed it on the table at Mr. Hawkins's place. The two were inseparable, more like sisters than mother and daughter.

"Mum, ye are so pritty. I luv ye so much. Wat would I do witout ye? Who woulde take care of me? I coulde not take care of miself."

"Do not fret, Darlin. I wille not be goin anywhar. Ye be mi pryde ond joi, ond I wille take care of ye 'til the day I die, ond I do not intende to leve ye soone."

With that, Mary smiled at her mother and seemed reassured. Jenny was truly a lovely young woman of twenty-eight; tall and slender, her light brown hair falling loosely to her shoulders. Her crystal-clear blue eyes sparkled when she smiled, especially when she gazed upon the face of her beautiful daughter. Yet she worried constantly about how she would be able to eke out an existence for the two of them, with so little money. At times, there was barely enough money to pay the rent, buy food, and put clothes on their backs. What little food they had, Jenny would give to Mary. Thus, Jenny was terribly thin and pale. Mary's clothing was a gift from their church. Jenny had no new dress in ten years.

Together, they lived in a dwelling on Drury Street, in the poorest part of London, several blocks across the Bridge from Hawkins's school. Three other families shared the three rooms in the old stone building which was a haven for rodents. There was no running water. It had to be carried by bucket from a well three blocks away in the center of their neighborhood. Public toilet facilities were in an old wooden building in that same area. Jenny and Mary made this journey for water early each morning so they would be able to wash themselves before the others awoke.

The children played in the alleyway, where piles of rotting garbage attracted every kind of vermin, as well as some shameful drunken men who preyed upon small children, especially girls. Jenny worried constantly about Mary's safety and would not permit her to play with the other children outside. They were both happy to escape this depressing environment each day when they journeyed to Mr. Hawkins's home.

Hawkins was a very kind and gentle man, and though he had little more than they, he was always willing to share his evening meal with them. After dinner, before he worked on his next day's lessons, he would often tutor Mary in reading and writing since she did not attend school. Fathers in England, who believed that girls needed no formal education, often sold them into slavery at an early age. Of course, kind Mr. Hawkins did not agree with this custom. Tonight, Jenny and Mary would have to leave early without sharing their meal with Jenny's employer, as they were going to attend a Bible class at eight o'clock at Saint Augustine's Catholic Church across the River Thames on Exeter Street. Still a bachelor at age thirty-five, Hawkins lived alone in a small, ivy-covered, three-room cottage on Exton Street, on the other side of the Bridge from where Jenny and Mary lived. At six forty-five, the clock on the desk in his study chimed at the three-quarter hour as Hawkins appeared at his front door; his slight build barely filling half of the doorframe. However, his deep baritone voice quickly convinced those near him that he was a dominating presence. Today, he announced his arrival with an apology.

"Jenny, Mary, I be sory thaet I be late this evning. Two of mi studene, who are preparen to take the entrance exam to Cambridge Universite in the spring, neede mi halp wit Latin.

They hav been werken their asez off to passe. In mi opinion, they wille niver be worlde shakers, but parhaps they wille be riche businessmon. We kan onle praye. Miracles do happene. I beleve Mary hath mor intelligents. O Jenny, afore I forgit, I hav somethin for ye."

Somewhat embarrassed, he pulled a long blue ribbon from a pocket of his long grey cloak and gave it to Jenny, who immediately made a bow and tied it to her hair.

"Thank ye, Meister Hawkins. I be gratfel. Meister Hawkins, sir, your stewe be on the tabel. Tiz oxtail stewe; your favourit. Thore be bread too, wit honey, for your sweet tuth. Plese sitte afore all git cauld ond ye git upset."

"Wille ye ond Mary joine me this evning? Thore be plente for us all. I do not like to eat bi miself." "No, Sir. We must leve. Bibel studie be at eighte houre, ond tiz importante for Mary to be properly educated in our Faith. I want hir to meet gude peple wit gude manneres," Jenny said as she refilled Hawkins's bowl with stew and moved the honey pot closer to the bread. "So somday, she wille marrie up in classe. Come, Mary, twille soone be late."

Hawkins looked at his pocket watch as the clock chimed again. It was seven forty-five. He knew that they must leave, but he was always sad to see them go. Tonight, however, he had an inexplicable feeling of deep sorrow.

"Be ye carefel, ladies. The air be cauld ond dampf ond a thikke fog be movin in. I worie about ye walken over the dark Bridge in this pea soupe. I wille walke ye across," he offered, as he rose from his chair and walked them to the door.

"Sir, thaet wille not be necessaire. We wille be fine. Tiz onle a ten-minute walke from hier to the Chirche. Gode wille halp us."

Until the fog enveloped them as they approached the Bridge, Hawkins stood in the doorway and watched them start across. Soon, he lost sight of the shadowy figures completely. Turning slowly, he closed and bolted the door behind him and sat at the table to finish his dinner, which had long since cooled. Yet he could not stop worrying about Jenny and Mary.

"I shoulde hav accompanied theim acros," he said aloud. "They be so vulnerable in this evil city. Ladies neede a mon to kepe theim safe. This night be darker than usual."

Jenny and Mary walked quickly through the fog and along the left side of the Bridge. The air was brisk, and they were not properly dressed for the cold, damp November night. Neither wore a coat nor shawl over their long shift-style dresses. Arm in arm, they huddled together to protect themselves against the bone chilling cold.

"Mum, do ye thinke Meister Hawkins hath a liken for ye?"

"O, Mary, where do ye git those idean? He be mi employer, nothing more. He be a very gude but lonle mon, I thinke. We be like familie to him. Faster, Mary, or we wille be late for Chirche. We do not want to miss anything. They be discussen the Godspel accordin' to Sanctus John, chapitre one, tonight. O Dear, someone be comen. Move over, Mary, ond let him passe. Thore be not much room on this side of the Bridge."

"Mum, I be afrayd. He be comen streght for us. Let us cros to the other side of the Bridge. I do not like the way he looke."

"No, Mary. This side be closer to the chirche. We wille be thore in a fewe minute. Tiz almost eighte houre. We wille be fin, Mary. Stay clos to me."

"Yes, Mum, but he be not movin over to let us passe."

"He wille. Holde tight to mi arm ond let him passe. Gode halp us. Plese, Gode, protect us from evil."

Having finished the last piece of bread and honey, Hawkins wiped his sticky mouth on his long puffed sleeve, pushed his chair away from the table, and stepped outside his front door to get some fresh air, which he always did before beginning work on tomorrow's lessons. Off toward the Bridge, he heard a great hue and cry – shouting, yelling, whistle blowing and footsteps running across. Soon, there were more shouts and loud voices. After a few minutes, an eerie silence pierced the heavy night air and his heart. The color began to drain from his face.

"They wille be fin," he told himself. "Gode wille kepe theim safe ond wille protect theim from evil."

But as the fog swirled around his feet and legs, a cold chill slowly worked its way along his spine. Shivering through his heavy monk-like clothing, he went inside, closed and bolted the door behind him, shutting out the outside world which frightened him.

A short time later, as he worked on his next day's lessons in his study, there was a loud, rapid, and persistent knock on his front door, disturbing his concentration. The candle on his desk flickered inside of its glass chimney as he looked at the clock.

"Who coulde thaet be, out on a miserabil night like this? Tiz late; almost nyne houre. Parhaps I shoulde not answer the dor. O, someone may be in neede of mi halp. I coulde na refuse a person in neede."

He stood up from his chair and moved toward the door. Very slowly and cautiously, Hawkins unbolted the door and opened it a crack just as the clock struck nine. Squinting slightly, he could make out the dark figure of a large man standing in the fog.

"Hawkins, wat be wrong wit ye? Tiz Adkins, your neighbour. Let me in. I be getten wet standen out hier in this cauld dampf air. I hav terribil nuz to telle ye."

"Wat is it, Adkins? I be werken in mi room."

Hawkins opened the door wide to let Adkins in. Terror gripped him as his eyes focused on a belt around Adkins's waist. Entwined around the belt was a wet blue ribbon tied in a bow.

10

CHAPTER 2

Dawn was just breaking over the beautiful Western New York community of Orchard Park, on a late September day in 2010. Inside the Albert Chapman home, the silence of that Monday morning was interrupted by punctuated blood curdling screams of sheer terror emanating from the second floor master bedroom.

"Halt! Halt! Plese do not hange me. I be sory for wat I don. Plese, halt! *Augh*..."

"Al, wake up! You're having a nightmare. Wake up! What's happening to you?"

"Oh, Karen, it was horrible. They hanged me."

"Who did what to you?"

"Sailors on a pirate ship, 'The Black Falcon', hanged me. They caught me stealing rum from the ship's hold one night, dragged me on deck, and beat me about my head. They bound me with rope and hoisted me up by the neck. I was kicking and screaming and telling them to stop what they were doing. But they didn't, and then I was swinging in the wind. Karen, I was choking and dying. I know it was 1448 and I'm too young to die. Everything was going black when you woke me up."

"How terrible. You're soaking wet. Even your pillow is wet, and your face is as white as a sheet. Get up and take a hot shower. Let the water beat on you. It will make you feel better. Take your time. You don't have to go to the 'Ralph' today. It was a tough game yesterday for you and the Bills against Miami.

You're probably all stressed out. I'll get the kids up and get breakfast started."

"I guess you're right; I'm pretty beat up. It was a dirty game, with lots of holding and bad mouthing. I just have no respect for those Dolphins. They're a good team, but they'll do anything to win. I've got to get over this bias I have against them. I need a change, Karen. Let's pick the kids up after school today and drive to the Falls for some sightseeing and then go to dinner at the Skylon."

"That's a good idea. Now, take your shower. Let it relax you. Try to forget that dream. That's all that it was—a dream. I'm looking forward to a wonderful family outing."

Al got out of bed slowly. His whole body ached from yesterday's game. He looked in the bathroom mirror and examined his neck for any rope marks.

"Don't be ridiculous—it was only a dream."

He ripped off his pajamas, left them in a heap on the floor, and stepped into the shower stall. A huge man, six feet four inches tall and weighing well over three hundred pounds, he was not too large as offensive tackles go. His head reached to the top of the showerhead. The hot water felt good beating on his neck and back.

"Karen was right—the hot water relaxes me."

His thirty-four-year-old body was tired. It now took him almost a week to recover from a hard-hitting game instead of one or two days when he was younger. He knew that he was nearing the end of his professional football career.

"I'm getting too old for this game. My body knows it and is trying to tell my brain to hang up my helmet permanently. Maybe my brain is already damaged."

Although football was considered a violent sport, Al was a soft-spoken gentleman who was greatly respected by his teammates and coaches as well as other players around the NFL.

Rarely did he let his emotions get the better of him during a game. He did not even use profanity except for an occasional "damn" or "hell." It was almost impossible for anyone who did not totally know Al to penetrate the protective outer shell that hid his true self. In mixed company, he was always polite and very formal in conversations. First impressions were that he was cold, humorless, and aloof; a sort of "leave me alone" guy. Even his more sociable wife, Karen, sometimes had trouble communicating with him. Introspective, not aloof; shy, not cold; quiet, not unsociable. These traits defined Albert Chapman. Seven times, he was selected by his peers to play in the Pro Bowl in Hawaii; an honor bestowed upon just a fraction of the players in the League. It was an honor well deserved by number 91 of the Buffalo Bills.

Karen quickly arose from bed, put on her robe and slippers, and walked down the hall to wake up the children.

"Melissa, Jonathan, it's time to get up for school. Get washed and dressed and come down to breakfast. Your father and I have a surprise for you."

Karen hurried down the stairs, put on a pot of coffee, and went into the lavatory adjacent to the kitchen. She looked in the mirror at herself and was pleased with her image. Just five-feet-two and weighing one hundred pounds, she was in sharp contrast to her husband's mammoth stature. Her green eyes stung as she splashed cold water on her face. At thirty-three, she often felt cheated, having married Al after graduating with a BA degree in English from the University of West Virginia. She always wanted to be an English teacher, but marriage at age twenty-two and giving birth to Melissa one year later put an end to any ambitions she may have had; a decision she never regretted.

"I am so fortunate to be married to Al and to have two beautiful children," she thought as she dried her face and brushed her shoulder-length auburn colored hair. "He is such a good family man. I never have to worry about him getting involved with another woman or in some scandal. Some professional athletes have so much violence in their personal lives—spousal abuse, rape, murder."

The O.J. Simpson trials had left the Buffalo Bills organization adamant in their desire to draft only men of high character as well as those possessing excellent football skills.

"Is it the game or the limelight that molds their behavior?" she wondered. "Perhaps athletes have too much too soon, and they can't handle the notoriety that is thrust upon them as soon as they enter the professional arena."

After completing her morning routine, Karen went into the kitchen, put a pound of bacon in a Teflon pan, scrambled a dozen eggs, toasted a half loaf of bread, and poured the orange juice and milk. Melissa, their ten-year-old daughter, was the first to the table.

"Good morning, Mom. What's the surprise you have for us? You know I'll be antsy if I have to wait too long to find out."

"Sorry, but you'll just have to wait until your father and Jonathan are here, Honey."

"Oh gee, can't you whisper it in my ear now? What's the secret?"

"No, Melissa. Be patient for a few minutes more."

Melissa, a small clone of her mother, slouched in her chair, her long, shoulder-length auburn hair covering her green eyes. A studious fifth-grade student at Saint Margaret's Catholic School in Orchard Park, she was usually a shy little girl, but on occasion, she would speak her mind in no uncertain terms. Karen encouraged both of the children to express themselves without being disrespectful. There were times, however, when they came close to crossing the line. Karen wisely recognized that this was all a part of growing up.

Jonathan, the eight-year-old third-grader, was the next to the table. He took his regular seat across from Melissa. Tall for his age, he appeared to be a chip off the old block, but his interest in football was minimal. Nevertheless, Al kept hoping that the powers of suggestion would work; often telling Jonathan that he was a natural linebacker. Jonathan was not studious like his sister, to say the least. Karen was often at her 'wits' end trying to get him to hand in his school assignments on time. He procrastinated, blamed his teachers, made excuses, and threatened to quit school whenever an assignment was challenging or took some time to complete.

"What's for breakfast, Mom? It smells like bacon frying. Are we having pancakes too?"

"Good morning, Jonathan. You are half right. It's bacon and scrambled eggs. I hope you have your usual growing boy's appetite this morning so you'll be alert for school."

At that moment, Al sat down at the head of the table. The smell of shaving lotion permeated the air. Karen loved that scent. She called it a real sign of masculinity.

"Good morning, kids. How are you this morning? I hope you slept well."

"Okay, I guess. So what's the big surprise, Dad?" Jonathan joked. "Are you raising our allowance?"

"Funny boy. Well, your mother and I thought we'd pick you kids up after school and take you to Niagara Falls for some sightseeing and then have dinner at the Skylon."

"Great. Cool," Melissa squealed excitedly. "Can we go to the aquarium? I heard they have a new dolphin, and the sea lions put on a spectacular show."

"We'll see, but I don't think that your father is ready for another dolphin today. It all depends upon how much time we have. We can't begin until after three o'clock."

"Great idea, Dad, but I have a paper due on the solar system today. I better get it finished or Sister Joseph will keep me after school."

"Jonathan, why can't you do your homework before the last minute? It would be so much easier for you," Karen scolded.

"Get a move on, Son, and get it done now, or we'll be getting a sitter for you while we go to the Falls."

Jonathan got up from the table. "Let's skip school today. I'd like the day off. Sister Joseph is always picking on me," he grumbled as he went into the den to work on his paper.

"I guess they're thrilled to be going, Karen."

"I agree, Al. Can you finish the bacon and toast? How about another cup of coffee?"

"Thanks, no coffee, but I'll finish up the toast and bacon. Too much coffee gives me heartburn. I'll help you clear the table in a few minutes."

"Melissa, we'll pick you up in front of the school at three o'clock. Get ready. The bus will be here soon."

"Okay, I'll be waiting."

"Jonathan, are you ready?"

"I just finished my report, Dad. I'm ready for school and the trip afterward."

At that moment, the bus pulled up in front of the Chapman's white colonial style house on Maple Road and the driver tooted the horn. The two children rushed out of the front door and down the driveway; book bags flying.

"We'll see you at three. Don't forget. Love you both. Do well in school today," Karen called, as they climbed aboard the bus.

"Love ya too," Melissa shouted back over her shoulder.

After doing the dishes, Karen and Al spent the remainder of the day reading the paper, chatting and waiting for the time when they would pick up the children.

"Al, how are you really feeling? Are you all right? That dream this morning was scary. You had me worried to death with your screaming and thrashing about in bed."

"I feel a lot better than I did after you woke me up. I think I'm okay now. A day at the Falls will be a good change for me. It's a beautiful day for a ride."

At 2:50 p.m., Al backed their green 2002 GM van out of the garage. Karen exited the house from the front door, locked it behind her, and slipped into the passenger seat next to Al. In less than ten minutes, they were at the school on Abbott Road. Melissa and Jonathan were already anxiously waiting in front for them. They quickly jumped into the back seat and fastened their seatbelts. When they were all ready, Al pulled away from the curb and headed toward the Peace Bridge and Niagara Falls, Canada, less than an one-hour drive from Orchard Park.

As they approached the Peace Bridge, Al alerted the excited children in the back seat. "Kids, listen up. When we stop at Customs, don't act smart. Answer the inspector's questions—nothing more. We don't want to be delayed for several hours while they check us out. Since 9/11, security has been very tight at the Bridge—understandably so, because it is an international border where terrorists might try to cross into the USA."

"Do you want me to tell them that I'm an adopted kid from Iraq?" Jonathan quipped.

"Jonathan, I'm tempted to let them keep you. Button your lip. Don't act wise at the Bridge," Al warned the children in a stern voice.

"Oh, Dad, I was only kidding."

"I know, but these Customs inspectors don't like kidders. They detain wise guys to teach them a lesson."

Traffic was not heavy, and after all of the lecturing by Al, they easily passed through inspection. All that Jonathan said was, "Orchard Park, New York, USA," when asked where he was born.

Upon leaving the Bridge, Al decided to go through Fort Erie, along the Niagara River, instead of taking the QEW, which would be faster. He knew that the river route was more scenic and safer than the high-speed super highway. Suddenly, led by Melissa, the family broke into song, singing, "Oh, Canada," the Canadian National Anthem as they cruised along the calm waters of the Niagara River at fifty kilometers per hour.

Karen interrupted the songfest to ask, "Did you get your science paper on the solar system in on time, Jonathan? Why can't you begin work on an assignment immediately after you are given it?"

"I don't know, Mom. I always think that I'll have enough time. I did manage to get it in on time, but Sister Joseph let her pet, Jim Martin, have another day because his dog ate his paper."

"Oh brother, that old chestnut. I used that excuse when I was a kid. How old is Sister, Jonathan?"

"She's old—about Mom's age. It's hard to tell because her hair is covered by her veil."

"I guess I might as well pack it in," Karen commented. "But I bet that Sister is closer to forty."

"I'm surprised that there are any nuns left. Their numbers are rapidly declining in the United States. It's a shame. They are marvelous teachers and disciplinarians. I can remember Sister John Luke whacking me across the knuckles just for turning around in my seat to talk to a friend. I still have the scars. But we kids learned how to behave ourselves and exercise self-control. The nuns were too strict, I know, but they gave us the foundation for a strong value system."

"What school did you go to, Dad? That sister would be charged with child abuse today," Jonathan remarked.

"Saint James on the east side of Buffalo. It was a wonderful school. I read in the paper recently that the diocese closed it because of declining enrollment. The neighborhood just deteriorated. There was so much vandalism that people sold their homes and moved away. Those who couldn't sell them just abandoned the houses. What a tragedy. I loved that old neighborhood. We had so much fun playing in the street—tag, baseball, football, roller skating, and even tennis. You don't see much of this comradery nowadays. It seems that it's everyone for themselves."

"You play a team sport, Dad. Don't the Bills stick together?"

"Yes, we do, but I credit Coach Schultz with teaching the young guys sportsmanship. Winning is important, Jonathan, but it isn't everything. Professional sports have gotten to be too violent. Kids see this on television and then they try to imitate the bad behavior. Many high school coaches around the country are making brutes out of their kids. I just don't like violence in sports. Remember that, Son."

"That was good advice your father just gave you, Jonathan. We're all lucky that he was brought up to be such a gentleman."

The Chapmans did not fit the mold of a typical, present-day American family. They were more a throwback to the Cleaver family of the *Leave It to Beaver* TV series of the fifties; doing things together as a family, respecting others, setting high standards for themselves, and openly showing love toward one another. It works well for the Chapmans, although by today's measure, they might be considered "square." Regardless, this family of four happily cruised along the Niagara River toward Niagara Falls, Ontario, Canada, without a care in the world. From this moment on, their lives would never be the same.

CHAPTER 3

As they drove along the Niagara River, lined with ugly chemical plants on the American side and beautiful homes on the Canadian shore, Al commented about the absence of birds on the river.

"I don't know what's happening to the ducks. The river used to be full of mergansers, old squaws, blue and green teals, and buffleheads. My eighth-grade teacher, Miss Webster, who was not a nun, would take us on field trips a couple of times a year to see the birds on the river. She would be shocked at how few ducks there are now."

"What's causing it, Al?"

"I guess it's a combination of factors: pollution, global warming, a change in migratory patterns. The State and Federal governments are attempting to clean up the river, but it may be too little, too late. Fortunately, we can still enjoy the outdoors."

"I've been thinking about where we should sightsee today. I wondered if you all would like to take the Maid of the Mist ride to the base of the Horseshoe and American Falls. I'm not sure if they're running this late in the year, but we could check it out."

"That's a wonderful idea, Al. The kids have never taken that trip. It's a beautiful day for a boat ride. We haven't taken it for almost ten years. I vote that we go for it."

"I second it," Melissa chimed in.

"I third it," added Jonathan.

"It's unanimous. We're on our way."

It was almost five o'clock when they reached the parking lot overlooking the Falls.

The lot was full of cars.

"We're in luck. They're still operating. I'll go and buy the tickets. Wait for me at the elevator entrance."

In American currency, adult tickets are $8.50 each; children's tickets are $4.50 apiece. They took the elevator down to the boat landing, presented their tickets, and were issued blue raincoats and hats according to their sizes. The Maid of the Mist was loading and almost full. It appeared to hold at least one hundred passengers. They boarded swiftly and made their way to the port side of the lower deck, just as the boat pulled away from the dock, and sailed quickly toward the base of the Canadian Horseshoe Falls.

"I can't believe that we made it with only seconds to spare," Karen noted. At that moment, the captain came on the PA system.

"Welcome aboard the Maid of the Mist, folks. This is Captain Burns. We'll be at the Horseshoe Falls in a few minutes. Prepare yourselves for a good soaking. Afterwards, we will swing over to the base of the American Falls, before turning back to shore. If you do not like water, you should have taken the camel ride at the Buffalo Zoo. From now on, you won't be able to hear much of anything except the deafening roar of the Falls. Enjoy the ride. See you later."

Water flowed down the faces of everyone as the mist from the Canadian Falls poured over them. They looked like someone had turned a fire hose on them.

"I'm soaked, but I love it. Isn't this cool?"

The roar of the Falls drowned out Melissa's voice. Suddenly, Al grabbed the boat's railing tightly. His knuckles turned white, his breathing became labored, and he gasped for air. Instinctively, he reached for Karen's arm.

"Karen, I'm not feeling well," he shouted.

"What's wrong, Al? You're as pale as a ghost," she yelled in his ear.

"I don't know. I feel like I'm going to pass out. My heart is racing and I'm breaking into a cold sweat. I've got to get off this boat."

"Sit on the deck and put your head between your knees. That should make the blood flow back to your head. We'll be at the American Falls in a couple of minutes, and then we'll turn for the shore."

Al was in obvious agony and held on to Karen and the railing as the boat turned away from the Falls and made its way toward shore. Five minutes later, they docked. Al stood up and rushed down the gangplank and past Captain Burns, who was getting ready to greet the disembarking passengers.

"Watch your step, folks. We don't want to lose you now. Hope you enjoyed the ride. Come again. Bring a friend."

Karen and the children chased after Al, who was already waiting at the elevator. They turned in their raincoats and caps and rode the elevator to the top level. Al surprisingly had enough stamina to hurry to the van while the others struggled to keep up with him.

"Al, what are we going to do? I think we should get you to a hospital right away. You're very sick and could be having a heart attack. A doctor should look you over."

"Nonsense. Whatever it was, it has passed. I'm fine now. It's getting late; almost six o'clock, and I'm hungry. Let's go to the Skylon for dinner like we had planned."

Karen did not argue with her husband. She knew it would not do any good. *He's a stubborn man*, she thought to herself as they drove the short distance to the Skylon's parking lot adjacent to the impressive Tower.

Al purchased four tickets for the outside elevator, which would take them 775 feet up the wall of the building. Karen and the children enjoyed the spectacular view of the Falls as they ascended to the revolving restaurant. Al stood at the rear during the fifty second ride, his view blocked by twenty other passengers. The maître d' greeted them as they emerged from the elevator and led them to a window table, where he handed them each a menu.

"Welcome to the Skylon Tower. John will be your waiter this evening and will be with you shortly. First, let me caution you not to place anything on the window ledge. The inside of the room revolves while the outside wall is stationary. It would take almost one hour for your things to return to you again."

"Isn't that cool, Mom?"

"Yes, Melissa, it is very cool."

They perused the menu, and in the end, they all decided to have the Pacific salmon with roasted potatoes and asparagus. Rolls and a small salad were included. After John took their order, they swiveled their seats around to face the windows as the Falls came into view for the first time.

"Wow! Look at that panoramic view. You can see way down the River toward Buffalo," Jonathan observed.

"It certainly is beautiful, isn't it, Al?"

He did not answer but remained motionless, looking straight ahead and away from the window and the outside view. He stared straight ahead without seeing.

"You're sick again, aren't you? Your face is starting to pale, and you have beads of perspiration on your forehead. I'm worried about you. Let's forget about dinner and go home. Kids, we're leaving. Head for the elevator."

"Aw, gee whiz. Can't we stay? I'm hungry."

"You heard me, Jonathan. We'll eat at home later."

They all rose from the table and walked to the elevator. John was just coming out of the kitchen nearby.

"Is something wrong?"

"John, my husband is not feeling well. I'm sorry, but we must leave. Can you cancel our order?"

"Your order hasn't been filled yet, madam, so there will be no charge. I hope you feel better, sir. Please come again."

"Thank you, John. You're very kind," Karen said as she slipped a Canadian ten-dollar bill into his open hand.

They entered the empty elevator and began the rapid descent. Al again stood at the rear, facing away from the fantastic outside view and staring straight ahead without seeing. On the ground, Karen rushed to the van and sat behind the wheel.

"I'm driving home, Al, and tomorrow, I'm calling Doctor Wilson to make an appointment for you to be checked over. We've got to find out what is causing these attacks you're having."

"No, I'm all right now and can drive. Move over. I probably have a bug. Tomorrow, I'll see Doctor Olsen, our team doctor, and see what he says about all of this."

Al's stubbornness won out as he took Karen's arm and directed her to the passenger seat.

They were home in about ninety minutes. It was almost eight o'clock when they pulled into the driveway. Since they hadn't had any dinner, Karen called Mario's Pizza Palace to have a large, family-size pizza with pepperoni and a bucket of medium hot chicken wings delivered. By ten o'clock, the weary Chapmans were all in their beds, sound asleep, except for Karen, who continued to have deep concerns about Al's health, although he seemed to have tolerated the spicy foods quite well.

Tuesday morning, Al appeared to be back to normal and did not want to linger over breakfast. He ate quickly and gulped down a cup of black coffee.

"Karen, I have to dash this morning. I want to get to the stadium before the team meeting so I can study the films of last Sunday's Jets/Colts game. I'll be home around five. Take it easy, Hon. You look tired. Yesterday was rough on you too."

"Don't forget to see Doctor Olsen."

"Forget about it, Karen. I feel fine today. It was probably the twenty-four-hour flu. You worry too much."

Al kissed Karen on the lips and went out the front door to the van, which he had left parked in the driveway last night. Melissa, who had skipped breakfast, claiming that she was still full from last night's pizza and wings, watched her father through the front window as he drove away. Karen returned to the kitchen and joined Jonathan.

"Is there something wrong with Dad, Mom?"

"I don't know, Jonathan. I hope not. I hear the bus. Don't forget your lunch. Melissa, the bus is here. Jonathan, give your sister her lunch. See you later."

The children rushed out of the house, leaving Karen standing alone in the doorway. She returned to the kitchen to finish her coffee, which had long since cooled. Against Al's wishes, she decided to call Doc Wilson's office as soon as he opened at nine o'clock. She continued to be concerned about the bad dream the night before and the attacks in Canada.

I know Al will be angry with me for making an appointment, but I don't care.

It had been over a year since any of the Chapmans had been in to see David Wilson, an old-fashioned family doctor who still made emergency house calls in the middle of the night. Karen knew that they could always depend on Doc. However, he did have a tendency to spend too much time chitchatting with patients while the waiting room overflowed with impatient people. Nevertheless, he was a kind and caring man.

At seventy-four, Doc was nearing retirement although maintaining that he would "die with my stethoscope on." As a young man, he was well over six feet tall. Now he was bent over by arthritis, which made him look four inches shorter. Doc was obese because he liked to over indulge himself with sweets that Molly, his secretary, kept on her desk. Never pausing to rest between patients, he huffed and puffed as he went from one examination room to another.

Dr. Wilson was not in his office when Karen called at nine. Molly took her call.

"Doc had an emergency at Mercy Hospital, Karen. We're running late this morning. I'll have him call you as soon as he has time. Is it an emergency?"

"Yes and no. It's Al. He's been having some kind of attacks. I'm worried."

"I'll have him call you the minute he arrives."

"Thanks, Molly. I'll be waiting at the phone."

The phone rang at nine-thirty. It was Doc.

"Hello, Karen, it's Doc Wilson. Molly told me that you called. Sorry I wasn't in the office. I had an emergency. Now, the office is jammed. What's the problem?"

"Oh, Doc, it's not me; it's Al. We went to Canada yesterday and took the Maid of the Mist ride."

"Isn't that a marvelous experience? I just love to feel the mist from the Falls on my face."

"Yes, it is. Anyhow, we were just at the base of the Horseshoe Falls when Al had some sort of spell—sweating, breathing heavily, heart palpitations. He was all right once we were on shore. Then the same thing happened when we were at the Skylon Tower restaurant."

"That is one wonderful place to dine, isn't it? The views are fantastic and you really get a great panoramic perspective of the Niagara gorge and surrounding region. Yesterday was such a gorgeous day."

"Yes, it was, but Al was really terribly ill—on the verge of passing out. He was okay again once he reached our van. He was fine again this morning. The night before last, he had a horrible nightmare that left him pale and perspiring. I'm very concerned. He's always been so healthy."

"It sounds like he's having some sort of anxiety attacks. I'd like to examine him before I draw any conclusions, Karen. Have him come to my office at six, tomorrow evening. I'll open up the office for him. I know he practices all day."

"He can be there at six. Thank you so much. I appreciate everything you do."

"No problem. By the way, how are those two beautiful children of yours? I haven't seen them in some time. Aren't they due for their annual checkups?"

"You are amazing. What a memory you have. They've been fine, but I'll make appointments for them when Molly comes back on the line."

"Here's Molly. Bye for now, doll."

"Molly, does Doc have Saturday hours? I need appoint-ments for Melissa and Jonathan."

"Yes, he does. I can give you back-to-back appointments at two and two-thirty this Saturday, September 27."

"That's perfect. Thanks for all of your help. Al will be in to see Doc at six, tomorrow evening, and Melissa, Jonathan, and I will see you Saturday."

That task completed, Karen sat back in her chair in the den and relaxed until it was time to prepare dinner, which she had decided would be meatloaf, baked potatoes, yellow beans, and strawberry ice cream for dessert. Exactly at five o'clock, Al returned home from practice and joined Karen in the kitchen. He was in an especially jovial mood.

"How was your day? We had a great practice today. I feel good about playing the Jets Sunday. Did anything earthshaking happen around here?"

"Nothing much, just the usual housewifely chores. Did you talk to Doctor Olsen?"

"No, I didn't want to embarrass myself by going in and talking to him when I wasn't sick. You're making a mountain out of a molehill, Karen."

"Well, you're going to be angry with me, because I made an appointment for you with Doc for tomorrow evening at six. He's opening up his office, especially to see you, so hurry home from practice."

"No way, Karen. I'm not going. I was fine today. It must have been a bug I had. I don't have any symptoms today at all. Call Doc back and cancel."

"No, I won't. Doc wants to check you over, and you're going."

"You treat me like a child, Karen. I'm in great shape. Cancel the appointment. Case closed. Last word."

Because of this disagreement, they sat in complete silence throughout dinner and the rest of the evening; a rarity in their marriage. The children did not want to ask questions but knew that there had been some sort of argument. After dinner, they both went to their rooms to work on their homework without being told.

Wednesday morning, Karen reluctantly called Molly to cancel the appointment.

"Molly, I'm so embarrassed. Al refuses to see Doc this evening. He says he's okay. Tell Doc that I'm sorry."

"Don't fuss, Karen. That's men for you. I'll tell Doc."

"Thank you. See you Saturday, anyway."

The rest of the week was uneventful, but an air of coolness remained between Al and Karen. Al seemed well and was focusing on Sunday's game with the New York Jets. He never took them lightly. They were a talented and well-coached team. Al always referred to them as the "New Jersey jets" because they played their games at the Meadowlands in New Jersey. Even the New York Giants played in New Jersey.

"The Bills are the only legitimate New York State team," Al maintained.

As game day approached, the Chapman family was returning to normal. The children had their physicals Saturday and passed with flying colors. Doc did not mention Al's cancelled appointment, for which Karen was grateful.

Saturday evening, Al and Karen finally relaxed together in the living room and discussed tomorrow's game.

"I'm a bit worried about the defensive line of the Jets. They have an excellent middle linebacker—Ron Jefferson. He's awfully fast and very strong and has five sacks of the quarterbacks so far. I'll have to be at my best to protect our quarterback, Adams. I just hope that I can measure up to the challenge."

"You'll do just fine, Al—you always do."

But deep down, Karen was worried. She prayed that the anxiety attacks were over and she could stop harping to Al about seeing the doctor.

He should be all right during the game because he is used to the game day tension and apprehension. No doubt, he won't even remember these episodes, but I certainly will. Al has never been sick before, not even a cold. That's important. He thinks that he may have had the twenty-four-hour flu. I just can't believe that you can recover from a flu bug ten minutes after an attack. Al believes that he's Mister Tough Guy, but deep inside, he's a softie with fears like everyone else. He was very frightened after the two attacks at Niagara Falls—I could see it in his eyes. If he has any more of these episodes, he's going to see Doc Wilson—like it or not. It's time I put my foot down and do what I know is the right thing. This is my solemn promise I am making to myself.

Al was having some doubts himself.

I know that Karen is very worried about me and the attacks I've been having. I'm very concerned too, but I can't let her know about my fears. I'll be okay. The important thing now is the game with the Jets. The attacks were probably just freak occurrences, and they won't happen again, I'm sure.

CHAPTER 4

Sunday was a gorgeous, warm, sunny day in October. The NBC sports commentators could not complain about Buffalo's weather because it was a perfect day for football. Seventy-five thousand screaming fans, bathed in sunshine, were anticipating a hard-hitting game between the Eastern Division American Football Conference rivals; the New York Jets and the Buffalo Bills.

In order to beat the traffic congestion caused by fans pouring into the Ralph Wilson Stadium parking lots for their tailgating parties, Al left home at seven o'clock. As he drove slowly along One Bills Drive, the aroma of grilling hot dogs and hamburgers permeated the air. Gourmet meals were prepared and served on tables set up and covered with white tablecloths. Steak, lobster, roast beef, and venison were often served. The beverages of choice served at these feasts were champagne, wine, and beer.

"They really start early here in Buffalo; five hours before game time," Al noted as he glanced at his wristwatch. It was almost eight o'clock in the morning.

Inside the stadium, in the locker room, the players were preparing themselves mentally for the game, gathering in offensive and defensive groups with their coaches, or just sitting quietly alone and meditating.

Al stood before his locker, putting on his pads and clothing according to a ritual he had established for himself when he played at the University of Virginia. Under his number 91 Bills shirt, he wore a favorite tee shirt given to him by Karen when they spent a weekend together at Shenandoah National Park before they were married. Inscribed on the shirt was the message, "Al, you'll always be number one with me." Beneath his Bills regulation red socks, he wore a pair of blue socks knitted by his mother. His left shoe was always put on before the right. And in his pants pocket, he carried a Saint Christopher medal, although Christopher had been removed from the Catholic Church's list of saints because no one could prove that he ever existed. Even though he did not consider himself superstitious, Al believed that the medal protected him from danger. As an offensive tackle, he was especially prone to injuries caused by charging opposing defensive men. Leg and head injuries were common. Al would only sit at the end of the bench facing toward the Bills' end zone. Each quarter, he would have to change ends.

Chapman was one of the best at his position in the NFL. More than that, his opponents respected him for his clean play and superb sportsmanship. He was the third player taken by the Bills in the 1999 college football draft because they needed a strong offensive line to protect their quarterback, Jim Adams. Opponents knew that they would have to double team Al if they were to have any chance of sacking Adams.

Although football is considered to be a violent sport played by violent men, Al was considered to be a gentle giant who often visited critically ill children at the Roswell Park Cancer Institute in Buffalo. On his day off, this hulk of a man could be found reading stories to the youngsters, many of whom were terminally ill. They adored him and looked forward to his frequent visits. Several times a year, he would come laden with toys and other gifts and pass them out to the children.

Often criticized by his coaches for failing to retaliate after an opponent's late hit on him, his standard response was "That's his problem, not mine."

Coach John Schultz never gave pregame pep talks to the players. His speech was brief but to the point.

"You fellows are all professionals, and by this time, you should know how to play the game of football. Don't play dirty. Now, go out there and win this game for all of those fans who paid good money to cheer you on."

Karen and the children attended all of the home games and sat with other players' families in the Paul McGuire suite, from which they had a perfect view of the game between the forty-yard lines. They arrived at noon, just in time to see the Bills warm up and to order a hot dog and a soda for each of them. At twelve fifty-five, the teams ran onto the field, took their places on their respective sidelines, and waited for the coin toss, which the Bills won. They elected to receive. Wind gusts were up to twenty miles per hour, so the Jets elected to kick with the wind during the first quarter of the game. With the wind at his back, Parker, the Jets' kicker, kicked the ball out of the end zone for an automatic touchback. It was the Bills' ball on their own twenty-yard line. The offensive unit ran onto the field amidst the deafening roar of the crowd. On the first play of the game, Adams rolled out to pass. Al saw the blitz coming and tried to block the charging middle linebacker, Ron Jefferson, who spun Al around and hit him across the back of his knees. Al crumpled to the ground, and as he lay there writhing in pain, with Jefferson still on top of him, he uncharacteristically shouted.

"You're a damned son of a bitch dirty player, Jefferson. Remember, what goes around comes around. Just you wait."

"Go to hell, Chapman," was Jefferson's response as he climbed off of Al.

A hush fell over the crowd. Al remained on the ground, his left leg twisted beneath his body. Karen let out a scream when the Bills' medical staff hurried onto the field to attend to Al.

"He's badly hurt, I know. Look at his leg. It's twisted. I've got to get down there to him. I have to help him."

Janet Adams, the quarterback's wife, restrained her.

"Stay here, Karen. You can't go on the field. Look. He's moving. They're getting him to his feet. He's going to be all right."

"I'm worried. He's limping off the field."

The crowd rose to its feet. Al hobbled to the end of the bench, where the trainer examined his leg. Melissa stared quietly at her father, watching him valiantly try to walk off the injury. Jonathan, on the other hand, had something to say.

"You dirty rotten player, Jefferson. My dad will get you. Just you wait. You're next."

"Jonathan, sit down and be quiet. You're not helping your father at all by acting this way. Behave yourself."

Jonathan sat down and mumbled to himself under his breath as the game resumed. The Bills failed to get a first down on their first series and had to punt. On their first possession, the Jets also had to punt. When the Bills' offensive unit came back on the field, Al was among them. Though limping slightly, he took his place on the left side of the line. At the first snap of the ball, Jefferson again outmaneuvered Al and sacked Adams. When Adams attempted to get up, Jefferson taunted him. In anger, Al grabbed Jefferson's facemask, swung him around by his head, and threw him heavily to the turf. The fans, who were cheering wildly a moment before, now fell silent. Jefferson lay motionless on the ground. Again, the medical staff ran onto the field and tried to stabilize Jefferson's head and neck. After fifteen minutes, they carefully lifted him onto a stretcher and into an ambulance which had been driven onto the field. Jefferson was still not moving when the ambulance left for Mercy Hospital in south Buffalo. Out of respect for the injured player, the fans stood and applauded Jefferson, watching the ambulance leave the playing field and exit through the stadium tunnel.

Before play resumed, the referee ejected number 91 from the game for unsportsmanlike conduct. Al did not protest the penalty and went immediately to the locker room, showered, got dressed, and waited for the Bills to come in at half time. By then, the Jets were leading the Bills 24 to 0. Coach Schultz went over to Al, who was sitting in front of his locker, his head in his hands.

"What in hell came over you out there, Al? You're not a dirty player."

"I don't know, John—I just lost it. I felt a sudden rage come over me and I just wanted to hurt Jefferson. I couldn't control myself. I did an awful thing. I'm so terribly sorry. How is he? Is there any word about his condition?"

"We don't know anything yet. When he left the field, he didn't have any feeling from the neck down. Sometimes that is temporary. Let's hope and pray that it is."

"God! What have I done to him? I'm going to the hospital to see how he is."

"I don't think that's wise. The family will be there and they certainly won't want to see you. Right now, they probably hate you. And the place will be crawling with reporters from radio and TV. They're going to crucify you on the air tonight. Stay away."

"I don't blame them after what I did. I just want to express my sorrow to the family."

"All right, Al. Do what you have to do but stay out of trouble. The league is going to come down hard on you for this. Let me know about Jefferson's condition when you know anything."

"I will, John. Please pray for Jefferson, and for me."

"I'll have the whole team pray for you both, buddy."

Al dashed out of the stadium and, unnoticed, entered his car and sped across Tim Russert Road toward Mercy Hospital. Upon arriving, he immediately went to the information desk, where he was told that Jefferson was not allowed any visitors; only family.

"What is his room number so I can send him a card?"

"It's room 507 South, but remember, you can't go up there."

Waiting until the on-duty guard was looking the other way, Al sneaked past him and entered the elevator, which took him to the fifth floor in the South wing. Once there, he had no trouble locating room 507. The door was closed, but he opened it and slipped inside. On the bed, his head stabilized by sandbags and in a neck brace, lay an unconscious Jefferson; pale and lifeless looking. As Al stood beside the bed staring at Jefferson's still figure, the door opened suddenly, and a pretty young black woman entered the room.

"Who are you? What are you doing in here?" she screamed, her dark eyes flashing as she looked directly at Al.

"I'm Al Chapman. Are you Mrs. Jefferson?"

"You're the one who hurt my Ron. Get out of here, you monster. Someone, help! Call security! Come in here and get this man out of here."

"Please, Mrs. Jefferson, I want to tell you how sorry I am and to ask for your forgiveness. I didn't mean to hurt Ron. What can I do to help him?"

"You can get out of here right now. I don't ever want to see you around here or my Ron again. You tried to kill my husband. Look at him—he's paralyzed and may never walk again."

Hearing all of the commotion, a nurse came running into the room.

"Is something wrong in here, Mrs. Jefferson? Do you need help with Mr. Jefferson?"

"Yes. Get this man out of here. He's an intruder. He's the one who injured my husband. Don't ever let him near my Ron again. Who let him in here?"

"I don't know. Sir, you'll have to leave, or I'll call security to have you removed."

"Mrs. Jefferson, I'm so terribly sorry."

Two burly looking orderlies entered the room, took Al by the arms and ushered him out of Jefferson's room and into the corridor. Al immediately left the hospital, fearing that he would be seen and recognized by reporters who were congregating in the lobby, waiting for news on Jefferson. Back in his car, Al put his head down on the steering wheel and sobbed uncontrollably; totally ashamed of himself for what he had done and wondering if Jefferson would ever walk again.

"What got into me? Why did I viciously attack this man? I've never done anything like this before in my life. That was not me on that football field today. Do I have two sides to my personality? Who am I? I'm no better than a wild animal."

Pulling himself together so he could drive, he found his way home, left his jeep in the driveway, and entered an empty house. Karen and the children were still not home from the game, apparently stuck in traffic. He did not know what to say to them when he saw them. He went into the den, sat down in his favorite chair, and turned on the TV, hoping to get a report on the condition of Jefferson. The game had just ended. The NBC sportscasters were summarizing the game, which the Bills lost to the Jets 34 to 3.

"The Bills played badly today after Al Chapman was ejected from the game. It looks like they are not a playoff contender while the Jets are beginning to surge."

"Tell us about Ron Jefferson's condition, you jerks," Al yelled at the TV set. The response from Geiberger was instantaneous.

"Ron Jefferson's condition is unchanged—he is paralyzed from the neck down."

CHAPTER 5

Immediately after Al was ejected from the game, Karen and the children quickly left. The exodus of disappointed fans from the stadium was massive. The Bills appeared to be headed for another defeat. Bills fans leave early if they see no hope for a victory.

Traffic was extremely congested on route twenty; slow-moving, with many fender benders. When they arrived home at three o'clock, they were surprised to see Al's jeep in the driveway. Karen rushed into the house and found Al in the den, slumped in his chair.

"Al, Dear, how are you doing? Is there anything I can do to help? I know how you feel. Would you like me to fix you something to eat?"

"I'm not hungry, Karen. And you have no conception about how I feel. I almost killed a man this afternoon. Have you ever done that? I went to the hospital to see Ron and talk to his wife, but she wouldn't even let me apologize or speak to her. She had me ejected from the room like I was a common criminal. That's getting to be a pattern with me lately. Right now, I need time to sort things out in my head."

"Calm down, Al. You're a good and loving man. I know that you didn't mean to hurt Jefferson. You have never been violent; it's not your nature."

"I'm not sure about that. I can't remember if I deliberately tried to injure him. For some reason, I guess I was out of control. I'm even a mystery to myself."

At that moment, Melissa and Jonathan entered the room and stood listening to their parents' conversation. Staring at their father, Jonathan interrupted.

"Dad, Jefferson had it coming to him. He's always been a dirty player and he got what he deserved. Someone had to stop him. Maybe now he'll think twice before he goes after you again."

"Don't talk to your father like that, Jonathan. A man has been seriously hurt and we must pray for his recovery," Karen scolded, raising her voice to make sure that Jonathan understood the seriousness of the situation. "Now don't bother your father. Haven't you any homework to do? There is school tomorrow. Remember?"

"I know, Mom. I'll keep my mouth shut from now on."

He turned and stormed up the stairs to his room. Karen heard the door slam behind him. She didn't like his attitude, and she intended to correct it soon.

On the other hand, Melissa did not say a word. She went into the living room, turned on the TV, and stretched out on the couch. Karen left Al and joined Melissa, who was staring blankly at the screen. A local sportscaster was updating Jefferson's condition.

"The latest report issued by Mercy Hospital on Ron Jefferson is not encouraging. He remains paralyzed from the neck down and has no feeling in any of his extremities. The doctors will not commit themselves to any prognosis."

On hearing this news, Melissa began to quietly sob and turned to Karen.

"Why did Dad do such an evil thing, Mom? I hate him."

Karen sat next to her daughter and tried to console her by stroking her long auburn hair and counseling her.

"Honey, don't talk about your father like that. We've got to stand by him. He's suffering too. It's not like you to act this way. Is something the matter? You've been very quiet lately. Aren't you feeling well? Is everything all right at school?"

"I'm fine, Mom. I'm just worried about what the kids will say in school tomorrow."

"It isn't going to be easy for you. Whatever they say, try to tune them out. They'll tire of the story quickly, and believe me, it will pass. Just imagine what your father is going through. You know that he hasn't been feeling well lately. I've been trying to get him to go and see Doc Wilson, but he refuses."

"Mom…"

"Yes, sweetie, what is it?"

"Nothing—it's not important."

"Everything you say is important to me, Melissa. You can always come to me with any problem. You know that."

"I know, Mom. It's just that I don't feel like talking right now. So much is happening in our family. I'm worried about Dad."

"What do you say that we go to the movies tonight, just the two of us? We'll let Jonathan and your father batch it at home together. I think we both need a break."

"I'd like that, Mom. There's a reissued movie playing at the McKinley Mall that I heard was cool. It's called *Sixth Sense*. Can we see it?"

"Is it R-rated?"

"No, it's PG-13, so it's okay for me to see. It's about people who see dead people. Some of the kids at school have seen it and they liked it. The ending is a surprise—nobody will tell me what it is."

"Melissa, that movie won't cheer us up. It will be depressing. Let's see a comedy or a nice musical to help get our minds off today's events."

"Please, Mom. I want to see *Sixth Sense*. I like movies like that. They relax me and make me think."

"All right, we'll see it. We'll catch an early show and get something to eat afterward. I'll check the paper for the show times now."

Karen returned to the den to get the movie section of the Sunday paper, which was still in its wrapper, unopened. The first show was at five o'clock. They could make it if they hurried. Al appeared to be asleep in his chair, so Karen approached him cautiously.

"Al, are you awake?"

"I am now. What's up?"

"Would you mind terribly if Melissa and I go to the movies tonight? You and Jonathan can order in and spend some father/son time together. I think you need to have a talk with our son. You know what I mean. I realize that it's difficult to get your mind off from everything that's been happening, but Jonathan needs his father, and our daughter needs her mother."

"That's okay with me. I'll try to do my best with Jonathan. Have a good time with Melissa, and don't worry about us. We'll be fine."

"The show is at five and we'll have to hurry. We should be home by eight."

"Don't hurry. Just enjoy yourselves."

It was ten after five when Karen and Melissa entered the darkened theater, carrying a bucket of buttered popcorn and two sodas. Coming attractions were showing as they groped their way down the aisle looking for two empty seats together. People were talking and not paying attention to the previews being shown on the screen.

"Here are two seats on the end, Mom."

"Good. Let's take them."

After their eyes became accustomed to the darkness, they realized that the theater was crowded, and they were lucky to have found two seats together. They couldn't resist the inviting smell of their popcorn and began eating.

"Melissa, isn't this popcorn luscious? I know it's full of cholesterol, but I don't care. We can cut back tomorrow, okay?"

"Right, Mom. We should do this more often. It's fun to be with you without Jonathan being around. Oh, the movie is going to start. Let's not talk during it, because I don't want to miss anything."

"Okay, I'll be quiet."

Karen was amazed by her daughter's maturity.

"She acts more like a young adult. How did she grow up without my noticing it? This movie is certainly not one I would have picked for a ten-year-old to see, but we're here," Karen mused.

The movie lasted over two hours. It was almost seven thirty when it ended. Surprised by the unpredictable ending, the crowd was silent as they left the theater.

"Let's go to McDonald's, Melissa. I'm famished and I'd like a cheeseburger."

"Good idea. I'd like a Big Mac, some fries, and a chocolate milkshake. The movie made me hungry. I feel like eating junk food tonight."

"After all of that popcorn, you're still hungry? That's a lot of food for a little girl."

"The popcorn was just an appetizer. I can handle everything."

They picked up their order at the counter and sat in a booth, providing them with a little more privacy than the tables which were close together.

"Mmm. This cheeseburger and the fries are fantastic—full of cholesterol, I know. How's your chocolate shake?"

"Thick and delicious. What did you think of the movie, Mom? Do you think that there are people like Cole, who can see dead people? Do you believe in ghosts?"

"I thought the movie was interesting, but I don't believe in ghosts. I've never seen one and I don't know anyone who has. The movie was just a story; pure fiction. Don't let it upset you, Melissa."

"Mom…"

"Yes?"

"I see ghosts; at least I think they're ghosts. I've seen a little blonde-haired girl standing around Dad, watching him. She was on the Maid of the Mist trip and in the Skylon Restaurant, and yesterday, she stood in front of Dad when he sat on the bench just after he was injured."

"Melissa, what are you talking about? It probably was your imaginary friend whom you had when you were four years old. What was her name?"

"Her name was Marie. No, Mom, this is not Marie I see. I've seen this girl hanging around Dad for a few months now. She smiles at him, and yet she seems sad."

"I know you wouldn't lie to me, but are you sure that your imagination is not running wild?"

"I'm sure, Mom. Sometimes she frightens me. She looks at me like she wants to say something to me, but she doesn't speak or can't. I almost feel like I know her."

"Oh, sweetie, I don't doubt you, but how do you know that she's a ghost?"

"Nobody else seems to see her—only me. She often vanishes before my eyes. Dad has never said that he sees her. And neither have you."

MARILYN FIEGEL

"Well, I don't want you to be upset over this. Let me know if she appears again."

"I will, Mom."

Having finished their meals, they left the restaurant, relaxed and quiet. When they arrived home, they found Al and Jonathan sitting together in the den, eating pizza and watching a movie.

"Hi, Mom. Dad and I are watching *Independence Day*. Dad rented it at Media Play. It's about aliens from outer space who are trying to invade Earth, and it's neat. You should see this movie. Do you believe in UFOs, Mom?"

"No, Jonathan, I do not. I never saw one, and I don't know anyone who has. How is the pizza? Did you guys have a nice evening together? Did you have a chance to talk to Jonathan, Al?"

"The pizza is great. And, yes to all of the questions."

"Good. Anyhow, it's a beginning, Al."

"Ghosts, aliens, UFOs. What's next?" Karen asked herself as she began picking up after her men. *"I wonder if there is any truth to this sixth sense business. Melissa certainly believes it, but she's only ten years old and is at an impressionistic age. And who is this little blonde girl she sees around Al? Why can't I see her? I wonder if Melissa is psychic. I once had an Aunt Kate who was clairvoyant, and I've heard that this ability runs in families. Maybe Melissa will outgrow this like she did her imaginary friend."*

It was after ten when the children said goodnight to their parents and went up to bed. Karen and Al sat in the den together, trying to sort out the day's happenings.

"Al, did you really have a chance to speak with Jonathan about his attitude?"

"I did, a little bit, but he was anxious to see the movie. I tried to assure him that I wasn't a dirty player, and that today was an anomaly. He knows how sorry I am for injuring Jefferson

44

and that I would have to live with that regret for the rest of my life with a blemish on my soul. I emphasized how important it was for us not to lose our tempers, because the consequences are often irreversible."

"That was good advice you gave him."

"I'm worried about what the kids in school will say tomorrow. Kids can be cruel bullies. I told Jonathan to bite the bullet, but I don't know if he can handle being taunted. I think that boys are worse than girls. How is Melissa doing? This is liable to affect her more than Jonathan. She keeps things more to herself."

"She'll be all right. I told her the same things you told Jonathan. Al, she is such a mature young lady, and I'm so proud of her. We have two wonderful children."

"I've always known that."

Karen decided not to say anything to Al about Melissa telling her that she sees a ghost; a little blonde girl standing near him sometimes. She kept her thoughts to herself.

He has enough to worry about without me telling him that a ghost is watching him. Melissa is not making this up, I know, but it is pretty far out. Maybe she is clairvoyant. That Sixth Sense movie seemed to give her courage to speak with me about this. I wonder if she is seeing a ghost or something else. What is a ghost anyway?

It was almost eleven o'clock when they stopped talking and went upstairs to bed. Al had Monday off, but he knew that the NFL Commissioner would make his decision quickly about his punishment. He was prepared for the worst and, in his mind, began guessing what penalty he thought the commissioner might impose.

I know I'll be fined—maybe $5,000, and probably will be suspended for one or two games. Whatever the penalty, I deserve it. This incident should be a wakeup call for other guys in the NFL who play to intentionally injure.

Karen was worried about the children at school tomorrow.
Melissa and Jonathan seemed to enjoy a night alone with us. I only hope that they can make it through school tomorrow without any incidents. It could be a very difficult day for them, especially Jonathan. He doesn't accept criticism well, preferring to run away from it and then lash out at someone or something. And he is developing a tendency to blame people without giving them a chance to explain themselves. That's what he does with Sister Joseph and is now doing with his father.

CHAPTER 6

Pat Rogers, the NFL Commissioner, was at the game Sunday at Wilson Stadium and observed the incident involving Al Chapman and Ron Jefferson. His decision came down to the Bills' front office on Tuesday. The penalty given to Al was harsh; a four-game suspension and a $50,000 fine—ten times what he guessed it would be. Al accepted the punishment without appealing. He knew it was just and well deserved. However, he would miss his teammates and the game tremendously.

Two days later, the news on Jefferson was encouraging. Some feeling was beginning to return to his arms and legs. The doctors were hopeful that the paralysis was temporary. His recovery would be lengthy, however. It was doubtful that he would ever play another down of football. His career apparently was over. Al had mixed emotions; happy that Jefferson would recover the use of his extremities, but sad that he had been responsible for ending a man's livelihood. All he could do was pray for Jefferson's full recovery.

On the home front, Jonathan wanted to change schools because his classmates at Saint Margaret's School were taunting him about his father.

"Your dad is a dirty player. Like father, like son. You're a chip off the old block, Johnny boy," they chanted, as he jumped off the school bus and ran into the house.

Karen, hearing what they were shouting at Jonathan, was at the door to meet him.

"Ignore their remarks, Jonathan. They're just trying to get a rise out of you."

"Well, they've succeeded. I want to go to public school. I'll have more fun there. They have swimming pools and all sorts of good things. I never want to go back to Saint Margaret's. I can't listen to what they're saying about Dad anymore."

"You're going to remain at Saint Margaret's, young man. They'll stop taunting you if they know that it doesn't bother you."

"You're a great one to be giving me advice—they're not taunting you."

"That's enough, mister. Go to your room and work on your homework. I'll call you when you can come down for dinner. You're grounded."

Jonathan ran up the stairs and slammed the door to his room. This was the youngster's way of handling adversity.

Melissa overheard the verbal exchange between Jonathan and her mother and confronted Karen in the kitchen.

"Mom, I think you were too hard on Jonathan. A couple of the girls in my class were at the game with their parents Sunday. They said that their parents said that Dad hurt Jefferson on purpose. It's all over TV and on the talk shows. I tried to stick up for Dad, but I think he did it deliberately too."

"Don't believe what those kids say. You know that your father is not like that—he's a good man. You must believe in him."

Al, who was sitting in the den, heard everything that was being said about him by his children. He went into the kitchen. Melissa, upon seeing him, left without speaking to him and went to her room.

"Well, Karen, I've really wrecked our family. Now, even my kids hate me. And I can't blame them for that."

"Stop that talk, Al. They don't mean what they say. They love you. They'll get over this in a few days. You'll see."

"Karen, let's go away. We need to escape from all of this hoopla around here."

"You know, Dear, I was thinking the same thing. I saw an ad in yesterday's paper for a seven-day trip to England. It departs from Buffalo a week from Wednesday. Let's go. I'll call the travel agency to see if they have room for us, and I'll ask my parents to come over and stay with the children. They'll be thrilled to spend the time with their grandchildren."

"Sounds good to me. I have almost four weeks left on my suspension. We can make this trip our second honeymoon. You know, my parents came from England before World War II began, and I'd like to see where they were born."

"I'll call the first thing in the morning. I hope they're not filled up. Keep your fingers crossed that they still have two spaces left. Maybe this trip will change your luck."

"I sure could use some of the 'good' variety; I'm overdue."

Early Wednesday, Karen called the World Travel Bureau. Luck was indeed with them. There were two spaces left for the England tour. They would be leaving in exactly one week. Their American Airlines flight to New York's Kennedy Airport was scheduled to leave the Buffalo-Niagara International Airport at eleven o'clock Wednesday morning.

Karen's parents, Joe and Evelyn Browning, were happy to stay with the children and were pleased when Karen asked them for the favor. There was so much to do to prepare for the trip: get passports, shop for food for one week, pack, and write out a list of instructions for the Brownings, Melissa and Jonathan.

"Al, are we crazy to be going on a trip on such short notice? There are so many preparations to make. Do you think we can get everything done in time?"

"Yes, I do, and it will be fun to do something spontaneous for a change. We certainly won't have to pack much for just one week. Should we tell the kids now that we're going on a trip, Karen? No doubt they'll be unhappy that they're not going with us."

"We can tell them in a couple of days. We don't want to give them time to think up some exotic illness to prevent us from leaving. By the way, Doc Wilson checked them over Saturday, and they are fine. He was glad to see them. What a memory that man has."

"That's good news. We certainly can use all that we can get right now."

When they did tell Jonathan and Melissa about their trip, they were very happy because they would have their beloved grandparents with them for one full week. It would be like a vacation for them, and they knew their grandparents would spoil them.

Somehow, all of the packing and preparations were completed, and on Wednesday morning, they kissed the children goodbye as they went off to school. The Brownings arrived early to drive them to the airport, so they would have plenty of time.

"We're on our way. Do you believe that we'll be in London tomorrow morning? It's only about a six-hour trans-Atlantic flight. Isn't that amazing? The world is getting smaller. Quite a change from the Queen Mary days, isn't it?"

"It sure is. How did we ever get packed in time, Al? I'm afraid that we'll get to London and discover that we have forgotten something important like money. Did you bring the traveler's cheques? Do you have the record sheets for them?"

"Certainly. I have them right here in my jacket pocket."

"Al, any pickpocket can steal them from that pocket. Put them in a safer place. Don't you have a zippered inside pocket?"

"No, I haven't. I'll put them in my shoe. That's a safe place unless we walk a lot and I wear a hole in my shoe."

"Don't be silly. Find another place, Al."

"You're the one being silly. Traveler's cheques can be replaced if they are lost or stolen. Stop worrying. We've barely left home. You'll be a nervous wreck."

"Okay, I'll try to calm down and relax on this trip. I'm putting you in charge of everything, Al, because I'm on vacation."

"Is that a promise?"

"Yes, it is. By the way, did you remember to call Coach Schultz to let him know where you were going? He'll wonder what you are doing."

"I thought I was in charge. Stop worrying. I called him, but it doesn't make any difference since I'm suspended and can't report for practice. Is that all, Karen?"

"Do you have our passports? Are they still valid? They're five years old."

"I give up. I thought we were on vacation."

CHAPTER 7

After changing planes at Kennedy International Airport, the England tour group took off at 6:35 p.m., heading east. It was a beautiful evening for flying; clear and starlit, with a first quarter moon rising in the east.

As soon as the plane attained cruising speed, the flight attendants took drink orders and then began serving supper, which was a turkey sandwich on whole wheat bread, carrot strips, and a bite-sized Milky Way candy bar.

"Remember, Karen. We're flying coach."

"That's all right. I need to lose some weight, and this is a good place to begin. Here, you can have my candy bar."

Exhausted from a full day of waiting in airports and traveling, Karen was soon asleep on Al's shoulder. With little room for his long legs, Al extended them out into the aisle, which made for hazardous walking for attendants and other passengers. Sleep was impossible. He kept replaying the Jefferson incident in his mind.

Karen awoke just as the plane was landing at Heathrow Airport just outside of London.

"Why didn't you wake me up, Al? Look at my hair. I'm a mess."

"It was more important for you to sleep."

"What about breakfast?"

"I saved you an orange and a sweet roll."

"What about my coffee?"

"I drank it. It was delicious."

"Oh, Al. You do take such good care of me."

"I try."

"Not hard enough."

After leaving the plane, the tour guide, Robert Allen, gathered the group together and directed them to the baggage area and then to Customs. By eight o'clock, they were checked through Customs and ready to board a bus which would take them to their hotel.

"'Listen up, everybody," Bob implored the excited group. "We will arrive at our hotel, the Lime Tree, in a few minutes. It is conveniently situated in the Westminster section of London, with easy access to shopping and many historical points of interest. Wait for me in the lobby. I'll give out the room assignments and keys there. Your luggage will be delivered to your rooms in about an hour. It is not necessary for you to wait for it. If you have the energy, you may want to spend the day exploring. Don't worry, you should have plenty of time before dinner tonight. We'll all meet here in the lobby at six o'clock for a short bus ride to the restaurant. Don't be late. We won't hold the bus for stragglers. Now, set your watches to London time. It is eight forty-five."

Bob was a small man, about fifty years of age. His black curly hair and dark eyes accented his square face which featured a jaw that jutted out beneath a sharp thin nose. His best feature was his very white and perfectly aligned teeth, which lit up his face when he smiled. He and his wife, Marge, owned the World Travel Bureau in Buffalo and took turns traveling overseas. Bob was leading this trip because he was British born.

The bus pulled up in front of a red brick structure that looked more like an apartment building than a hotel. Inside, the Chapmans were given two keys to Room 405 at the rear of the hotel, on the fourth floor. Their room overlooked a small garden which still had a few blooms left on some plants.

Their room was small but adequate. There was a round table with two chairs along the wall and two easy chairs. The room appeared to have been recently redecorated; the scent of fresh paint permeated the air. One negative was the tiny bathroom, which had a small walk-in shower stall. They also could have had twice the number of towels than were provided, but they decided not to complain.

The luggage arrived in their room at nine-thirty. Al helped Karen unpack and hang up their wrinkled clothing on a small clothes rack in the corner of the room.

"Everything will straighten out in this damp air in a couple of hours, Al. We're fortunate that it isn't raining."

"Actually, my suits are relatively wrinkle free. It pays to buy good fabrics."

Al sat down at the table and began examining the itinerary which Bob had handed out in the lobby.

"Listen to this, Hon. Tomorrow morning, we're going to the Changing of the Guard at Buckingham Palace, and then in the afternoon, we'll visit Parliament. Look at all they have planned for us—a bus tour of London, the Tower of London, Westminster Abbey, a boat trip on the River Thames, and a side trip to Stonehenge, whatever that is. We'll have some free time on Tuesday for shopping and meals on our own. I'm looking forward to everything, aren't you?"

"Al. This is the trip of a lifetime—the history, pageantry, the tradition. I'm so happy we came. Guess what, Dear? I'm hungry. Let's go down to the little restaurant near the lobby and get something to eat."

"You still have your orange and sweet roll."

"You know what you can do with those, Mister Chapman."

They rode the lift down to the lobby and entered the restaurant, which was serving lunch. A pretty young waitress seated them and introduced herself.

"My name is Betty, and I'll be your waitress. We have one luncheon special today—a roast beef sandwich on rye. Would you like to look over the menu for a few minutes?"

"I'm going to have the beef sandwich and a cup of tea, Betty. I don't need a menu."

"I'll have the same," Al added.

"Very good. I'll be back shortly."

Betty returned in a few minutes with their sandwiches and a pot of hot tea, which she poured for them.

"I like the sandwich, Karen, but it can't compare with Anderson's beef on weck."

"You've got that right, Al. But remember, this is jolly old England, and they're not known for their culinary skills."

"Karen, are you up to walking around the area? We can pick up a map at the desk."

"Would you mind if we went to our room and just relaxed before dinner? Suddenly, I feel tired."

"Not at all. I think you're suffering from jet lag. It may be twelve-thirty here, but it's seven-thirty back home. The kids are having breakfast, I hope."

"You are so smart, Dear. I think I'll keep you."

Back in their room, they rested, showered, dressed, and were ready by 5:40.

"Let's go down early, Al. You heard Bob say that the bus wouldn't wait for latecomers. I don't want to be left behind on our first evening here."

"Oh, Bob was just trying to scare us. That's an old school-teacher ploy. Maybe he used to be one. He kind of looks like a teacher."

Everyone was at the curb waiting for the bus at six o'clock, anxious to go to dinner.

The twenty-five people in their group were driven to an old English pub, Mead's Ale House, which was over the

Westminster Bridge on York Street. Bob obviously had eaten there before because he recommended the sizzling steak, fries, and a small salad. For himself and Karen, Al ordered a tankard of ale. It was unusual for him because he rarely took a drink of alcohol.

"I don't know why, but I just had an urge to order ale for us. I think some of the men on our tour know who I am. They're staring at me like they know what I did to Jefferson. I'm not comfortable in this pub. I have a funny feeling about this place."

"Al, you're letting your imagination run wild. I think you're getting a little paranoid. These are all nice people. Loosen up and enjoy your ale. It tastes good to me."

"Okay, I'll try, but I don't want to get cozy with anyone. We can be civil, but nothing more. Let's just try to keep to ourselves. You're right—the ale is good, and so is the food."

"Attention everyone," Bob bellowed, tapping his water glass. "Tomorrow morning, we are going to Buckingham Palace for the Changing of the Guard. We cannot tour the palace because the Queen is in residence. Be at the curb promptly at ten-thirty and dress warmly. The weather forecast is for a cold rain, and we will be outdoors for the entire ceremony. After lunch, we will proceed to the Houses of Parliament and sit in on a session in the House of Commons. I am certain that you will find the session most entertaining. As you can tell, tomorrow's schedule is very full. It is almost ten o'clock. Finish your dinners—our bus is waiting."

Karen still could not get used to the five-hour time difference.

"It's ten o'clock here in London. The kids are sound asleep. It's three in the morning at home. I hope my dad remembered to lock up the house properly and set the alarm."

"No, Karen. It's five o'clock back home. They are probably having their dinner now with your parents. Let me remind you again. We are five hours ahead of Buffalo time."

"I get it, Dear. I'm not used to this time yet. I'm so excited about tomorrow. I probably won't sleep a wink. I'm not sleepy. That ale must be a stimulant for me."

"You're not used to alcohol. Try to sleep anyhow. It will be morning before you know it. Goodnight, Hon."

"Al, do you have your raincoat ready? Bob said that it will be rainy tomorrow, and we'll be standing outside for over an hour."

"Yes, Hon. I hung it up. Don't worry about me. I'm not Jonathan. I'm perfectly capable of taking care of myself. You don't have to act like a mother hen in England."

"Do you think we'll see Queen Elizabeth? Wouldn't it be thrilling if she left the palace while we were standing there? Do you think she drives her own car around the palace grounds? It should be safe for her on her own property, don't you think?"

"Silly questions. What's going on with you, Karen? I'm no expert on royalty. Guys don't care about seeing queens. We just go along to please our wives."

"Oh, that must be like wives having to watch sports on TV because their husbands have control of the remote."

CHAPTER 8

After reliving the past two weeks in his mind and thinking about the next day's activities, in the early morning hours, sleep finally visited Al, but it was a disturbed sleep. Another dream was invading his subconscious, and as he tossed and turned, he was experiencing another horrific nightmare.

He was dining alone in a popular restaurant in Salisbury, England; the Lion's Tavern. At the top of the dinner menu, he could see the date: April 15, 1564. The dining room was crowded with weary businessmen. When the waiter came to take his order, he selected the roast ox with boiled potatoes and carrots and then tied a large white napkin around his neck. When his food was served to him, he picked up the knife and fork from the table. The meat was not especially tender. The piece which he cut was too large. Nevertheless, he put the meat in his mouth and began chewing. Suddenly, upon taking a breath, the meat was drawn into his throat and became lodged in his windpipe.

Not being able to breathe or talk, he thrashed his arms about wildly, grabbed his throat, and badly cut his head on the corner of the thick oak table as he fell to the floor, unnoticed. The diners were too engaged in noisy conversations to see what was happening near them. No one saw that he was choking, bleeding heavily, and dying. Nobody came to his aid.

At three o'clock, Al's kicking and choking noises awakened Karen. "Al, stop kicking me. Wake up! What's wrong? Are you okay?"

"Oh, Karen, it was another nightmare. I was in a restaurant in Salisbury, England, and I choked on a piece of roast ox. I couldn't get anyone's attention. All I could do was wave my arms about wildly. You woke me up as I was dying on the floor. Everything was going black."

"You're trembling, Al. Sit up. You're having another anxiety attack. I'll get you a glass of water. What should we do?"

"I don't know Karen—the dream was terrifying."

"These nightmares are becoming frequent and very frightening. You've put it off, and I let you, but when we get home, you're going to see Doc Wilson."

"I'll do what you say, Karen. I'm beginning to get more concerned, myself. Let's just try to enjoy our vacation and forget about this dream. Now, get back to sleep. It will be daylight soon."

Al got out of bed and went for a glass of water which Karen had forgotten to bring him. He felt better for the time being and sat up in bed for a while, wondering why he had experienced another scary dying dream.

Why am I dreaming about dying so often? he asked himself.

The ringing of the travel alarm clock awakened Karen at seven. She quickly turned it off so Al could sleep a little longer, got out of bed, and went into the bathroom to shower. Afterwards, she dressed and awakened Al, who was snoring loudly.

"Rise and shine, Al. We have a full schedule today. I'm finished in the bathroom—it's all yours. I need my morning cup of coffee, so don't be too long. What do you think we'll have for our first breakfast here?"

"I don't have a clue. As you know, my folks are British. Mom isn't much of a cook, and her idea of a breakfast is a piece of toast and jelly. Dad used to eat breakfast on his way to work each day."

Al was ready in fifteen minutes.

"How do you feel, Al? Have you recovered from that terrible dream last night? If you don't feel up to it, we can skip the tours today."

"Oh no, I want to go. I think I'm all right now, but I was scared last night. I was actually dying. It was so real. I even knew my name—Thomas Bentley."

"That's really weird. Let's forget the dream and go to breakfast."

"I'm famished. I think I burned up a lot of calories in that dream. Now I'm ready for my coffee."

They took the lift to the lobby and entered the restaurant that they had lunch in yesterday. First in their group to arrive, they gave their names to the hostess and were seated at a table reserved for them. Betty was again their waitress.

"Good morning, Mr. And Mrs. Chapman. How nice to be your server at the Lime Tree again. Would you like some coffee or tea to start your day?"

"We'll have coffee, Betty. Do we order breakfast?"

"No, sir. It is preordered for you. I'll bring it to your table in a few minutes."

"Thank you, Betty, but please bring our coffee now."

"Yes, madam. Right away."

"Don't expect a five-course meal, Karen. Remember, this is England."

Betty brought their coffee and, shortly afterward, a tray overflowing with plates of food: breads, eggs, turkey, sausage, bacon, cheeses, muffins, toast, jellies and jams.

"Al, do you believe this? Have you ever seen so much food? It's unbelievable."

"I think I'll eat my crow first. I don't think my mother is English."

They ate heartily but left much uneaten food on their plates. Karen suggested that they make sandwiches with the ham, cheese, and rye bread and have them for their supper later, instead of going out to eat.

"I'll ask Betty for a doggie bag."

Betty returned from the kitchen with two well-filled bags. "You had better tip Betty well, Al—she's a gem."

"I plan to. Let's finish our coffee and go back to our room until it's time to catch the bus. We'll have to rest a bit after eating all of this food."

After freshening up a bit and relaxing for a couple of hours, they were downstairs again at ten-thirty, eagerly looking forward to the Changing of the Guard at Buckingham Palace.

During the short bus ride, Bob stood at the front of the bus and used a microphone to give them some historical background about Buckingham Palace. Just as Al had guessed, Bob told them that he was a high school history teacher from East Aurora; a charming village not too far from Orchard Park. He seemed to enjoy treating the members of the group as students. He began his lecture.

"Buckingham Palace is a red brick structure with a white stone face located on a forty-eight-acre garden."

Bob's talk was cut short because the bus was already parked and ready to unload the passengers. Rain was gently falling as they waited for the ceremony to begin. Promptly at eleven o'clock, the new guard appeared, marching behind a brass band and moving to the forefront of the palace gate. The military pageantry was magnificent and lasted about half an hour. After the change was completed, and the new guard, in their bright red jackets, black trousers, and tall fuzzy black hats, were positioned, they stood erect and motionless. Some jokesters in the group were unsuccessful in their attempts to make the guards laugh or speak.

"Wasn't that thrilling, Al? And they're so tall."

"Yes, I was impressed by it all. And what discipline they exhibited. Nobody was able to get them to change their stoic expressions."

It was almost noon when they boarded the bus for lunch. Their destination was another pub called "The Cow." There, they had English ale and ox tongue cooked in milk.

"Eating ox tongue was not on my list of foods I want to eat on this trip, but I must say, it was very good," Al remarked. "I sure am getting my fill of ox on this vacation—awake or asleep."

Aboard the bus, Bob again addressed the group before their next stop.

"Let me have your attention everyone. Our next stop will be the Houses of Parliament, just a short ride from the palace. We have tickets for a session in the House of Commons today, which I thought you would find more interesting than the House of Lords. I know you will enjoy the session tremendously. Compare it with our Congress."

Their pre-purchased tickets enabled them to avoid standing in line to the Strangers Gallery of the House of Commons. The debate, which began at three o'clock, was about spitting in public. One speaker after another rose and shouted at his opponent at the top of his lungs. After one hour of listening to the unresolved oratory, the group left.

"Well, that certainly was different, wasn't it, Al? I think I like our congressional debates better, although they can be pretty heated at times too. At least they don't threaten one another."

"Oh, I kind of liked the cursing. And what did you think about the spitting demonstration? That was a riot, wasn't it?"

"It was gross. I guess they leave their manners at home."

After taking a short bus trip to view some historical points of interest in London; Big Ben, Saint Paul's Cathedral, and the Bank of England, they returned to their hotel room, weary but happy.

"I enjoyed everything today, Al—visiting and seeing all of those famous historical places we could only view on TV at home. But I'm very tired now. Let's stay in tonight and eat our leftovers from breakfast."

"Fabulous idea. Ham and cheese on rye sounds great. I guess age is beginning to catch up with us. We've done a lot of walking today. Maybe it's still jet lag."

"That's a good reason. What was your favorite part of today?"

"I'd vote for the House of Commons. Although they are rude to one another, it's still democracy at work. What did you like best, Karen?"

"I definitely would pick Buckingham Palace and the Changing of the Guard, even though we didn't see the Queen, I was impressed by the guards, who must stand at attention for long periods without moving a muscle. What do they do if they have to sneeze, I wonder? Did you see any pockets in their jackets where they could keep a handkerchief, or do they use their sleeves?"

"You're too much. How do you come up with these questions? It's a good thing that nobody else can hear you."

After all of this banter, they opened their doggie bags and were surprised to find that Betty had given them fresh rye bread, more ham and cheese, an apple, and a lemon pastry.

"Al, we have enough here for two more meals. By the way, did you know that the sandwich was invented in England by the Earl of Sandwich?"

"Stop it. Enough already."

"What kind of cheese is this, Al?"

"Gouda."

"I know it's good. I meant, where is it made?"

"We're beginning to sound like Abbot and Costello. Gouda cheese is made in the Netherlands, I believe."

"You're so smart. By the way, did you tip Betty well this morning?"

"'I already tipped her for the week."

"You're really a step ahead of me. I'm glad I brought you along and made you the boss. It gives me more time to needle you."

After finishing their meal, they settled in the easy chairs and turned on the telly. The subtle British humor had them laughing uncontrollably.

"I think these programs are a riot. The actors are so poker faced, that it takes me a while to get the jokes."

"Several British shows are on Fox at home, Al. When you retire, you'll have time to watch them with me."

"We'll see. Don't push me. I may have other plans."

"I like staying in at night instead of going out to dinner with the group, Al. Where are we scheduled to go tomorrow?"

"Let's see. Saturday, it's Westminster Abbey in the morning and the Tower of London after lunch. Sounds like another big day of walking for us. We better get to bed. It's almost eleven o'clock."

"I am a bit tired, but it's only 6:00 p.m. back home. Hope the kids are working on their homework."

"You finally got the time right."

"I did? That was a lucky guess. Goodnight, Al. Pleasant dreams."

"I certainly hope they are. Good night, Karen."

CHAPTER 9

Time was passing quickly. It was already Saturday. Everyone was on time for the bus which would take them for a visit to Westminster Abbey, a symbol of English history. With great anticipation of where they were about to tread, they entered the shrine where rulers such as William the Conqueror, Henry VIII, Queen Victoria, and Queen Elizabeth II were crowned. It is here that rulers from Edward the Confessor to George VI are buried. The poets Chaucer, Shelley, and Milton are also entombed here, as well as the scientists Newton and Darwin. Many of the tourists found themselves reliving the English Literature, History, and Science classes of their high school and college days. Subjects that were boring to them then now held their undivided attention.

"Karen, I never liked reading about these old boys, but being here where they are buried has revived my interest in them. I'll appreciate Chaucer more now than before when I slept through English Lit class."

"I feel the same way, Al. I'd like to read about Darwin's theory of evolution when we get home. This tour really rejuvenates the brain and makes one think."

Lunch was at Le Gavroche, where they were served lobster in champagne sauce, roasted herb potatoes, white asparagus, and chocolate mousse, accompanied by French cookies.

"I think I died and went to heaven. This is a gourmand's dream."

"Watch it, Karen, I'll do all of the dying for us on this trip, but I kind of miss the ox."

The next stop after lunch was the Tower of London, which is not one but many connecting structures. The highlight for Karen was a visit to the Jewel House, where they waited in line to see royal robes, swords, and crowns studded with precious gems. The Imperial State Crown, worn by Queen Elizabeth II to State affairs, contains thousands of diamonds and other jewels. Karen was thrilled to be so close to the Crown worn by British royalty, past and present.

"It's so beautiful, but it must weigh a ton. How can the Queen hold her head up without tipping over?"

Bob overheard Karen's question and answered: "Practice."

Afterward, they were guided through the different towers and were shown various torture instruments used on prisoners over the centuries. There were plaques marking the spots where famous historical figures were executed. Al became more and more uncomfortable as the tour continued along dark stairways and corridors. He leaned against a stone wall for support as the group was shown the spot where Anne Boleyn, one of Henry the Eighth's wives, was beheaded.

"Hon, I feel sick from all of this gory stuff. It gives me an eerie feeling to stand here where people were executed centuries ago. It's like déjà vu. I need to get some fresh air."

"This is becoming all too frequent with you, Al. Your face is losing its color and you're perspiring. Let's get out of here and find a place for you to rest."

After walking a few minutes, they found a bench to sit on.

"Here we go again, like a broken record. We must find out what's causing these attacks. By my count, there have been five—two dreams, the Maid of the Mist, the Skylon, and this one today. Thus far, you have bounced back quickly from each of them, but I'm worried that you're paying a price, either physically, emotionally, or both. You said that today's episode was like déjà vu. What did you mean by that?"

"When we walked along the corridors, into dungeons, and up and down stairs, I felt the horror and pain that the prisoners must have experienced."

"That's awful. Just try to forget about these things until we get home and see Doc. Look, our group is boarding the bus. Let's go. We don't want to be left behind."

"I'm right with you. This is the last place on earth where I want to be stranded."

In their hotel room a short time later, they discussed their plans for the evening.

"Al, I'm still full from lunch. Let's skip dinner tonight and go shopping instead. We must buy something for my parents and the kids. I've heard about a department store called Harrods, which is supposed to be terrific. They have a wide variety of quality merchandise spread over several floors. There will be lots to choose from. Did you know that the British invented the department store?"

"No, I wasn't aware of that. You are just full of little facts unknown to others—a virtual encyclopedia of trivia."

"Okay, mister wise guy, let's find out how we get to Harrods."

Betty was working at the desk in the lobby and gave them directions to the store. "You're within walking distance. Turn right out of the hotel and keep walking. You'll be there in about ten minutes Be careful—you can spend a small fortune there."

Betty's directions were perfect. They were inside of the store in less than ten minutes, but once inside, they did not know which way to go.

"This place is huge—I could spend days here. It's a shopper's dream."

"Don't get carried away, Dear. What are we looking for?"

"I'd like to look for cashmere sweaters for everyone. We should get great buys on them here. They're so expensive in the States—probably twice what they are here."

They walked for about fifteen minutes and, after taking the escalator, finally located the sweater department on the third floor. Karen found exactly what she was looking for; cardigans for her mother and Melissa and pullovers for her father and Jonathan.

"Just feel of them, Al—they are so soft. Aren't the colors and patterns gorgeous? Everybody should be thrilled with what we've selected. Let's each get a sweater for ourselves too."

"I've had my eye on this brown pullover. It should go well with my tan slacks."

"And I love this lovely pale blue cardigan that will complement my navy blue skirt."

"Is that all we need, Karen?"

"No, not quite. As we came in on the first floor, we passed the ribbon counter. I'd like to get a variety of colored ribbons for gift-wrapping our Christmas packages at home."

The ribbon counter was on the first floor near the entrance. Karen knew exactly what she wanted and selected several rolls of satin ribbons: red, green, gold, blue, and silver.

"These are wonderful for making bows. Before we know it, Christmas will be here."

"Are we finished now, Karen? It's getting late—almost five-thirty."

"Yes, I think so. We can check out now and walk back to the hotel."

They paid for their selections, and after one and a half hours, they were back in their hotel room, where Karen surprised Al by announcing:

"You aren't going to believe this, but I'm getting a wee bit hungry. It's almost six o'clock, and I've worked up an appetite walking. How would you like to go someplace just for dessert?"

"Dessert sounds great. I was wondering when you were going to bring up the subject of food again. I'm ready. Let's go looking for a place."

Within ten minutes, they were outside hailing a cab without knowing where they were going.

"We can ask the cabbie for a good place to get a pastry or some ice cream," Al suggested as a cab pulled to the curb to pick them up. They climbed into the back seat and Al leaned over the seat to ask the driver if he knew of a place that had just desserts.

"I sure do, mister. There's a place not too far from here called 'Nico Central' that has all kinds of desserts. It's a favorite of a lot of tourists."

"We'll try it. Take us there, please."

Nico's was crowded; they waited for a table for fifteen minutes. A waitress wearing a tight black mini skirt and a long-sleeved white blouse showed them to a marble-topped table and handed them one huge menu.

"Al, this is fantastic. Look at the choices; every flavor of ice cream, eclairs, tortes, French pastries. That cab driver knew what he was talking about. What are you going to have? Pick something exotic that you'd never get at home."

"You know I'm an ice cream guy. I like the sound of the nougat ice cream with almonds, blackberry sauce, and whipped cream."

"I'd like to try a French pastry. The caramelized lemon tart with lemon sauce and a meringue topping sounds intriguing."

Shortly after their order was placed, two monstrous servings were brought to their table. Wide eyed, they couldn't wait to try what they had selected.

"This is heavenly, Al. Take your spoon and try mine. I've never had anything quite like this before. This pastry is so delicate—it melts in your mouth."

"All right, if you'll try my ice cream. Give me your spoon. You'll have to help me eat this eventually, since you're the one with the sweet tooth."

"How many calories do you think are in these two desserts?"

"Thousands, Karen."

"We can diet when we get home. Enjoy this moment. Which do you like better?"

"Mine—yours is too tart."

They went on gorging themselves without giving any thought to the horror experienced by Al earlier in the day. At least, neither let it be known to the other that they were thinking about it. After finishing every bit of their desserts, they called a cab and returned to their hotel, exhausted and ready for bed.

"Tomorrow, we have an all-day trip to Stonehenge. Are you sure you're up to it, Al? If not, I can take the bus alone. I've been looking forward to this ever since I saw it on our itinerary, and I don't want to skip it."

"Sure, I'll go with you. What is Stonehenge? I never heard of it."

"You never heard of Stonehenge? It's an area near Salisbury where there is a mysterious arrangement of huge stones which date back thousands of years. No one is certain of their meaning or how the stones got there."

"Sounds like nothing I'm interested in, but I'll keep you company. Did you say it was near Salisbury? Now I'm getting worried. Remember in my dream? I died there."

"Don't worry about it; we're not going there."

"I hope not; that choking experience was too real to be just a dream."

"Everything will be all right, you'll see. I'm just thinking about seeing Stonehenge and am anxious to see those stones close up. This will be another highlight of the trip."

"Maybe I'll learn something tomorrow just to please you, Karen."

It was eleven-fifteen when they turned out the light and said goodnight. Karen prayed that Al would have an uninterrupted night's sleep. She didn't want him to know, but she was very concerned.

That dream Al had last night was terrifying for him. And then another anxiety attack at the Tower of London frightened both of us. I don't want to push him tomorrow at Stonehenge. Maybe the bus ride will be restful for him, and if he's not interested in the stones, I'll let him wait for me in the bus.

CHAPTER 10

It was a beautiful warm sunny Sunday in October; a perfect day for a bus ride to Wiltshire County, in south central England. About twenty people on the tour were making the trip to Stonehenge; those tourists who knew about the mysterious stones.

Al and Karen tried to relax amidst the unending chatter of the people. It seemed to the Chapmans that the group became noisier the longer the tour lasted. The bus traveled west from London, through areas which could not be described as breathtakingly beautiful. However, the fossil-bearing cliffs of the region kept the tourists' interest. The bus entered Salisbury, a city that Bob told them could trace it's origin back thousands of years and which boasted the famous Salisbury Cathedral. It was evident that the city was of major significance as their bus meandered along its charming narrow streets. Hundreds of tourists walked along the sidewalks, admiring the ancient architecture, and shopping for souvenirs. Al was quiet as usual. All of a sudden, he cried out.

"Karen, this is it—the place I dreamt about. I saw it in my dream. The restaurant was in that building along that side street over there. I'd recognize it anywhere."

"That's weird, Al. The dream was a déjà vu experience all right. This proves it."

Bob interrupted with an announcement from the front of the bus. "Folks, we're stopping here for lunch at the Lion's

Tavern on Dover Street, a short walk from where our bus will let you off. I've reserved a private room for our group. As usual, the meal has been preordered. Wait inside for me."

"We're going to the restaurant in my dream, Karen. I remember it was called the Lion's Tavern too. I don't want to eat here. I'm afraid to go near the place. You go in and eat—I'll wait in the bus."

"No, I think we should go in there together, and you should confront this fear head on. I'm with you and you are going to be extra careful eating. Nothing is going to happen to you. I won't let it. Just remain calm."

"You're right, but I'm still anxious about going in there."

Inside, just beyond the entrance, they could see the main dining room with old oak tables and chairs. Paintings of the Renaissance period adorned the walls. The waiters were dressed in black trousers and white shirts open at the neck. There was nothing medieval about their garb, and they all had short hair.

"This is it, I'm sure. That's the dining room, just like I saw it in my dream."

Just then, Bob appeared at the door.

"Okay, everyone, follow our host to the dining room."

A small balding middle-aged man ushered the group to a modem looking room with maple wood tables covered by red tablecloths. Al was relieved to be in unfamiliar surroundings, and had no trouble downing the roasted partridge served to him.

"Chew your food thoroughly, Al, and don't talk with your mouth full."

"Yes, Mother Karen, I feel fine. I even like the food this time."

Their young waiter was very friendly, speaking to everyone in a casual manner, as he refilled the water glasses. He looked at Al and addressed him.

"Are you enjoying your visit to England, sir? Is your group going on to Stonehenge?"

"Yes, we are looking forward to it," Karen answered, because she knew that Al was not paying attention.

"It's a bit spooky up there, you know. It makes you wonder about the ground you walk on every day. I don't know if I believe any of those things they talk about there."

"I'm sure it will be very interesting anyway. I've read a lot about the stones, and I'm very anxious to see them for real."

Without any more interruptions, they finished their meal and, after one hour, were on the bus again. Once again, Bob stood up and gave them additional information about Stonehenge as if he were lecturing a high school class of teenagers.

"Folks, Stonehenge is an ancient monument made up of huge stones, placed in various positions. It was thought to have been built in stages, starting in 2800 B.C. There are many theories about who might have arranged these mammoth monoliths and why. Some archaeologists believe that there is a religious connection. Perhaps ancient druids might have used the structure as a temple. A few scientists have theorized, however, that the stones represent some sort of astronomical instrument, because of the way the sun shines through the gaps between some of the stones during the equinoxes and solstices. But it has been almost 5,000 years since its construction, and the earth's orbit has shifted slightly, thus negating this theory. The stones could have been used to predict eclipses, or perhaps they were some type of calendar. No one living today really knows. You will see that the four series of stones are enclosed by a circular ditch about three hundred feet in diameter. Within one of these series, there appears to be an altar stone. As you walk around the site, ponder this question. 'How did these ancient people, lacking our present technology, lift and arrange these huge stones; some weighing forty tons and standing five feet high?'"

"It seems to me, that the same question is asked about the pyramids in Egypt."

"You are paying attention, Al. I'm proud of you."

The bus arrived at the Stonehenge parking lot. Bob again spoke to the group. "We'll get off the bus here, folks. You can walk the short distance to the stones, examine them, and be back here in one hour."

"Al, let's hurry over there. Isn't this exciting?"

"You go ahead and I'll catch up with you at the stones. I don't like crowds."

Karen was able to get a close up look at the monoliths and was amazed at their enormous size. She was gazing up at one of the larger ones, when Al joined her. They walked together a bit and were looking at one of the altar stones when a heavyset gray-haired woman in her sixties approached them and spoke.

"Excuse me, folks. My name is Myra Johnson and I'm on the tour with you. I've seen you in the hotel and on some of the trips, and I just wanted to tell you how pretty I think your daughter is. Do you hire a sitter when you go out late in London?"

"What are you saying, Mrs. Johnson? Our daughter is not with us. She's back home in Orchard Park with her grandparents," Karen responded sharply.

"Oh, I'm so sorry. It's just that I've seen a little blonde girl standing with you. She was here a moment ago, sir, but she's gone now. I must be mistaken. Perhaps she's with another group."

"You certainly are mistaken, lady. Please leave us alone and stop watching us," Al shot back at her rudely.

Surprised by Al's behavior, Karen had a sudden flashback. She remembered that Melissa had told her about a little blonde girl whom she had seen near her father at the Skylon and again at the last football game.

"Could this Johnson woman be seeing the same girl? Who was she, and why was she following Al? Could she possibly be British? And why couldn't she and Al see her?"

Karen temporarily put these thoughts out of her mind, as she and Al then decided to return to the bus. Not surprisingly, they were the first aboard for the trip back to London.

During the ride back to the Hotel, Karen sat silently, thinking about Al's déjà vu experience at the Lion's Tavern, Myra Johnson, and the little blonde girl. Al seemed unperturbed by the day's events. But he continued to avoid the others in the group in an unfriendly manner, which Karen was beginning to get used to. Strangely, Myra Johnson was not on the bus, and Karen could not recall ever having seen her at the hotel or on any of the trips either.

When they were back in their hotel room Al suggested that they order a fish and chips dinner from 'Chippies' around the corner from the hotel. Karen thought she would like to try it, so Al called the desk and asked to have the meals brought to their room.

"Of course, Mr. Chapman, we'll order them right away and have Betty bring them up to you in about twenty minutes."

Within fifteen minutes, Betty was at the door carrying two meals wrapped in newspapers. With a smile on her face, she handed them to Al.

"Thank you, Betty. Please put these on our bill."

Al tipped her three shillings. She gratefully smiled again.

"Thank you, Mr. Chapman. I hope you and the missus enjoy your fish and chips."

They were anxious to remove the newspapers. Inside were two greasy brown bags containing large Icelandic codfish, fried potatoes, gravy, peas, and a pickle.

"What do you think of this, Al?"

"Well, it sure isn't like Schwabel's Friday night fish fry, is it?"

"No, it isn't. How do you like these mushy peas?"

"They're okay, but I miss coleslaw and macaroni salad, Karen."

"And pumpernickel bread and butter and dessert. This is okay, but we've done it now. Once is enough for me."

"Do you think we're being too picky?"

"I don't think so. It's probably because we're getting a bit homesick. Where are we going tomorrow, Al? I hope it's someplace where we can sit back and relax. We've been on the go constantly. You can look at just so many ancient buildings and relics before you get tired."

"I'm surprised to hear you say that, Karen. I thought you liked relics. Let me check our itinerary. Tomorrow, we're taking a luncheon boat cruise along the River Thames to Greenwich and back. We'll see a lot of the same buildings again, but this time, from a boat. I think I'll like that better than riding in a bus and looking out of a window."

"This should be a restful trip though. And we're going to Greenwich, where every new day begins in the western hemisphere."

"You know, Karen, it's another boat ride. Remember the last one on the Maid of the Mist? I was terribly sick and thought I was dying."

"Yes, but that was in rough water. We'll be seated on this boat, and it will be moving slowly along the shore. There is no comparison between the two. Don't worry about it."

"I hope you're right."

"I am," Karen emphasized. "This is the River Thames, not the Falls."

But now she too was apprehensive about another boat ride and worried to herself.

It seems to me that we have a crisis every day on this trip so far, either a nightmare, an anxiety attack or a strange woman seeing a strange invisible little girl. This trip is beginning to turn into one long nightmare. I just can't wait until it's over and we're safely home, and Al can see Doc.

Al looked over at Karen. He could read the worry on her face, and thought to himself.

I know I'm keeping Karen from having a good time on this trip. Tomorrow, I'm going to try and enjoy myself. I'm glad that we'll be going home in three more days. What would we have done if this had been a two-week tour; a fortnight?

CHAPTER 11

Monday morning was cloudy, cool, and misting slightly; the way London weather is supposed to be. After a leisurely breakfast of scones, jellies and jams, and coffee, there was some time to read the morning papers. At eleven forty-five, the anxious travelers boarded their bus for the luncheon cruise along the River Thames. Big Ben was just chiming twelve noon as the bus pulled up to the Westminster Pier, where a sleek motor launch, the Silver Bonito, was docked. Al and Karen walked up the ramp of the boat and took two seats on the starboard side for the downriver trip. At approximately twelve fifteen, the boat pulled away from shore and began the four-hour cruise which would take them to Greenwich and back.

Soon after, lunch was brought to them on trays, airline style. The Chapmans were not surprised to see roasted chicken with herb sauce, parsley potatoes, yellow beans, brownies with anglais sauce, and a pot of hot English tea.

"This is a pleasant way to enjoy the beautiful view of some of London's historical landmarks, isn't it, Al? And we don't have to walk in and out of buildings."

"It certainly is much more comfortable than sitting on a bus for several hours just to get to see some rocks. And the food isn't bad either."

Off in the distance, on the port side, as they passed beneath the Waterloo and Blackmar Bridges, they could see Saint Paul's

Cathedral coming into view. A short time later, the Bank of England appeared.

"We saw Saint Paul's Cathedral and the Bank of England on our bus tour of London the other day. Remember, Al?"

"I don't remember much about that ride. I must have been daydreaming, or else my eyes were still recovering from the dazzle of the crown jewels."

"Or maybe you had other things on your mind, like the nightmare the night before."

"Could be."

They sat quietly, taking their time eating, and enjoying the scenery and smooth ride. Farther along, Bob directed the group's attention to certain points of interest, as the boat approached them.

"Folks, coming up on the left is the new London Bridge. Its predecessor now resides in an Arizona desert—just the place for a bridge. And beyond that bridge is the Tower Bridge, which you saw the other day.

"Look, Al, there's the Tower of London. It looks a lot less threatening from this boat, than it did when we walked about it."

"I disagree. Those dungeons and plaques marking the spots where people were executed were not on my list of ten best things to see in London. Why do people enjoy that stuff? It's sickening."

Karen remained silent as the boat wove its way along the ribbon-like river route, heading for Greenwich, about four miles from Westminster. East meets West at the Greenwich meridian: zero degrees latitude and zero degrees longitude. Bob mentioned that, on New Year's Eve, there was a huge millennium celebration there because it was the first place in the Western Hemisphere to reach the year 2000. After being told the correct time, everyone set their watch to Greenwich time. At that point, the Silver Bonito slowly turned and began its upriver trek toward Westminster. Now, Al and Karen would have the sights on their side of the craft, although Al apparently cared little about seeing anything. He was getting a little fidgety and stood up to stretch his legs.

"Karen, I'm thirsty. There's a cash bar aft. Would you like something?"

"No thanks. I'm okay. Get a drink for yourself. You look like you could use a pick-me-up. It's been a pretty rough week for you."

Al left Karen and headed for the bar. Since there were no other customers, the redheaded young bartender was eager to take Al's order.

"Good afternoon, sir. What can I get for you?"

"I feel like having a 'Rusty Nail,' lad."

"Coming right up, sir. You're an American, aren't you?"

"Yes, I am. How did you know? My accent? Clothing? Haircut?"

"Yes, all of those, but we call this drink a Kilt Lifter, a name coined by our Canadian cousins."

"I like that name better. I'll remember it the next time I'm in Canada. It's only an hour from Buffalo, where I live."

"Oh, I know about Buffalo; the Bills lost four Super Bowls in a row."

"That's right—the home of the Buffalo Bills."

Al began sipping his drink. He glanced out of the window and looked up just as the boat was passing beneath the Waterloo Bridge for the second time on the trip. Suddenly, his hand began to tremble and some of his drink splashed down the front of his jacket. As with all previous attacks of this nature, it was difficult for Al to breathe, and perspiration began forming on his forehead.

"Mister, are you all right? You look like you've seen a ghost. Lord knows we have plenty of them in England, although I haven't seen any aboard the Silver Bonito. Anything is possible, I suppose. Here, mister, use some of these cocktail napkins to wipe your jacket."

Al did not answer. He took a handkerchief from his jacket pocket and wiped beads of perspiration from his brow. Then very abruptly, without saying a word, he left the rest of his drink on the bar, walked away, and returned to Karen.

"What took you so long? How did your jacket get so wet?"

"I was talking to the bartender when the boat lurched and I spilled my Kilt Lifter."

"You spilled your what?"

"My Kilt Lifter. That's what they call a Rusty Nail in England. The young bartender told me that the name originated in Canada."

"That's a riot. I'll have to tell the gals in my bridge club that one."

Al remained quiet for the remainder of the trip back to the Westminster Pier, staring out of the window but focusing on nothing in particular.

The Silver Bonito docked at four-thirty. Everyone was happy as they boarded their waiting bus for the ride back to the hotel. By five o'clock, the Chapmans were in their room, discussing plans for the evening.

"Karen, I want to go home. Let's skip the rest of the trip and try to catch a plane out of here tomorrow morning. There's something about England that makes me feel uneasy; the dream, the déjà vu experience, Myra Johnson, the Tower of London. It's all so weird. I'm apprehensive about every place we visit."

"Do you know what you're saying? We have only one more day here. We'd have to pay full price for two one-way airplane tickets, and all flights are probably booked anyhow. Can't you stick it out just one more day?"

"I don't care about the money. I just want to get out of here now. One more day here could be my last. I'm going down to the lobby and talk to Bob. All right?"

"You're the boss. Remember?"

"That's right. I'm the boss, and we're going home."

Al caught sight of Bob as he was about to leave the hotel. "Bob, wait up. I have a favor to ask of you."

"Sure, Al, what's up?"

"Could you possibly get us seats on a plane back to New York tomorrow morning? I'm not feeling well, and I want to get back to see my doctor as soon as possible. I know it's an impossible request, but maybe we'll get lucky."

"I doubt whether I can get you anything on this short notice. All flights are probably booked solid, but I'll do my best. We might get a last-minute cancellation if a couple decides to extend their vacation a few more days."

Behind the reservation desk, Bob began calling every airline without success. "As I thought, they're full up, Al."

"Damn, I thought we'd be lucky."

"Just a minute. British Airway's line was busy. I forgot to call them back. I'll try them again."

He dialed the number and heard the voice at the other end say, "Cheerio, British Airways. May I help you?"

"I hope so, sir. Would you perhaps have two seats on any flight leaving for New York City tomorrow evening?"

"No, sir. All flights out of here for tomorrow are completely booked. However, a gent just called and cancelled two tickets leaving tonight at seven, but they're $2,000 a seat."

"They have two seats for $4,000, leaving at seven tonight. You'll have to hurry to make it."

"I'll take them. Are the seats gold plated?"

"No, they're first class. You'll be in New York in about five hours. It's very deluxe. You'll love it."

"Here's my credit card, Bob. Tell them to hold the seats. We'll be there as soon as we can pack and get a cab."

After all arrangements were finished, Al thanked Bob for all he had done for them.

"You've been magnificent, Bob. I'm sorry to have to leave the tour early."

"I'll have a cab waiting for you at six. Is there anything else I can do for you, Al?"

"Well, do you have $4,000? Karen is going to kill me when she finds out what I paid for the tickets."

"Good luck, Al. I can't help you there. Have a safe trip. It's been a pleasure having you and Karen on the tour. Hope to see you again."

Back in the hotel room, Karen was waiting anxiously, when Al returned all excited.

"Start packing. We leave at seven tonight, and we have until six o'clock to pack and be downstairs to catch a cab."

"Tonight? How much did it cost?"

"We'll be in New York at about 7:00 p.m."

"That's fine, but how much is it costing?"

"I paid $4,000."

"You paid $4,000 for two one-way tickets." Are you crazy? You just paid a $50,000 fine to the NFL. The yearly tuition for both of our kids at Saint Margaret's is $4,000. Why in the world do we have to rush out of here like a hurricane is coming?"

"Karen, I have the feeling that I'll die here if I stay one more day. Let's pack."

"What about my parents? Shouldn't we call them to let them know of the change?"

"I'll call them as soon as we reach New York. No need to worry them."

Somehow, they got everything packed and were at the curb waiting for the cab at ten minutes to six.

"Do we have everything?"

"I hope so. It's too late to go back now. Here's our cab."

There was little traffic to Heathrow Airport. At six-thirty, they were at the British Airways desk checking their luggage and picking up their tickets. After passing through the security check, they walked to British Airways Gate 43, where passengers were already boarding. A flight attendant greeted them and took their tickets.

"Welcome aboard, Mr. and Mrs. Chapman. You have seats four and six on the left, up in front. Put your carry-ons in the overhead," she informed them.

"How did she know our names, Al?"

"They're printed on the tickets. Gee, Karen, the seats are soft leather and very comfortable, but I would think that for $4,000, I would have had more leg and shoulder room. It's a bit of a disappointment. I'll have trouble sleeping."

"For $4,000, we could sleep at the Ritz for a week. You're a huge man, Al."

Before takeoff, a young black-haired flight attendant introduced herself to them.

"Good evening, Mr. and Mrs. Chapman. I'm Jackie, your flight attendant. We will be airborne in a few minutes. Please fasten your seatbelts. Would you like to order a cocktail before dinner?"

"Yes, Jackie, I'd like a Kilt Lifter, please."

"The same for me," Karen replied, trying to stifle a big grin on her face.

"I will bring your drinks and some hors d'oeuvres as soon as we have reached our cruising altitude," Jackie said, as she went to her takeoff seat behind the pilots' cabin.

"Hold on, Karen. We're taking off."

"Oh, Al, I'm scared. I can't move. I'm pinned in my seat."

The plane climbed steeply, almost straight up, after they left the ground. They felt the pull of gravity holding them back in their seats. Cruising speed was attained within minutes. They were then able to relax and enjoy the flight.

"Wasn't that something, Karen? I felt like an astronaut going up in a rocket."

"Well, I won't forget that for a while. And I'm the one who is afraid to go on a rollercoaster. That was some takeoff."

True to her word, Jackie returned with their cocktails and a tray of unbelievable appetizers; shrimp, stuffed mushrooms, and assorted softened French cheeses. She placed the food on a linen-covered tray between them.

"Al, just look at all of this food. Eat, drink, and be merry, because for the rest of our lives we will be eating macaroni and cheese."

"Oh, things aren't that bad. We'll be okay, even if I retire."

They finished their drinks and ordered another as the plane sped toward New York.

Jackie appeared again at eight o'clock to announce that dinner would be served in a few minutes. She placed a hot wet linen towel on their trays for them to use to freshen up.

"Would you like wine or champagne with your dinner, Mr. Chapman?"

"We'll have the champagne, Jackie. Do you have Moet et Chandon?" Al asked.

"Yes, sir—vintage 2000. Will that be all right?"

"That will be fine. You may bring it now, please."

"Where did you learn about French champagne? All we've ever had is New York State's finest at eight dollars a bottle."

"I look at all of the expensive champagnes when I'm shopping at Premier Liquors, and I remembered this name. It's about forty dollars a bottle."

"You are brilliant for a football player."

Jackie brought the champagne, showed it to Al for his approval, uncorked the bottle, gave Al the cork to smell, and poured a sample for him to taste.

"This will be fine, Jackie."

They toasted one another, sat back and relaxed, sipping their champagne and waiting for their dinners to be served. Once again, Jackie appeared but this time brought their hot dinners to their seats.

"Be careful, madam and sir, the plates are very hot."

She uncovered the plates and placed them on their trays. Then she poured each another glass of champagne from the bottle she was keeping up front.

"Please put your light on if you need anything. Enjoy your dinners."

"Thank you, Jackie. Everything is just fine," Al responded.

"Duckling with orange sauce, wild rice, white asparagus, and a small salad of hearts of artichoke on a lettuce leaf with poppy seed dressing. I guess this will just have to do."

They both savored every mouthful. Seeing that they were finished eating, Jackie returned to refill their champagne glasses once more, and asked.

"Would you like dessert now? We have Bananas Foster and Chocolate Mousse."

"I think I'll have the Chocolate Mousse, Jackie, to satisfy my craving for something sweet, and with coffee, please," Karen stated.

"No coffee for me, Jackie," Al added. "I'd just like a Hennessy cognac."

After she had finished the last spoonful of chocolate mousse and the last sip of coffee, Karen emoted. "Divine, absolutely divine. Everything was perfect. This flight has been an unforgettable experience. It's a wonder I'm not dancing in the aisle."

"May I have this dance, my Dear?"

"Remember, Gene Kelly, you're seeing Doc as soon as he can take you."

"I will. I promise you."

It was now 3:00 p.m., New York time. As their plane continued westward, Karen was asleep. Al remembered that they hadn't called Karen's parents. It was almost dinner time and he didn't want to worry them, so he decided to wait until they were in Buffalo and then call from the airport. He stretched his legs out in front of him the best he could and reclined his seat, but he could not sleep. At six-thirty, he awakened Karen to let her know that they would be landing at Kennedy Airport in half an hour. Jackie brought them each a cup of hot coffee and a croissant with assorted jellies and jams. Karen was not in the mood for more food.

"My stomach isn't ready yet. I'll just have coffee, Jackie."

"I'll eat yours, Karen. I'm a bit hungry. It's our dinner time here now, you know."

"Be my guest, but our diets start tomorrow."

The plane landed at 7:00 p.m., New York time. They passed through Customs without any problems and immediately went to the US Airways desk to get tickets to Buffalo. Luckily, the next flight out was scheduled to depart at 8:00 p.m. Al paid for the tickets with his charge card, hoping there was enough money in his account to cover their cost. There was no problem. With a little time before their flight, they decided to get a snack at a McDonald's restaurant on the way to their departure gate. Karen was now hungry and ordered coffee and a cheeseburger. Al just had coffee. It was eight o'clock when they walked to the Gate and boarded US Airways Flight 650 for Buffalo.

"We'll be in Buffalo in forty-five minutes. I'll call your parents from the plane."

Chapman home at eight-thirty, and Evelyn answered.

"Hello, Evelyn, it's Al. We're on our way home from New York and will be landing at Buffalo Niagara International Airport at eight forty-five."

"What's wrong, Al? Are you and Karen all right?"

"We're fine. We just missed you and the kids and decided to cut our trip short and come home. We'll catch a cab at the airport and should be home about nine-thirty. Don't tell the kids. We'll surprise them. How are you all?"

"We're all okay. The children have been wonderful. We'll be waiting for you."

At nine forty-five, the taxicab pulled into the Chapman's driveway. The front door of the house flew open, and Jonathan and Melissa ran out to greet their parents. Evelyn and Joe stood inside in the doorway.

"Why aren't you kids in bed?" Karen asked.

"It's too early for bed," Jonathan answered.

"We were watching a movie with Grandpa," Melissa explained as she hugged her mother. "It was called *Casablanca*, and it was pretty good for an old movie."

The Chapman family was together again, and Karen just had to say, "There's no place like home."

CHAPTER 12

Joe and Jonathan helped Al carry the luggage inside while Evelyn and Melissa held open the door. There were smiles all around.

"Oh, Al, why did we leave our beautiful home and family? I'm content to stay home until the kids put us in a nursing home."

"No nursing home, Karen. We'll hire help to care for us in our old age."

"After what we spent on this trip? Dream on."

"No more dreams."

After all of the luggage had been carried inside of the house, everyone had questions to ask the weary travelers.

"How was England? Did you get to see the Queen?" Evelyn asked.

"No, we didn't, but we saw the Changing of the Guard at Buckingham Palace."

"Mom, you're home a day early. What happened? Are you sick?"

"No, Melissa, we got homesick and missed you kids. We're okay; just tired." Jonathan stood by waiting his turn to speak.

"What did you bring us?"

"Jonathan," Al scolded, "can't you wait until we at least have our coats off and have unpacked? Stop thinking of yourself."

"Karen, your father and I must be going. We have things at home to attend to," Evelyn interrupted.

"Oh, Mom, I'm sorry. In all of this excitement, we didn't give you a chance to tell us anything. Were there any problems? Did the kids behave? Are you and Dad all right? You must be exhausted. They're a handful to take care of, I know."

"The children were wonderful. We enjoyed being with them. And they were a big help to us. You should be very proud of them."

"I'm relieved to hear that," Al commented. "They were a big help? How did you manage that?"

"We just asked them, and they were happy to help the old folks, as Jonathan called us. We're going to miss being with them."

"We really appreciate what you did, Mom and Dad. We couldn't have gone on the trip without your help. I'll bet that you've spoiled them rotten."

"That's what grandparents are for," Joe added. "It was a pleasure. You know that we love the children and don't see them enough. Now, we really have to be going."

"But we have gifts for both of you."

"Keep them. Bring them over later in the week. It will give us a chance to talk."

"Did you hear that, Melissa? Secrets. They can't talk in front of us."

"I think you're right, Jonathan. Now we really can start worrying whether one or both of our parents is sick and dying."

"Don't be ridiculous, kids. There are no secrets. Mom, I'll call you. Thanks again, for everything. We love you both."

"Bye-bye. We love you too."

They left the Chapmans standing in the doorway, and waved, as their blue 2000 Buick Riviera backed down the driveway and onto the street.

"Okay, gifts were mentioned. What did you bring us?"

"Well, Jonathan, here you are—a beautiful cashmere sweater. And, Melissa, here's one for you. They'll be perfect for school."

"Is that all?" Jonathan groused.

"It's beautiful, Mom and Dad. Thank you so much. I love it."

"You're welcome Melissa," Karen responded, as Melissa hugged and kissed both of her parents. Jonathan stood watching.

"And, Jonathan, do you like your sweater?" Al asked.

"Clothes are not presents. Toys are presents," Jonathan complained and stormed upstairs and slammed his door.

"Isn't it great to be home, Karen? Nothing has changed, has it?"

"I guess not. Melissa, what did you do while your grandparents were here? I'll bet they spoiled you. Did you do your homework every day?"

"We had to do our homework right away when we got home from school. Then, we'd have supper, do the dishes, and sit in the den and watch movies that Grandpa had rented. Oh, and we'd have ice cream or popcorn during the movie."

"It sounds like you had a good time."

"Yes, it was fine, but we missed you, Mom and Dad."

Quietly, without being noticed, Jonathan had returned to the living room, feeling sorry for the way he had acted, and joined in the conversation.

"I tried on the sweater, Mom and Dad, and I like it. It looks great on me. Thank you very much. It's better than toys."

"You're welcome, Jonathan," Karen answered. "Now I want to go upstairs and unpack and then do the laundry. Al and Jonathan, bring the bags upstairs, please."

"No problem, Mom."

Karen started to unpack when she remembered that she had to call Doc Wilson. It was almost ten o'clock, but she hoped he would still be in his office. Jonathan had gone downstairs again, and so she called from the bedroom.

"Doctor Wilson's office," Molly answered.

"Hello, Molly, it's Karen. You're still in the office? I hoped you would be. We just returned from our trip to England because Al wasn't feeling well again. Can Doc possibly see him? I hope he's not upset with Al for canceling last time."

"Oh, Doc doesn't hold grudges. Let me check his schedule. We've been awfully busy, Karen. There's a lot of flu going around. That's why we're working late tonight, but I know Doc will want to see Al. We can squeeze him in tomorrow morning at ten."

"He'll be there, Molly. I promise. Thanks for being so understanding."

Al brought the rest of the luggage into the bedroom and placed it on the bed.

"Al, I just called Doc's office. You have an appointment with him at ten tomorrow."

"Thanks, Karen. I want to get this over with and find out what is wrong with me."

Tuesday morning, they all had breakfast together and the children went off to school as usual. Al moped around the house until it was time for him to leave for his appointment. It was nine-thirty when he went to the door to leave.

"Are you sure that you don't want me to go with you, Al?"

"I'm not a baby, Karen. I want to go alone."

"Okay, have it your way."

Doc was a little behind schedule, but he was able to see Al at ten-fifteen.

"Hi, big guy. I hear that you have a problem with some sort of anxiety attacks." "I've had better days, Doc. How are you?"

"Just fine. We have a new grandson. My son is living in Los Angeles now and is the executive producer of the late-night show, *Political Parties*."

"Congratulations, that's a lot to be proud of."

"You bet. Now, let's get down to business. Karen told me a little bit about you a few weeks ago, but now I want to hear it from you directly. Tell me exactly what you have been experiencing; the time of day, duration of the attack, the exact symptoms, and any after-effects."

"Doc, for several weeks, I've been having what Karen describes as anxiety attacks. I've had two horrible nightmares and several episodes of rapid heartbeat, cold sweats, and difficulty breathing. I thought I was dying. The episodes only last a few minutes, but I'm fine afterward. It's a frightening experience."

"That's interesting. Try to be more specific about each incident, Al."

Al related, in some detail, the hanging and choking dreams, the Maid of the Mist, Skylon Restaurant, Tower of London, and Silver Bonito incidents while Doc sat and listened attentively, writing an occasional note on his memo pad. Finally, he checked Al over physically. After completing his examination, he removed his glasses and looked directly at Al, who had a worried look on his face.

"I can't find anything physically wrong with you, Al. I could run some more tests, such as a CT scan, but I'm fairly certain that your problem is more psychological."

"Are you telling me that I'm crazy?"

"Of course not. The mind is very complex, and we still don't know everything about it; especially the subconscious. This is out of my field, Al. Therefore, I would like you to see a psychotherapist who might be able to determine if something in your subconscious is causing these attacks."

"You want me to see a 'shrink', Doc? Give me some pills to stop these attacks. That's all I need."

"No, Al, I want you to see a specialist, whom I believe can help you. Her name is Dr. Elizabeth Sawyer, and her credentials are excellent. Pills aren't going to attack the cause—they can only treat your symptoms, and you would still have the problem. Give Dr. Sawyer a chance. You'll like her. She's a brilliant woman."

"Okay, I'll go and see what she says."

"Good. Molly will set up an appointment for you with Dr. Sawyer. Next time, don't stay away so long, Al."

"I won't, Doc. Thanks."

Al stood by Molly's desk while she called Dr. Sawyer's office and made an appointment for him to see her the following Monday morning at nine.

"You're going to like Dr. Sawyer. Doc thinks highly of her, and she's very well respected nationally."

"You and Doc have both convinced me, Molly. I'll give her a chance."

Al left the office quickly, being anxious to get home to Karen. He sped down Delaware Avenue and onto the Sky View Bridge which crossed over a part of Lake Erie. He looked down at the dark water and felt a chill come over him. From there, he was home in fifteen minutes. Karen was waiting for him at the door.

"How did it go, Dear? Did Doc find out what is wrong?"

"I'm fine physically, but he thinks I have a mental problem and he's sending me to a psychotherapist, a 'shrink'—Dr. Elizabeth Sawyer. I'll go, but I'll quit if I don't like her."

"Don't be so negative. Think positively. Give this doctor a chance. Doc wouldn't be sending you to see her if he didn't think she could get to the bottom of what's causing your attacks. One thing is certain—you cannot go on the way you are now."

"You're right. I know I can't."

"Al, you've had an exhausting day so far, and I don't feel like cooking tonight. When the kids get home from school, let's go to Anderson's for a beef on weck and a sundae."

"Did anyone ever tell you that you had a sweet tooth?"

"Just you. It's good to patronize all of the great places we have to eat in Western New York. I wonder what their special ice cream flavor is today. Hope it's banana."

"You never stop thinking of food, do you? And yet you still keep your youthful figure. What's your secret?"

"I have three people living with me that I have to care for—one adult and two children. I still haven't figured out who the adult is though."

"The one who pays the bills, of course."

While they waited for the children to get home, Karen's thoughts wandered to Al's first appointment with Dr. Sawyer.

I wonder what she looks like. I hope she's old and ugly. Al probably won't want me to go with him. I'll have to wait here and then question him when he gets home.

Al watched TV all day, and then, at ten minutes after three, called out from the den, "The kids are home. I'll back the car out of the garage."

Karen greeted them at the door before they could take off their jackets.

"Put your book bags down, kids. We're going to Anderson's for beef on weck for supper. Get in the car. You can do your homework when we get home."

"Hooray! I was hoping that we'd go out for supper. Can we have a sundae too? I want a hot fudge sundae with cinnamon ice cream," Melissa shrieked excitedly.

"Cinnamon ice cream? That's gross. You only have vanilla or chocolate ice cream with a hot fudge sundae, Melissa," Jonathan piped in.

"Don't knock it if you haven't tried it, Jonathan. It's super."

"I might try it, Melissa. It sounds delicious," Karen chimed in supportively. After finishing their roast beef sandwiches, they ordered their sundaes.

"Melissa, I love this cinnamon ice cream with hot fudge. You are a dessert genius."

"Thanks, Mom. I knew you'd like it."

"I would never have anything but chocolate ice cream with hot fudge," Jonathan added. "Right, Dad?"

"Right, Jonathan. Real men prefer chocolate."

CHAPTER 13

Day after day, Al moped around the house, waiting for Monday and having second thoughts about keeping his appointment with Dr. Sawyer. Fear was beginning to grip his consciousness. He knew Karen would not permit him to back down.

"I wish I could find a way to get out of this, but I promised Karen I'd go, and I can't disappoint her," Al mumbled to himself.

Jonathan tried to get his father to take him to the Bills game Sunday, but Al refused, saying he wasn't feeling well. The Bills were playing their old nemesis, the New England Patriots. It was an important division game.

"Gee, Dad, you want me to get interested in football. How can I when you don't want to take me to a big game?"

Al ignored Jonathan's question, just thinking his own thoughts and shutting out the outside world and his family.

Melissa had overheard her parents discussing Al's forthcoming appointment with a psychotherapist and was curious.

"Mom, what's wrong with Dad? He's been acting funny lately, and he doesn't have much to say to us. Does this have anything to do with why you returned from your trip to England early?"

"Yes, Honey, it does. Your father is not feeling well. Do you remember what happened to him on the Maid of the Mist and at the Skylon—how sick he was?"

"Yes, I do, Mom. He was so sick that he almost passed out."

"Well, he had a couple more of those attacks on our trip that frightened us both. We returned home early so he could see Doc Wilson, who has recommended that he see a psychotherapist who may be able to find out if there is something in his subconscious that may be the cause of these episodes."

"Could that little blonde girl who keeps hanging around Dad be upsetting him? She's upsetting me."

"Oh, Melissa, he doesn't see any little blonde girl, and neither do I. I'm not doubting you, Honey. It's just that I'm having trouble understanding something that I cannot see."

"But, Mom, she's there. All she does is stand there and watch Dad. She doesn't even speak. Usually, when she knows that I'm looking at her, she disappears. Mom, there's something familiar about her. It's like I know her."

"Let's not tell your father about this girl. It's our secret, but let me know if you see her again."

"I will, Mom, but I wish you could see her."

"I do too. Now get ready for dinner, and remember, mum's the word."

"Okay, Mom."

"Al, Jonathan—dinner is ready."

"We're coming. What are we having tonight?"

"Roast chicken, stuffing, salad, carrots, and deep-dish apple pie. Does that suit you, Jonathan?"

"Yes, they're all my favorites, especially the apple pie."

As they were quietly finishing their dinner, Al made a proposal.

"How would you all like to go to the hockey game tonight? The Sabres are playing the Detroit Redwings. It should be a good game. We haven't been to a game in a couple of years, and I feel like getting out around people."

"What are we, Al? Chopped liver?"

"Oh, you know what I mean, Karen."

"You bet, Dad. Let' go. I hope that my Dominik Hasek shirt still fits me. You gave it to me when I was a little kid."

"Jonathan, Hasek is retired now. I'll have to buy you a Ryan Miller shirt now."

"Fantastic! Miller is a star since the Winter Olympics in Vancouver."

"Dad, do you mind if I don't go to the game with you? I'm invited to a slumber party tonight at Faye's. You know that I don't care much about hockey."

"That's all right, Melissa. Do you need a ride to Faye's?"

"Yes, I do. Could you drop me off at six o'clock?"

"That's good. Now, everybody, get ready. The game starts at seven, and I want to get a good parking place."

They left at 5:50, dropped Melissa off, and then drove to the HSBC Arena, where Al was able to get a good parking space close to the entrance. He purchased three lower level seats at mid-ice. The puck was just being dropped as they arrived at their seats. An excited Jonathan remarked, "Dad, these seats are great. Maybe we'll catch a puck here."

"I hope not. Those pucks are made of hard rubber and can seriously injure a person."

No pucks were shot their way, however. The game was exciting, and Miller showed why he is considered one of the world's best goalies. The Sabres shut out Detroit 4 to 0.

After the game, they hurried to the car to beat the traffic. No one was surprised when Karen asked, "Would anyone like to stop at Fowler's on the way home for an ice cream sundae?"

"Karen, how do you do it? You're always coming up with places that have sweets."

"I just know where all of the good places are."

As they were sitting at a table eating their hot fudge sundaes, Jonathan made an announcement. "Dad, I want to be a hockey player. Hockey is safer than football."

"Jonathan, you don't even know how to skate."

"That's okay, Dad. I'll be a goalie like Miller."

"Well, you've certainly picked a good role model, Son."

Karen was delighted to see Al and Jonathan getting along so well.

It's a relief to see Al relaxing for a change, she thought.

Al was anxious about his appointment tomorrow and complained to himself.

I wish I could get out of going. I don't like the idea of a strange woman probing my subconscious and inner thoughts. I don't even tell Karen everything I'm thinking. I suppose there will be a couch for me to lie on while she's picking my brain.

At the same time, Karen was having her own thoughts about Al's appointment.

Sometimes I just can't figure Al out. He knows that he has a problem that keeps reoccurring. Yet he keeps trying to avoid going to doctors. He'd be happy if there was a blizzard tomorrow. Then he could stay home. Men—they're like children. They want a magic pill for everything that ails them.

"Karen, what time is my appointment tomorrow?"

"Nine o'clock. You'll have plenty of time to get there if you leave about eight-fifteen. The Doctor's office is at Delaware and Allen. Traffic shouldn't be heavy then."

"I guess that should give me enough time."

"Do you want me to go along with you?"

"Absolutely not! I want to do this alone. If you're there with me, the doctor will think that I have a domineering wife."

"Well, haven't you?"

"There have been times when I thought you were one."

"I'd like to listen to your remarks about your possessive wife."

"I was just kidding, but I want to do this alone."

"Okay. I'll wait at home and worry about you on that couch."

CHAPTER 14

Exactly at nine o'clock, Dr. Sawyer personally ushered Al into her office. She looked nothing like he had imagined. She was much younger than he had pictured her to be; about thirty-five, he guessed. A pretty, petite, brown-eyed brunette, she projected a business-like image. Yet she warmly extended her hand to greet Al and smiled broadly, revealing a set of perfectly even white teeth.

"Good morning, Mr. Chapman. I'm Dr. Sawyer. I'm pleased to meet you. My secretary had an emergency and I apologize for not properly admitting you, but I understand that you are Dr. Wilson's referral."

"Yes, I am, Dr. Sawyer. I'm very glad to meet you."

"He has given me a brief description of your problem, but I want you to tell me, in your own words, exactly what has been happening to you."

"I'm a little apprehensive about this visit. I've never been to a shrink before." Al knew immediately that he shouldn't have said 'shrink.'

"Mr. Chapman, I am a psychotherapist—in particular, a hypnotherapist. I use analytical therapy to find the root cause of a problem. In other words, I will hypnotize you in order to probe your subconscious. Perhaps the cause of your outwardly expressed symptoms may lie there. Once we find the cause, you hopefully will be cured. Undoubtedly, it will take several sessions under hypnosis. Do you have any questions about what we'll be doing, Mr. Chapman?"

"Will I be asleep? Will I be able to hear everything and be able to speak?"

"Your body will be relaxed, but you will not be asleep. You'll hear everything and will be able to respond to questions I might ask you. My questions will be brief, but your responses may be lengthy."

"Can you make me say or do anything against my will?"

"No, you will be in complete control of your actions. Anything you deem inappropriate will force you out of the hypnotic state."

"I'm very strong willed. I don't think you will be able to hypnotize me, Doctor."

"Most of my patients believe that too, but the odds are that you can be hypnotized. I have found that intelligent people are the best subjects."

"Will you record everything?"

"Yes, and I will replay everything for you, if you wish. I'm going to try to get you to recall past events which may be buried deep inside of your subconscious. Recordings are often very useful in uncovering tiny bits of information which may be overlooked during a session."

"Will anything I say be made public or end up on the internet? I'm a well-known professional football player."

"No, sir. We have a doctor-patient relationship. What takes place here is private and protected. I cannot be forced to reveal facts about your case to anyone. It's similar to priest-confessor or lawyer-client confidentiality.

"What team are you with, Mr. Chapman?"

"The Buffalo Bills. And please call me Al."

"I don't know much about football, Al, so please forgive me if I don't recognize your name. Sports have never been important in my life."

"That's okay. There aren't many women who understand the game of football, including my wife, Karen."

"Now, let's begin. From what Dr. Wilson told me, you are having some kind of anxiety attacks. I want you to tell me everything that you remember about these attacks."

Al went into a lengthy discourse about the hanging and choking dreams and how he felt during them. He recounted the Maid of the Mist, Skylon, Tower of London, Silver Bonito, and Salisbury incidents and described them in detail.

"What were your symptoms during each of these events? Were there any similarities?"

"I had intense fear in each case. I broke into a cold sweat, had a rapid heartbeat, and had difficulty breathing. My wife, who observed most of these attacks, said that my face turned white. In the hanging and choking incidents, I experienced dying. Everything went black. It was like a dark curtain came down over my eyes. It was very frightening. Karen awakened me each time."

"It's obvious to me that these dreams are very realistic and you suffer greatly in them. I want you to go home and try to remember every detail about each episode. Write everything down on paper. I want to see you next Monday at nine, and every week until we solve this mystery. Will scheduling be a problem for you, Al?"

"Well, I'm suspended for two more weeks. After that, Tuesday will be my day off."

"Why were you suspended? This might be relevant."

"I'm ashamed of what I did. I totally lost my temper and tried to intentionally injure another player. I tried to twist his head off. I don't know why I did it. I couldn't control myself.

His injury is so severe that his football career is probably ended. I'll have to live with this for the rest of my life. It tears at my soul."

"Have you ever been violent before?"

"Never. I'm known for never retaliating against an opponent. This was unlike me. This player taunted me, and I took the bait. I guess he pushed my monster button."

"We'll have to investigate this behavior also. There might be a triggering mechanism in your past. Well, that's enough for today. Go home, relax, and carry on with your normal activities. I'll see you next Monday at nine, Al."

"Okay, Doctor, and thank you for seeing me today."

Driving home, Al felt good about the session with Dr. Sawyer. He was confident that she would be able to help him. Nevertheless, he was not looking forward to being hypnotized. He still had fears about that procedure. As usual, Karen was waiting for him. She wanted to find out what had taken place in Dr. Sawyer's office.

"How did the appointment go?"

"I like her. I think she'll be able to help me. But, she's going to hypnotize me, and I'm not happy about that. However, I don't have a choice in the matter. She probably won't be able to do it to me anyhow because I'm so strong willed."

"When is your next appointment?"

"Next Monday at nine."

"Was there a couch for you to lie on?"

"I didn't see any—just a recliner, which I sat upright in."

"How old is she?"

"I don't know, maybe in her thirties."

"Is she pretty?"

"I can see where this questioning is going, Karen. Are you jealous?"

"Maybe. I don't want any woman going after my man, especially when he's on a recliner and hypnotized."

"Karen, she's all business, and I will have complete control over my actions when I'm under hypnosis."

"I hope so."

Karen was ashamed of herself for thinking that Al could get involved in an affair. She realized that the green-eyed monster was taking control of her emotions.

I must stop this. There is no reason to act this way. I don't even know this woman, she told herself. "But Al is very handsome and vulnerable, alone with a pretty doctor."

"Don't you trust me?"

"I trust you completely, and I know that I never have to worry about you straying from the nest."

Al was upset by Karen's jealous behavior.

She should know that I'm not like the other guys. I appreciate a pretty face, but that's all. I would never risk losing my beautiful family because of an affair, he assured himself.

"I'm sorry, Al. That was stupid of me."

"Apology accepted."

For the rest of the day, they both busied themselves about the house and stayed out of each other's way. Al began to wonder if he had made a mistake in agreeing to participate in this "experiment," as he called Dr. Sawyer's sessions.

I wonder what secrets of my past she can uncover. There are some things I don't want anybody to know about. But I understand that if I don't like the questions, I can refuse to answer them. And what's with Karen? She's never been jealous before. She doesn't even know Dr. Sawyer. But the doctor is very attractive, and I'm just a normal guy who likes a pretty face. Karen should know that I can be trusted.

CHAPTER 15

The rest of the week was normal, but Al was still anxious about being hypnotized. He worried about losing control of his free will. The idea that a woman psychotherapist would be probing minute details of his past and his private life made him uncomfortable. Finally, Monday arrived. As usual, Karen wanted to accompany him, but as usual, he went alone.

Like the week before, Dr. Sawyer took Al exactly on time. This time, he examined the room more thoroughly, looking for the customary couch that psychiatrists are supposed to have their patients lie on. Indeed, there was none, only a large leather recliner which he was certain he would be sitting in shortly.

"Good morning, Al. I hope you had a pleasant but uneventful week without any more anxiety attacks."

"No, there are no more dreams or other episodes to report."

"Did you remember any more details of the previous events that we discussed last week?"

"No, I couldn't recall anything more other than what I told you."

"Well then, let's begin. I want you to sit in this chair and relax. You may recline if you wish. Just be comfortable."

Al preferred to remain upright in the chair, but he did extend his legs.

"I know that you're a little apprehensive about being hypnotized but let me assure you that you will be awake and aware of everything going on around you. You will be in complete control of your thoughts and actions. Are you ready to proceed, Al?"

"I'm as ready as I'll ever be. I'm eager to get started and I'll try to be a cooperative patient for you."

The doctor pulled up a chair directly in front of Al. She was dressed in a black suit and a tailored white blouse, open at the neck thus partially exposing her breasts. Al could see that she wore tiny ruby earrings, although they were somewhat hidden by her long brown hair which reached to her shoulders. He could smell the faint scent of a very pleasant perfume that she was wearing. His mind began to wander.

Be careful, he warned himself. *Don't start window-shopping. Remember what Karen said. Don't add fuel to her fire.*

Dr. Sawyer brought him back to reality.

"Al, I want you to follow the motion of this small pendulum I'm swinging. Count backwards from five."

Al was certain that he could not be hypnotized, but he began counting.

"Five, four, three, two…"

Contrary to what he believed, he was quickly in a hypnotic state, although awake.

"Can you hear me, Al?"

"Yes, I can hear you. Do you want me to try again?"

"No, Al, you're fine. Just relax. I want you to go back in time and try to recall a very painful or terrifying experience. Can you recall any life-threatening event?"

"Yes, I can remember one."

"Tell me where you are."

"I'm on my boat off the coast of Maine, in the Atlantic Ocean."

"Describe your boat."

"It's a rowboat with two oars."

"What are you doing?"

"I'm picking up lobster traps. I'm a lobsterman."

"What is your name?"

"My name is Stanley James Morgan."

"How old are you Stanley?"

"I am twenty years old."

"What is today's date?"

"It is August fourteenth, nineteen hundred and twelve."

"Are you married, Stanley?"

"No, I am single and live alone in a rooming house in New Harbor, but I have a girlfriend, Ellie."

"How far from the shore are you in your boat?"

"I'm close to the rocky coast—just a couple of hundred yards out."

"Why are you so close to the coast?"

"I dropped my traps here and have to pick them up."

"What do you do with the traps?"

"I remove the lobsters and measure them. If they are too small, I throw them back in the ocean. Then I bait the empty traps and drop them overboard."

"What is the weather like?"

"It has been sunny, but the wind is picking up. The sky is getting very black. A storm may be coming. I must hurry."

"Is everything all right?"

"No, a storm blew in suddenly, and I'm unable to return to shore. The wind is dashing my boat against the rocks. The boat is taking on water and breaking up. I am frightened."

"Stanley, are you all right?"

"No. I'm in the water. I cannot swim. The force of the water is too great. My head is smashing into the rocks. *Oh My God!!*"

"Stanley, what is happening to you?"

"A very sharp metal strip just slashed against my lower body. God help me. I've been castrated. My lungs are filling with water, red from my blood. I'm drowning. Everything is going black."

Realizing that Al was experiencing extreme trauma, Dr. Sawyer brought him back to the present.

"One, two, three… Al, you're back in Buffalo. It's 2010. You're safe."

"That was awful, Doctor. I was really drowning. I couldn't breathe. It was so real. How could it be 1912? I wasn't born until 1976. And who is Stanley Morgan?"

"You went back in time to a past life and relived a very traumatic experience. In that life, you were Stanley Morgan, not Al Chapman. Al, do you believe in reincarnation?"

"That nonsense? No way. We only live once, and that's it. I don't believe in any of that Hollywood stuff that Shirley MacLaine preaches."

"Please try to keep an open mind about everything we're doing, Al. Don't criticize the process. Something is causing your anxiety attacks, and these regressions may help us find out what that something is. I know that this is difficult for you but give it a chance."

"I'm a Catholic. Reincarnation is not one of the Church's teachings. We live once and no more. End of discussion."

"You are a bit misinformed, Al. Catholics believed in rein-carnation before 553 A.D., but then the belief was dropped from the religion, and it became a sin to believe in it."

"Why was it dropped?"

"I understand that the hierarchy wanted a more autocratic control over their flock. The idea of heaven and hell gave them more power. However, reincarnation remains a fundamental teaching of Eastern religions such as Hinduism."

"How does all of this drivel tie in with my case?"

"It's too early to tell, but you must go through these regressions, whether you believe in them or not. By the way, as a child, did you ever have a close call while swimming?"

"Yes, I did. I remember, when I was about five years old, having a little backyard pool that I splashed around in. One day, Kevin, a neighbor, who was seven, pushed my head underwater and held it there. Luckily, my mom saw what he was doing and saved me. Since then, I've been afraid of the water."

"Do you own a boat?"

"No, I've never been fond of them. A lot of my teammates own boats and have invited me and my family to go sailing with them, but I have always made some excuse not to go. Even as a child, I never liked boats or the water."

"There have been a few connections to water in your anxiety attacks, but I can't draw any conclusions without more information. Today's session has been traumatic for you. I don't want to put you through anything more now. We'll call it a day, and I'll see you next week. This is just the beginning, Al. It's a new experience for you, I know."

"I am a bit shaken and upset by everything. It is a lot for me to digest in one day."

"That is to be expected, Al. Go home and relax, and please don't discuss today's session with your wife or anyone else. I don't want any outside influence creeping into your subconscious."

"I understand, Doctor Sawyer."

Al left the doctor's office and drove directly home over Delaware Avenue and the Skyview Bridge. He expected Karen to be waiting for him, and she was. She would want to know everything that went on in the doctor's office, but Al was determined to hold his ground and tell her nothing. However, Karen kept pushing.

"Please, Al, what did she do?"

"Karen, stop. I am not going to tell you anything now. Give me a break and butt out. I don't even want to think about it anymore today. I'm going into the den to watch the news on TV, and try to relax."

"Okay, Mr. Chapman, I'll butt out."

Karen was terribly hurt by Al's refusal to take her into his confidence. She knew that he was a very private person. It was difficult for him to talk about his personal life. Nevertheless, she followed him into the den and kept needling him.

"Did you lie on the recliner?"

"No, it was very comfortable. I put my feet up and sat up in the chair."

"Did you go to sleep?"

"No, I was awake the whole time."

"I'm glad to hear that, anyway."

"That's it, Karen. No more questions. I'll tell you something when I think you should know it. Don't bother fixing lunch for me—I'm not hungry."

That exchange ended the conversation between the two of them for the rest of the day. Karen busied herself in the kitchen baking and preparing a roast leg of lamb for dinner while Al watched TV. The dinner hour was unusually quiet except for Jonathan's complaining about Sister Joseph picking on him.

"Jonathan, are you getting your homework in on time?"

"Yes, but Sister still picks on me, Mom."

"What do you mean that she picks on you?"

"She keeps calling on me in class to see if I know the answers to questions she asks."

"That's not picking on you, Jonathan. Sister is showing concern for you and wants you to learn. That's good teaching."

"Oh, you always take Sister's side, Mom."

"Give it up, son," Al added angrily.

CHAPTER 16

The Buffalo Bills were struggling. With half of the season over, they were four and four. They still felt that they had a shot at the playoffs; a long one. Al was anxious to get back in the game. He worked out alone daily at the Ralf because he wasn't allowed to practice with his teammates. Much of his time was spent in the weight room, building up his strength. He could easily bench press two hundred pounds and could run twenty miles on the treadmill and an additional ten miles riding on the stationary bike.

On Thursday, Coach Schultz came in to talk to Al, sat next to him on a stationary bike, and tried to keep pace.

"Al, you'll be back practicing with the team next week. Your absence has really severely hurt us offensively. Of course, reoccurring injuries haven't helped either. Tell me how you are going to handle playing again. Will you be aggressive, or will you be afraid to do what is necessary to protect our quarterback?"

"John, I've given that question a lot of thought. Once I take that first hit, I think I'll be all right. I'm eager to get back in the game and make contact with the defensive guys opposite me. Fear should not be a factor with me. And I can be aggressive."

"That's what I wanted to hear, buddy. I hope you can put the Jefferson incident out of your mind on game day and not let it eat away at you. By the way, he's out of the hospital and in therapy. A full recovery is possible, but it's going to take time."

"That's good news about Jefferson, but I will hate myself for the rest of my life for what I did to him. John, I'll prepare myself mentally, on game day, as I always have in the past. But I will never play the game with a killer instinct. That is not me. You know I'm not like that."

"That's good enough for me. We surely will be glad to have you back. Play the kind of game you are capable of, and you'll be fine. And so will the Bills."

Karen was happy to have Al go to the stadium each day to practice. He had been bored and had been getting on her nerves. The long wait was almost over. He would be back at work in another week.

Sunday, the Bills were playing the Oakland Raiders at home. Al suggested that they all go to the game and sit in the Paul McGuire suite. He had never sat anywhere but on the field with the team before, and it was a new experience being with the players' families. It bothered him to be a spectator and not a player. On the other hand, Jonathan was glad to watch the game with his dad and seemed to be taking more of an interest in football than before. That pleased Al.

"Dad, do you think that the Raiders play dirty? Don't they have that reputation?"

"They used to be that way, son, but they're a new team with a new coach now."

"Does the coach teach the players to play dirty, or are the players just that way?"

"A little bit of both. I've heard it said that some coaches pay the players if they injure certain key players on a team. Coach Schultz doesn't want this kind of a player on the team. He will get rid of any player who gets that reputation around the league."

Melissa was getting restless watching the game, which the Bills were losing 21 to 7 at the half. She was not a football fan. On the other hand, she was becoming a tennis enthusiast, having recently discovered Rafael Nadal. Although she did accompany her mother and brother to the Bills' home games, she would just sit quietly and watch her father's every move.

"Dad, could I go and get a hot dog and some hot chocolate? I'm a little hungry."

"Me too, Dad."

"I'll go with you kids. Al, do you want one too?"

"I don't know what I was thinking of. Of course, we want hot dogs. They're the best around. Get me three dogs and a Genny. Here's fifty bucks, Karen."

"That's a lot of money for six hot dogs and drinks, Al."

"It's a business—supply and demand."

Al sat alone, wishing he could be on the field helping the Bills and blaming himself for their poor record. A woman approached him. He pretended not to know her. She addressed Al and spoke to him nevertheless.

"You don't remember me, do you, Mr. Chapman? I was on the England trip with you and your wife. I'm Myra Johnson. I spoke to you both at Stonehenge."

"I remember you, Mrs. Johnson. You're the lady who mistakenly thought we were there with our daughter. We told you that our daughter was home in Orchard Park."

"That's right, Mr. Chapman. I'm sorry that I upset you, and I'm a little embarrassed to have to say this to you, but I see that same child standing near you now and watching you. I have a strange feeling about her."

"I have a strange feeling about you too, Mrs. Johnson. That's my daughter over there getting some refreshments with my wife and son. I don't see any other girl here."

"This is another little girl—the same one I saw at Stonehenge. She's about the same age as your daughter, I would guess. She's very pretty and is smiling at us."

"Lady, please leave me alone. I don't want you bothering my family or me. Now, please leave. Frankly, I think you're a tad nuts. Go find the man in the moon."

"Forgive me, Mr. Chapman. I won't bother you again. You are a very rude man. I was only trying to alert you about this girl." Having said her piece, Mrs. Johnson turned and walked away.

"Who was that lady you were talking to, Dad?"

"I didn't see any lady, Melissa," Karen interrupted.

"Oh, she was someone your mom and I met on our trip to England. She just stopped by to say hello."

"Mrs. Johnson, Al? Where is she? Where did she go?"

"I don't know, Karen. I got rid of her by being rude. I don't like that woman. She keeps turning up like a bad penny. I hope I never see her again."

The Bills lost the game to the Raiders 24 to 14. The ride home was not a happy one.

"The Bills played awful today, Dad. They need you in there to protect Adams."

In the back seat, Melissa alerted Karen to what she was seeing in the car ahead.

"Mom, do you see her?"

"Who, Melissa?"

"That little blonde girl. She's riding in the car ahead of ours and is looking out of the rear window at us. Do you see her, Mom? She's waving at us."

"There's nobody in the back seat of that car, Melissa. I don't see anyone waving."

"Well, she's there looking at us. She was in the suite today watching Dad too. Mom, she scares me. You told me to tell you if I saw her again."

"Shush! Don't talk about that now. We'll discuss it later. I don't want to upset your father. He has enough to worry about right now."

At home, they continued the conversation in the kitchen while preparing supper. "Melissa, how is that little girl whom you keep seeing around your father dressed? Can you describe her clothing? Maybe it's a style we're familiar with."

"Well, she looks kind of poor. She wears a long brown loose-fitting dress with a round neckline. The dress has three-quarter length puffed sleeves. It's old-fashioned looking and reaches almost to her ankles. And her shoes are funny. They have buttons on them, and the tops of her shabby-looking shoes just touch the hem of her dress."

"That doesn't sound like any of our modern clothing. I think tomorrow I'll go to the Orchard Park Library and look for some books that have pictures of dresses from other time periods. I'll bring the books home and we can look through them."

"I'm sure I can recognize the dress from a picture. Then, maybe you'll believe me."

CHAPTER 17

D r. Sawyer was an hour late for the second regression session with Al because she had an emergency at the Buffalo Psychiatric Center where she is Chief of Psychiatry; a very prestigious position. At times, she was run ragged trying to balance her office practice with the care of hospital patients.

"I'm sorry to have kept you waiting. An emergency came up which needed my immediate attention. We're short-handed at the center due to more New York State cuts. I'll give you your full hour nonetheless."

"No problem, Doctor. You have quite a few current magazines in your waiting room. I became interested in an article about Shirley MacLaine and her beliefs about reincarnation. She's from another planet, isn't she?"

"She's quite a character. But I'm in agreement with more of her ideas than not. She has quite a following, and I am certain that she is sincere in her beliefs. Al, I've listened and re-listened to the previous tapes. I'm beginning to think that there is a water connection in some of the episodes you have experienced. Of course, water was absent in the Salisbury and Tower of London incidents. We'll have to wait and see how everything plays out as we proceed. Let's get to work and see what we can uncover today. I'm going to ask you to relax and look at the swinging pendulum again while you count backwards from five."

Once again, Al was easily hypnotized.

"Al, I want you to go back in time to the nineteenth century—the 1800s. Are you living then?"

"Yes, I am."

"Try to relive an unforgettable occasion—one that made an indelible impression on your subconscious. Perhaps a traumatic incident. Where are you?"

"I'm in a hotel room in San Francisco."

"What is the name of the hotel?"

"It's called the Olympia Hotel."

"Can you give me the address of the hotel?"

"It is on the Bay at 1400 Market Street."

"What class of hotel is it?"

"It's not very good—mostly for low class people."

"What is your name?"

"My name is Jane Dawson."

"How old are you Jane?"

"I am thirty years old."

"Do you know today's date, Jane?"

"Yes. It is Wednesday, April third, eighteen hundred and twenty-five."

"Are you married, Jane?"

"No. I'm a widow."

"What happened to your husband?"

"He died of a heart attack in his sleep two years ago. I found him dead in bed when I returned home from work."

"How old was your husband?"

"He was much older than me—forty-five."

"Do you have any children?"

"No. Two died in childbirth."

"What are you doing in the hotel today?"

"I am a housekeeper. I'm cleaning Room 307."

"Are you alone?"

"Yes. I have the door closed. Oh, there is someone knocking on the door. I am opening the door to see who is there."

"Who is there, Jane?"

"A strange man."

"What is he doing?"

"He is pushing his way into the room and forcing me onto the bed. He's on top of me and is tearing off my clothing. Stop! Stop! God. I'm being raped. He is hurting me. He is slapping me and punching me in the head. I'm trying to get free."

"Are you fighting?"

"Yes, but he is so strong. I'm scratching, kicking, and fighting as hard as I can. No! No!"

"What's happening?"

"He is choking me. I can't breathe."

"Can you get free?"

"I'm using my last bit of strength. He is relaxing a bit. I am able to squirm free and run to the door, but he catches me and is dragging me across the floor to the open window."

"What does he do next?"

"He is picking me up and is pushing me out of the window. I am falling three stories and screaming all of the way down. I hit the ground. All is black."

Seeing the agony Al is experiencing, Dr. Sawyer brings him back.

"Al. One, two, three, four… You're in Buffalo. It's November 2010. You're safe."

This horrific regression leaves Al physically and emotionally drained.

"This is getting to be too much for me to handle. I keep suffering and dying in my dreams, and now, in these sessions, I feel terrible pain and suffering. How much more of this must I endure? What does it all mean?"

"I'm not sure yet. It's going to take more time. Just try to hang in there. You're doing remarkably well so far. Today, we discovered that you were once a woman living in the nineteenth century. That is strange indeed."

"That's ridiculous. Look at me. I'm a man—a big normal man. Do I look like a woman to you? I don't believe any of this."

"You are a man in this lifetime, but in the nineteenth century, you apparently were a woman. Sex changes do occur from one life experience to another. It is necessary for our souls to experience both male and female lives."

"Why, Doctor?"

"It is part of your karma—a debt you owe from a previous lifetime. Perhaps it is to pay for some sin you may have committed."

"Please don't start with that again. You know that I do not believe any of it. What good is it doing for me to keep choking and dying?"

"You've hit on something—choking. That seems to be another link—hanging, choking on a piece of steak, and now this incident. I think we're making progress."

"That's right. Choking has occurred often if you count the dreams. It seems that every time I die, I suffer tremendously, but at the moment of my death, there is no pain—just blackness."

"That's interesting. You don't go through a tunnel toward a lovely peaceful light that many people have described after they have had a near-death experience?"

"No. All goes black. I fall into a deep black abyss."

"I'm all goosebumps, Al. This is very surprising. Let's stop at this point. You must be exhausted—I know I am. Go home now and rest. Try to clear your mind of today's revelations. Next week, as I remember, we will meet on Tuesday. I suppose you will be happy to be back playing again."

"That's right. My suspension is over. Now I can practice with the team again. I can play on Sunday if all goes well and I pass my physical."

"Just be careful. You don't need any more injuries or problems. Who are the Bills playing Sunday?"

"We're in New Jersey playing the New York Jets again—Ron Jefferson's team. And I will be extra careful. The ref will be watching my every move."

"Good. Don't lose your cool."

"Oh, Doctor. I almost forgot to mention this to you. Karen and I met a strange woman at Stonehenge who claimed that she was seeing a little blonde girl standing near me and watching me. We couldn't see anyone. She upset me terribly, and I was rude to her. But Sunday, this woman came over to speak to me at the game. She told me the same thing as before. The little girl was standing near me and staring at me. I think she's crazy. I don't ever see any girl nor does Karen. What do you make of it?"

"I don't know. It could be important. Who is she?"

"Her name is Myra Johnson. She just appears, says her piece, and then goes. Of course, I must admit, I am rude to her and ask her to leave me alone."

"We'll have to wait and see if she pops up again. You are right to tell me everything that happens to you, no matter how strange it may appear. These supposedly strange things could turn out to be relevant. Write things down so you don't forget details. Okay, Let's call it quits for the day. I'll see you next Tuesday. I'll try to be on time."

"Don't worry about it, Doctor. See you next week."

Karen was waiting at the door to greet Al when he arrived home at almost noon. She was anxious to pump him about the session with Dr. Sawyer.

"You're late today, Dear. I was getting worried. Lunch is ready. How did your appointment go today? Are you going to tell me any secrets or do you want me to think that you and Dr. Sawyer are having an affair? What's going on in these sessions?"

"Silly woman. Can't I at least sit down and have lunch? You certainly are nosey. But, I will tell you that I told her about Mrs. Johnson and the little blonde girl."

"Good, but wait until you hear this. Melissa told me that she has seen that same child near you on several occasions over the past months. She saw her watching you yesterday at the game."

"Hon, I'm going to call Dr. Sawyer. She told me to tell her everything that happens. This is important."

"Chill out, Al. Eat your lunch. Wait until next week to tell her. I'm going to the library today to get some books on dress styles over the centuries. There should be some pictures. Perhaps Melissa will be able to pick out clothing similar to what this girl is wearing. She has described the dress and shoes to me."

"All right. We'll talk to Melissa after you get the books. Why do you suppose that Melissa can see this girl and we can't?"

"I wish I knew. Some people apparently have a special gift. I guess that we don't have it. I'm beginning to think that Melissa and Mrs. Johnson are seeing a ghost."

"Wow. This is really getting spooky. And I was so rude to Mrs. Johnson."

"Melissa is going to be a great help to us in solving this mystery, Al. She is getting to be a very astute and mature young lady."

"I'm proud of our daughter. I guess the nuns are doing a good job with her. Now, I wish they'd work harder on Jonathan."

"He'll be all right, Al. You know that boys mature more slowly than girls. Look at you. You're coming along just fine for your age. I'm going to go to the Orchard Park Library now and then shop for something for dinner tonight. What would you like?"

"It's been a hectic day for me and it will be late when you get home from the library. Why don't we go to La Nova for wings tonight?"

"You know, Al, that I'd rather go out to eat than cook. Sometimes you come up with some great ideas. I think I'll keep you a while longer."

"I'm glad to hear that. I thought you were tiring of me and were going to turn me in for a more mature model."

"No way. I'm just getting used to you. Now, you relax. I'm going to the library."

Right on time, the children came bursting into the house at three fifteen. Karen was not yet home from the library.

"Start work on your homework right away, kids. When you're finished, we're going to LaNova for wings tonight. Your mom will be home shortly. She went to the library to pick up some books."

It was like someone fired a starting gun. They threw off their jackets and enthusiastically greeted their father.

"I did my homework at school, Dad," Melissa announced. "I'm ready to go now."

"I don't have much homework tonight. I can have it done in about an hour. Just mention wings and I'm ready to rumble, Dad," Jonathan announced.

At that moment, Karen pulled into the driveway and entered the house carrying two heavy-looking books.

"Did you get the books we talked about, Mom?"

"Yes, Melissa, I selected two that seem to be pretty good. We'll look at them tomorrow after the game. Tonight, let's have a pleasant family dinner without any extra little blonde girl intruding. She's beginning to get on my nerves. Where's Jonathan?"

"He's working on his homework upstairs."

"I hope he won't be too long. I can't wait to bite into those La Nova wings."

"Chicken wings are full of fat and high in cholesterol, Mom. We should eat more fruits and vegetables. Wings are very bad for our arteries. I'm going to have a big salad."

"Melissa, I think you should be our family nutritionist. You are so well-informed, but could we start on our low-fat diet tomorrow?"

"Okay, Mom. But remember, we are what we eat."

"We'll keep that in mind," Al commented from the den. Jonathan entered the den to speak to Al.

"I've done all of my assignment that I can for now, Dad. My computer's down; no telling for how long. We might just as well go for wings now."

"And when we get home, you will go upstairs and finish your homework, Jonathan."

"Yes, Dad. I will."

CHAPTER 18

The Buffalo Bills were in New Jersey Sunday to play the New York Jets again. Karen and the children were going to watch the game on CBS at one o'clock. The reception that the Jets fans would give Al worried Karen.

"Those Jets fans will be looking for revenge. I'm afraid that Al is going to get a raucous greeting. I hope he holds his temper in check today."

Al had practiced with the team all week and declared himself to be in good shape and ready to play, yet his mind was in overdrive.

"I'm ready, but am I able? The Jets are going to come after me from the get-go. They'll be after my blood today. No matter what, I cannot lose my cool. Commissioner Rogers will be watching this game and me. One false step and I'll be out of football for good."

The weather was cold and rainy, but the Bills felt good about their chances, because Al Chapman was back. The players were anxious for the game to begin.

As the players were introduced over the PA system, Al was very apprehensive. There were seventy thousand screaming people in the stadium; mostly Jets fans hoping to get revenge for Ron Jefferson. When Al's name was called, he ran onto the field to a chorus of boos. Fans began throwing things at him from the stands. A plastic bottle hit the nose guard of his helmet. Coke ran down his face and into his eyes. Ignoring all of this,

Al took his regular place on the bench, knowing that he had to keep his temper in check.

"This is getting really nasty. I need a suit of armor for protection."

An announcement was made warning the fans that the Jets would forfeit the game if the demonstrations did not cease. Rioting fans were being ejected all over the stadium. Order was eventually restored, except for the chant that was being shouted in unison.

"Killer. Killer. Killer Chapman," they repeated over and over.

Al tried desperately to tune the noise out, but he couldn't. The jeering continued. Then the fans spotted Ron Jefferson sitting in the owner's box. He stood up from his wheelchair and acknowledged the fans. That sparked another chant.

"Payback. Payback. Chapman's back."

Despite all of this, the Bills won the coin toss and elected to receive. They began their first series of plays on their own twenty-five yard line. Al lined up opposite the Jets' defensive end, Lou Chaffee. The badmouthing began immediately.

"Watch your back, Chapman. Your days are numbered. We haven't forgotten what you did to Ron."

Al did not respond. He got down in his stance and stayed focused. On the first series, the Bills made a first down on three running plays. On the next play, Chaffee ran around Al and sacked Adams for a six-yard loss. On second and sixteen, Adams rolled out to pass. Al was hit from behind and pounded into the turf by Chaffee. Al's helmet was knocked off and another Jet player angrily kicked him in the head. He lay motionless on the field. A hush fell over the crowd as the medical staff ran onto the field. Slowly, after several minutes, Al began to regain consciousness. He was able to be helped off the field and onto the bench, where the team doctor stood before him and interrogated him.

"What is your name?"

There was no response from Al.

"Your name is Al Chapman."

"Yes. That's who I am."

"Where are you, Al?"

"I don't know. I can't remember."

"How old are you, Al?"

"I don't know. My head hurts."

At this point, Dr. Olsen called for the cart to take Al into the locker room for some head x-rays. The fans were cheering and waving white towels as he was driven off the field.

"We're glad you're hurt. We're glad you're hurt."

This angered and motivated the entire Bills team. They gathered on the sideline, raised their fists in the air, and promised that they would win the game for Al.

Karen and the children watched the game at home in horror. Karen screamed as she saw Al lying unconscious on the field. She jumped up out of her chair and called the stadium, whose number was in the address book on the telephone table. After several long minutes of waiting on the line, Dr. Olsen came to the phone to speak with her.

"Mrs. Chapman, I understand your concern about Al. Our preliminary tests show no skull fracture, but it looks like he has a slight concussion. Right now, he's resting in the locker room. We have him under constant observation. I think he's going to be all right and will be well enough to come home with the team on the plane tonight. Someone will drive him home from the airport. I'll call you if there is any change in plans. Stop worrying."

Reassured, Karen thanked Dr. Olsen and hung up the phone. She went to the kitchen, sat at the table, put her head down, and cried.

"I wish Al would retire. He's getting too old to play anymore. There are too many head and back injuries."

Melissa heard her mother talking to herself and joined her in the kitchen. Not knowing what to say, she blurted out, "That blonde girl was there with Dad again, Mom. She was standing next to him at the bench. She was smiling as he was taken off the field and seemed happy that Dad was hurt. And she was doing something funny with her fingers, like she was counting on them."

"I wonder why she keeps watching your father. And what about those fingers?"

"I don't have any idea, Mom. Is Dad going to be all right?"

"The doctor said he thought so. He'll be home tonight. In the meantime, let's look at those books I brought home from the library while we have some time. There are lots of pictures in them of dress styles over the centuries. Maybe you'll be able to pick out that girl's clothing from a picture."

"Get the books, Mom. I'll look through them."

For over an hour, Melissa thumbed through the pages of the two books. She literally looked closely at hundreds of dresses; women's and children's alike. Then, her face suddenly lit up. She screeched and pointed to a picture of a dress worn by a child.

"This is it, Mom. I'm sure. It's just like that little girl wears. The dress and even the high button shoes."

"Melissa, this clothing is from the Renaissance period, maybe fifteenth century England. This particular loose-fitting dress with the rounded neckline is called a shift. It has no belt. Notice the three-quarter length puffed sleeves, which you described to me before. This is something we will have to show to your father when he gets home, if he's able."

At that moment, Jonathan came running into the kitchen, shouting, "Guess what? After Dad was hurt, the Bills tied the Jets and won the game in overtime by a field goal. Those Jets fans really got the Bills agitated. The Jets couldn't stop them."

"That's good news, Jonathan. Dad will be very pleased."

The plane, with Al aboard, landed at Prior Aviation at eleven o'clock. Coach Schultz, who lives near the Chapmans, drove Al home. Looking tired and pale, Al walked very slowly into the house. Not thinking about his injury, Karen opened the door, grabbed him, and hugged him.

"Oh, Al, are you all right? We've been so worried about you."

"Karen, get him to bed right away. What he needs most now is rest. Just let him sleep. He cannot go to practice this week. Whether he plays next Sunday or not will be up to Dr. Olsen to decide," Coach Schultz remarked.

"I'll be fine—just a little tired from the plane ride."

"Al, you are going straight to bed. Coach, maybe you could help me get him upstairs and in bed."

"Glad to, Karen."

Together they slowly led Al up the stairs and got him undressed and into bed. He was asleep and snoring as soon as his head hit the pillow.

"Thanks, Coach, I'll be able to handle everything from here on."

"Call me if you need anything. I'm close by and can be over in a minute. By the way, Al's car will be driven from the airport to your house by one of our office staff, probably tomorrow morning. Stop worrying. Al's tough. He'll be okay."

Karen showed Coach Schultz to the door and then went upstairs to bed beside Al. She was happy to listen to his snoring all night long.

It was three o'clock Monday afternoon, when Al awakened.

"Wow! What a headache. What did I have to drink last night? Where was the party?"

"There wasn't any party, Al. You received a concussion in yesterday's game with the Jets, and you've been pretty much out of it since. Welcome back, Dear. How are you feeling? Are you able to come downstairs for an early supper in a while, or do you want me to bring it up to you in bed?"

"I'll come down. Give me an hour to shower, shave, and put myself together."

"I'll begin getting dinner ready. We'll eat early today. You haven't had anything to eat since yesterday morning. You must be starving."

"Not really. Just fix something light for me."

Karen went down to the kitchen. The children had just come home from school and were anxious to know how their father was.

"Mom, the kids are all upset that Dad was hurt yesterday. How is he?" Jonathan asked.

"Yes, Mom. Is Dad okay?" Melissa repeated.

"He's a lot better today. He'll be down shortly for an early dinner. I'm about to get something ready now. Take it easy with him. He's very tired."

Karen decided to make a large julienne salad, and began boiling some eggs and chopping some sliced ham. She put a variety of different types of greens in the salad bowl. With Melissa looking on critically, she began slicing some rye bread.

"Mom, let's make a fruit plate with yogurt for dessert. I can help you with it. Lots of protein and vegetables and fruit will be good for us all."

It was four-thirty when Al appeared in the kitchen and took his place at the table. Karen poured him a cup of black coffee. The children sat quietly observing him but saying nothing.

"What's wrong with you guys? I'm all right. I'm not broken—just bent a bit."

Melissa was the first to speak as she handed Al a huge handmade get-well card with a big picture of Al in his football uniform on the cover.

"All of the kids in my class signed this card for you, Dad. They feel terrible that you were hurt in the game yesterday."

"That's so nice. Thank them for me, Melissa."

"And my friends want you to get better soon so the Bills can make the playoffs," Jonathan commented.

"I feel pretty good today, kids. Karen, how is supper coming?"

"Coming right up. We're having a light, nutritious meal this evening. It will be good for us all. Melissa, I guess we're starting our low-fat diet today."

"Ladies, everything is delicious. Thank you for taking such good care of us all."

After supper, Jonathan went to his room to work on his homework without being told. Melissa offered to do the dishes. Karen and Al went into the den to talk alone.

"Karen, I'm convinced that my Saint Christopher medal saved me yesterday from a more serious injury. He still helps me, even though the Church has disenfranchised him."

"I think so too. Now, listen to what I have to tell you. Melissa saw that little blonde girl near you again at yesterday's game. When you were injured, she seemed happy. Also, she was doing something with her fingers, like she was counting on them."

"Gee, what's going on? Why can't I see her too?"

"There's more news about that girl. Melissa and I looked through the books I brought home from the library, and she identified the clothing the girl wears as being from fifteenth century England—the Renaissance period."

"I'll tell Dr. Sawyer about this tomorrow. She'll figure out how all of this fits into the puzzle."

"Only if you are well enough to drive tomorrow. You can't rush things. When are you going to tell me what's been going on in these sessions?"

"When the time is right, Karen. We've really only just begun. Wait until we know something definitive."

"I'll try to be more patient."

"I'm sorry. I don't want you to think that I don't trust you, but Dr. Sawyer has sort of put a gag order on me not to discuss what we're doing with anyone. She feels that outside input could influence what I'm revealing in these sessions. I want to follow her instructions."

"That's good enough for me."

Al was surprised by Karen's change in attitude, but he knew that it would not last long. He therefore made a prediction.

I'll give her two weeks before her curiosity will get the better of her again, and she'll be back quizzing me about the sessions.

Karen left Al and went to the kitchen to put away the dishes, which Melissa had washed and dried and left on the table. She mentally planned her next move.

I'll give Al some peace and quiet because he's been hurt. In a couple of weeks, I'll question him again about his sessions with Dr. Sawyer. He should know by now that I don't give up easily.

CHAPTER 19

After breakfast Tuesday morning, Al was feeling much better; his headache had subsided. Therefore, he pronounced himself well enough to keep his appointment with Dr. Sawyer and braced himself for an expected verbal onslaught of objections from Karen.

"You're supposed to be resting for a few days. It has been less than two days since your concussion. You know that you're not allowed to practice this week, so I don't think you should go today. I'll call and cancel your appointment."

"No, don't! I'm okay, and I'm going. Drop it, Karen."

That said, he quickly kissed Karen goodbye and was out the door before any more argument developed.

He was a few minutes early for his appointment, but Dr. Sawyer was waiting for him. Her secretary showed Al into the office. The doctor was aware of the seriousness of Al's injury and brought it up immediately.

"I saw the whole tragedy on TV Sunday, Al. I'm very concerned about this head injury, which the sportscasters described as a mild concussion. Are you positive that you are all right to proceed with our session today? Don't you still have a headache?"

Al minimized the headache pain he was still experiencing.

"My head feels pretty good, so I want to go ahead with today's session as scheduled. But first, I have a couple of things to tell you."

"It seems that my daughter, Melissa, has been seeing that strange little blonde girl who apparently has been hanging around me for some time, although I can't see her. She saw her watching me at the game Sunday. When I was injured, she seemed happy about it. Melissa saw her smiling when they helped me off the field. She appeared to be doing something else that was weird; she was counting on her fingers. Well, last night, Karen and Melissa looked through a couple of books on dress styles over the centuries which Karen had brought home from the library. Here's the shocker. Melissa picked out an outfit commonly worn in England during the fifteenth century. It was identical to the clothing worn by this little girl. What do you make of all of this? Are these things relevant? I think this is getting spooky."

"I have to be honest with you. This case is getting very complicated. I can't be certain where it's headed. How this girl fits in, I don't know. Yet I have a gut feeling that she is a major player in this story. She appears to be another common thread in the mystery, but we still need more information. There are many zigs and zags in this case. I told you that it wouldn't be easy. Now, getting back to the present, are you ready to confront another life today, if we find one?"

"I believe I am, but I'll admit, I'm scared every time we do this. These regressions take a lot of energy out of me. Afterwards, I have to rest for a time in order to recover physically. And emotionally, I'm drained for days."

"That's to be expected. It is an emotional and physical ordeal for you. All right, relax. Take a deep breath. Look at the pendulum and begin counting backwards from five."

The method never varied; only the length of time it took Al to be hypnotized. He began counting, and his response was almost instantaneous.

"Five."

"Al, I want you to go back to the eighteenth century. Are you living in the 1700s?"

"Yes, I am."

"What is the date?"

"It is January ninth, seventeen hundred and seventy-six."

"What is your name?"

"My name is John Francis Mason."

"John, I want you to relive the events leading to your death. Where are you?"

"I'm in a tent with three men."

"Who are these men?"

"They are soldiers in the Colonial American Army."

"Are you also a soldier in the Colonial Army?"

"Yes, I volunteered to fight."

""Who are you fighting?"

"We're rebelling against the British. We want to free ourselves from British rule."

"How old are you, John?"

"I'm nineteen, but I'll be twenty in April."

"Are you married?"

"No, I am single. I have no family. My parents are deceased."

"Who is the leader of the American Army?"

"General George Washington."

"Where is he?"

"His headquarters is at Valley Forge, Pennsylvania."

"Where is your camp, John?"

"We are about five miles from Valley Forge."

"At the moment, is anything happening with you?"

"Yes, Captain Michaels is telling me to get on my horse and take an important message to General Washington. I'm to wait for a reply from the general and then hurry back with it and give it to the captain."

"What does the message to the general say?"

"I don't know. The envelope is sealed."

"What are you doing now?"

"I'm on my horse, and I'm riding over a narrow wooden bridge that crosses a wide stream."

"Tell me everything that is happening, John."

"Another rider is coming toward me on the bridge. There is no room for two horses. I am pulling on the reins. My horse is rearing up. I'm being thrown headfirst over the side of the bridge and into the icy water below. My head hits a log which is wedged in the partly frozen stream. I'm dazed and have broken through the ice. I am in the water and don't know how to swim. It is so cold. I am going under. My lungs are filling with water. I cannot breathe. I am drowning. All is black."

Once again, a concerned Dr. Sawyer knew that it was time to bring Al back to the present.

"You're Al Chapman. It is 2010. You're in Buffalo, New York. One, two, three, four, five."

It took longer to bring Al back this time.

"Oh, Dr. Sawyer, it has happened again. It's always the same—darkness and death. When will this end?"

"I don't know, Al, but we have another water link as there was with Stanley Morgan in Maine. You were a pirate at sea when you were hanged. And your attacks on the Maid of the Mist, Skylon, and Silver Bonita were on or near water. John Mason and Stanley Morgan were both non-swimmers, and you do not like the water. However, there was no water connection at San Francisco or Salisbury."

"Remember, I choked at Salisbury and was choked somewhat in San Francisco, and my hanging. And isn't drowning a way of choking?"

"That's correct, Al. There is more of a connection than I had thought. I want to replay all of the tapes again at home to see if I missed anything. But now, you must go home and rest.

You've been through a lot in the past two days. You're doing well so far, Al. As I've said before, let me know if you remember anything more about your dreams or attacks. Everything, no matter how insignificant it may seem, can be a potential clue. By the way, are you cleared to play Sunday?"

"I haven't been examined by the Bills' doctor yet. I'll know Thursday when he checks me over. Karen wants me to retire, and I'm seriously considering it. Injuries have taken a huge toll on my body, especially my head. At my age, it takes more and more time to rebound from any injury."

"Is Karen still bugging you about our sessions, or has she given up?"

"She sure is. So far, I haven't told her anything, but she keeps probing."

"Well, keep mum. In due time, we'll let her know everything. In the meanwhile, you must stay focused on what we're doing."

"I think Karen is jealous of you. That's part of the problem. It's so unlike her to behave this way."

"Oh, that's pretty common with spouses of my patients. Don't let it bother you. Tell her about professional ethics and the doctors' oath not to cross that line. This is always a very delicate matter."

"I'll try again to convince her. Sometimes, she can be unreasonable."

"If you'd like, I'll speak to her."

"No, thanks, I'll handle it. She'll be all right."

"If that's all, I'll see you next Tuesday at the same time. Take care of yourself and stay out of trouble this week, Al—and protect your head."

"That's good advice. I'll wear my helmet around the house."

On the drive home, Al decided not to say anything to Karen about what Dr. Sawyer told him regarding professional ethics. He was upset enough about the latest regression and his death as John Mason. All he wanted to do was go home and rest. To his great surprise, Karen was not at the door to greet him and did not ask him about the latest session when he came into the house. Al was suspicious of her behavior.

I wonder what she's up to—probably using a little psychology on me. That's all I need—another psychologist.

"What would you like for lunch today?"

"I don't care. I'm not very hungry."

"Go into the den, stretch out, and relax. You must be exhausted. I'll call you when lunch is ready in about fifteen minutes."

Al breathed a sigh of relief.

"She's off the jealous track for the time being. I wonder what she's up to."

In the kitchen, Karen was up to something. She was form- ing a plan in her mind.

I've been pretty pushy with Al lately, trying to find out what's been going on in those sessions with Dr. Sawyer. I'll just cool it for a while and let him tell me when he's ready. If I know Al, and I do, he'll confide in me soon.

Karen put the finishing touches on a chicken salad and removed warm rolls from the oven. She called to Al, "Lunch is on the table, Al. Come and eat."

CHAPTER 20

After a long day of seeing patients at the Psychiatric Center, and afterwards at her private office, Dr. Sawyer packed her brief case and left for home at five o'clock. With her, she took the tapes of all three sessions with Al, intending to listen to them again. Perhaps she would be able to find a common connecting link, which may have been overlooked before.

A divorced mother of two girls—Candace, five; and Amy, seven, she was having a difficult time balancing her career with her family life. Her divorce, due to irreconcilable religious differences two years ago, was ugly. Her husband, James Stein, also an MD, was unhappy with the settlement, which gave Elizabeth custody of the girls, but he had no intention of contesting it. Stein saw his daughters two weekends a month, two weeks in the summer, and certain religious holidays such as Hanukkah, since he was Jewish.

Born in 1971 she received her Bachelor of Arts degree from Harvard in 1991, and her Doctor of Medicine degree in 1995 from Georgetown University. Her residency in psychiatry was done at New York's Mount Sinai Hospital. Despite having a full professional schedule, she managed to give birth to her two daughters, Amy and Candace, in 2003 and 2005 respectively. Although she had been practicing for only ten years, her reputation as an outstanding analyst was rapidly spreading.

Every case was treated as though it were the most important one she had. Taking work home did not interfere with the precious time she wished to spend with her daughters. She simply worked well into the night, long after they were asleep in bed.

Every day, at three o'clock, the girls would return home from Maple Road Elementary School in Williamsville, a village just east of Buffalo. Always waiting for them at the door was the housekeeper, Rosie Maxwell, a seventy-year-old widow and retired fourth-grade schoolteacher. Rosie was a substitute grandmother to the girls, whose maternal grandparents lived in Florida and came north only for short visits once or twice a year. Candy and Amy dearly loved Rosie because she played games with them, helped them with their homework, made them laugh, and took care of them in Elizabeth's absence. Standing only five feet tall and weighing less than one hundred pounds, one might be led to believe that she wasn't strong. Not so! While performing her cleaning chores, Rosie easily moves heavy furniture around in the eight room Victorian house on Reist Street. Elizabeth considered herself fortunate to have Rosie as a friend and helper.

Dinner was ready and on the table Tuesday at six o'clock. The doctor had already arrived home at five forty-five. Rosie had prepared a pot roast with roasted potatoes and mixed vegetables. Her special dessert, which the girls loved, was brownies with chocolate sauce and whipped cream. Brownies never lasted long in the Sawyer-Stein household.

"Rosie, you spoil us so. What did we ever do without you before you came into our lives? You are a part of our family."

"Oh, Doctor Elizabeth, I appreciate that, and I love you all dearly. As you know, my own children are grown up and live out of New York State, and you are aware that I only see them once a year at Christmas," she said, her kindly blue eyes filling with tears.

"Rosie, this is your home for as long as you want."

"Thank you, Doctor. I am so grateful to you, and I am thankful for your kindness and generosity."

After dinner, everyone went into the living room for a customary hour of reading before the fireplace, where Rosie had made a roaring fire to take the chill off the room. Amy sat in her mother's lap in a large stuffed chair; Candy with Rosie on the couch. Rosie and Elizabeth took turns reading to the girls. On occasion, Amy would show off her reading skills while Candy impatiently sat and listened. Sometimes, however, she would interrupt Rosie if she saw a word in the book which she knew.

"Look, Rosie, this word is 'rabbit'," Candy pointed out.

"That's correct, darlin'." You are so smart," Rosie responded and went on reading.

"Let me read now, Mom," Amy pleaded.

Elizabeth recognized the attention ploy being used and let Amy read for a while.

"Rosie, you read better than Amy, and make the stories more fun. You make all of the people in the book seem real," Candy interrupted.

"Amy, you are a very good reader, but your mother will have to finish the book now, because it's getting late."

"Girls, do you have any homework to do before bedtime? I don't want you to be unprepared in school."

"Mom, I just remembered that I have to bring some colored leaves to class tomorrow," Amy, the second-grader, remarked.

"Amy, how are we going to get leaves now? It's dark out and the middle of November. How long have you had to get the leaves?"

"We were supposed to be collecting them for a few weeks."

"Not to worry, Honey. I'll let you borrow my scrapbook of leaves which I used when I taught school. I didn't teach forty years without collecting things."

"Rosie, I have to bring in some pumpkin seeds tomorrow," Candy added.

"Oh, you kids will be the death of me. Well, it just so happens, that I have a pumpkin in the garage which I have been saving for a pie. I'll cut it up tonight and save some of the seeds for you, but you'll have to dry them on paper towels yourself in the morning. I guess we'll have pumpkin pie for dinner tomorrow."

"Thank you, Rosie. We love you," the girls said in unison.

"I love you, too, kiddos, but you take advantage of me. Now, there's a Charlie Brown Thanksgiving TV special on at eight tonight. You can watch it before you have to get ready for bed."

"I'll turn it on, Rosie. What station is it on?"

"CBS, Doctor. I'll watch the program with the girls. You can go to your office and work. When the girls are in bed, I'll call you to tuck them in for the night."

"Thanks. Rosie. I do have a lot to do tonight."

Elizabeth went to her office, which was adjacent to the living room, and again began listening to the tapes of Al's regressions. She played and replayed them before Rosie called her at nine-thirty.

"Doctor, Candy and Amy are in bed and waiting for you."

The girls were lying in their twin beds waiting for their mother. Elizabeth was smiling as she entered their shared bedroom.

"Let's say our prayers together," Elizabeth began.

"Our Father, who art in heaven…" they recited together. "God bless Mom and Rosie and Dad," Amy continued.

"And everyone in the whole world," Candy added.

"'That was very nice, girls. God always listens to our prayers." Elizabeth then tucked them in their beds and kissed each goodnight. "Good night, Candy. Good night, Amy. I love my little angels."

"We love you too. Mom. Good night."

Rosie was already in the kitchen cutting up the pumpkin for tomorrow's pie. Elizabeth turned out the lights and returned to her office to begin listening to Al's tapes again.

"Al has dreams or regressions into at least five centuries. I wonder how that little blonde girl fits into all of this. And why does she keep popping up around Al? Based upon the style of the girl's clothing, she possibly could have lived in the fifteenth century. Al's death aboard the pirate ship took place in the 1400s. And how does that woman, Myra Johnson, fit into this? As the pattern seems to be developing, there has apparently been one incarnation a century. As yet, however, there is no seventeenth century life. It appears that Al may have to endure two more regressions to reach the fifteenth century, and perhaps, the little blonde girl. So far, there are more questions than answers."

It was already one-thirty when Elizabeth decided to call it quits and retire for the night. Wednesday, she had other important cases to work on and hospital visits to make. Sleep did not come easily. Her thoughts turned to Al.

"He is still resisting accepting the theory of reincarnation because of his Catholicism, but I think that he slowly is becoming more receptive to the belief. It's just a matter of time before he embraces it," she hoped. "His wife is affecting his thinking, but I cannot force this concept on him. Regardless, reincarnation is the vehicle that is going to carry Al toward an eventual cure. I am certain that his memories of past lives are real. He is such a fine man. My heart goes out to him."

Then she remembered what Al had told her about Karen's suspicions about Al and herself.

And what about his wife? Apparently, she's jealous of me. There is really no reason for her to be. I've been very professional with Al in all aspects of our sessions. I must admit, though, that I find him extremely attractive. He's so different from James. What am I thinking of? I can't jeopardize my career by breaching my code of ethics. I'm satisfied with things as they are. The girls mean everything to me, and I do not want to get involved in another relationship for a long time.

It would be a very short night. She had to be at the Psychiatric Center by eight o'clock and would have to be up at six, but still, she tossed and turned as she dreamt. It was not a nightmare but more like a déjà vu dream; not her life, but her stepfather's.

In the dream, her stepfather, Uday Kareishi, was a British soldier named Robert Smythe, living in the American colonies during the Revolutionary War. She saw him on a horse, riding over a narrow bridge toward another rider, whose horse threw him over the bridge and into the half-frozen stream below. Uday made a futile attempt to save the life of the American by jumping into the stream after him. But he could not save the man who slipped beneath the ice and drowned. Elizabeth awoke and sat up in bed in disbelief.

My God, it was all true. As a child of eleven, I would sit by his side and listen to stories he would tell about his past lives. I never believed his claims of living as a British soldier in the colonies during the 1700s. My father tried to save John Mason. I'm stunned. This can't be happening. Maybe this might explain why I feel such an attraction for Al. In a remote way, I am connected to a life lived by Al Chapman. God, do I have a conflict of interest in this case now? This is bizarre!

CHAPTER 21

Al was not cleared to play in the Monday Night Football game in Denver, since he was experiencing dizzy spells. During his football career, including high school and college, he had four concussions. The doctors did not want to risk further injury. Head injuries sustained by athletes can cause permanent neurological damage. Al didn't want to tell Dr. Sawyer because he was anxious to continue with the sessions. He was fearful that she would cancel the appointment, fearing a malpractice suit. He also just wanted to see her. He had missed her more than he wanted to admit, and he cautioned himself.

I've got to push her image out of your mind; I'm a happily married man.

Karen was still pressing him to retire this season, but Al wanted to finish the year and then play one more season. The money was good. They wanted to have enough saved for the kids' college educations and their own senior years; barring any major catastrophe.

Although he did attend team meetings, his week was spent mainly resting. Karen suggested that they go out to lunch Monday; just the two of them. She was hopeful that Al would be in a good mood and would confide in her. He had always refused to tell her anything in the past. She thus had to plan carefully.

"Let's go to the Red Lobster for lunch today, Al. We haven't had any seafood in some time, because the kids always turn their noses up at it. What did children eat before pizza and hamburgers? Or didn't they eat when they disliked something?"

"They ate what was placed before them on their plates, or they went to bed hungry. Things were much different in the old days—the thirties and forties."

"What do you know about the old days, did you? You weren't even born yet."

"My parents told me about the Great Depression and how there were bread lines for the starving people. This was not the land of plenty for them then."

"But you never went without, did you, Al?"

"What a beautiful day it is—just right for going to the Red Lobster."

They arrived at the restaurant at noon. It was surprisingly busy for a Monday. Both ordered the shrimp scampi, garlic mashed potatoes, and a Caesar salad.

"These hot cheese biscuits are delicious. Why is everything that tastes so good so fattening? I'm glad Melissa isn't here to see this. She wouldn't let us have a bite of anything. Let's not tell the kids."

Al nodded in agreement.

"What's the matter, Al? Are you down in the dumps again?"

"Oh, it's a lot of things—not being able to play tonight on Monday Night Football, the upcoming session with Dr. Sawyer, my future. I wish this ordeal was over, and soon. I have many doubts about myself."

"You know, if you would confide in me about those sessions with Dr. Sawyer, I might be able to help."

"I don't know about that, Karen. It's a private part of me that I am reluctant to share. Dr. Sawyer has given me strict orders not to discuss anything with anyone—not even you."

"We're married, or have you forgotten—through thick and through thin? The whole enchilada. Don't you trust me? Aren't we supposed to share the good and the bad—the beautiful and the ugly? This is the ugly, isn't it?"

"Yes, it is. I'm just afraid that you won't understand this stuff that Dr. Sawyer is uncovering. Some of it is quite shocking. You might not be able to handle it."

"Try me—I'm a good listener."

"Well, you know some of the things already—the dreams, the anxiety attacks at the Maid of the Mist and the Skylon, Salisbury, and the Tower of London, and of course, the little blonde girl."

He failed to mention the attack aboard the Silver Bonito, which Karen never knew about. That was something he didn't want to tell her.

"Dr. Sawyer has been hypnotizing and regressing me to past lifetimes, and it has been very traumatic for me."

"Are you kidding? You don't believe in that stuff, do you? We're Catholics, not Hindus. This is dangerous territory you're getting into."

"I knew you wouldn't understand. That's why I didn't want to tell you anything. Dr. Sawyer warned me that this would happen, and she was right."

"Oh, Al, I'm sorry. I shouldn't have commented. Won't you please continue with the story? I'll be good."

"Dr. Sawyer has taken me back to former lives in Maine in 1912, San Francisco in 1825, and Valley Forge in 1776. She is trying to find connecting links which are common to the dreams, the anxiety attacks, and the regressions. So far, water and choking seem to be the most promising common threads. The doctor is attempting to identify more of these connections. Then maybe she will be able to figure out why I'm having these attacks."

"What about that little English girl? How does she fit into all of this, or doesn't she? Did you discuss her with Dr. Sawyer?"

"The Doctor knows about her, but right now, she's baffled. There may be a connection, but we don't know what it is yet. It's going to take time to sort all of this out, but I have complete confidence in her."

"What are you doing in tomorrow's session? Are you anxious about it? Does the doctor let you know what is coming next?"

"I don't know, probably another regression. Maybe there will be a clue hidden someplace. Yes, I'm full of anxiety every time I sit in that recliner."

"Can I go with you? Maybe it would help."

"No, it's not allowed. There is a strict doctor-patient code of ethics which cannot be violated. Now, no more questions. I've said too much already."

"Well, I tried anyway. Whatever happens, you have my total support. If you need a shoulder, I have two ready for you."

"Thank you—I appreciate that. Now, I'm worried because I have broken the doctor's orders not to tell anyone about our sessions."

"Don't fuss, Al—I won't tell anyone."

They finished eating and drove home to be on time to greet the children when they arrived home from school. Right on time, at ten after three, the yellow bus pulled up in front of their house. Jonathan and Melissa came running into the house, book bags flying, as usual.

"How was school today, kids? What did you learn, Jonathan?"

"Same old stuff. Sister Joseph is harping on grammar lately—boring."

"Good, you need to speak and write correct English."

"We're studying about the American Revolution, Mom. It's very interesting. Those colonists were our first heroes, I think.

We wouldn't be as free as we are today if they hadn't fought and died for freedom."

"That's right, Melissa—we owe them a lot. By the way, I haven't anything prepared for dinner. Dad and I went out to lunch today, so we're not hungry. Would you like macaroni and cheese and tomato soup?"

"That will be fine, Mom."

"What about you, Jonathan?"

"That's okay with me."

The Chapmans watched Monday Night Football. The Bills lost to Denver in overtime, 17 to 14. Jonathan was allowed to see only the first half because of the late hour while Melissa preferred to read a book about the American Revolution. Both were in bed at ten o'clock. Al and Karen viewed the rest of the game together.

"Well, it looks like the Bills are definitely out of the play-offs. We should get a pretty high draft choice this year with our bad record," Al predicted.

Then he became pensive and confided in Karen one more time.

"Karen, I'm afraid to go through another regression tomorrow. It's very traumatic. All I do is suffer and die a different way every week."

"Don't you think that is significant? No two are exactly alike? It seems to me that many people, who have anxiety attacks, have recurring dreams which often have one commonality. Apparently, you are made ill by several things."

"I think you're on to something. I'll run this by the doctor tomorrow. Maybe you should hang out your shingle."

"No, I don't believe in reincarnation. It's against our belief in the resurrection."

"It's hard to accept, but I can see some advantages to it. Sometimes it seems so right. It sure beats the Catholic version—threatening us with hell and damnation after one life."

"Please Al, don't discuss reincarnation anymore. It's against the teachings of the Church, and we're still practicing Catholics. You are sinning if you believe in it."

"Says who?"

"The Pope."

"He does not. He never says anything about it. It's not in our catechism. I'm not buying into all of it—just the parts that may help explain my attacks. Now I'm sorry I told you anything. Please don't criticize anything that Dr. Sawyer is trying to do."

"Okay, you and your dear doctor can have your secrets."

"What is that supposed to mean? I've told you—nothing is going on between us."

CHAPTER 22

As usual, Dr. Sawyer was waiting for Al when he arrived at her office at nine o'clock on Tuesday. Both were eager to begin the session, but first, Al wanted to share with the doctor his and Karen's conversation the previous day.

"Doctor, I have a few things to tell you about since our last session. You're going to be angry with me, but last night, Karen and I discussed my case. She pressured me so much that I finally gave in and told her that I was being regressed to former lifetimes. She hit the ceiling when I told her that the concept of reincarnation was involved."

"Why doesn't this surprise me, Al? Remember, I warned you about sharing these sessions with her. Unwittingly, she could influence what you recall in future sessions. She may already have damaged the case. Do you realize the implications of this?"

"Yes, I do. I'm terribly sorry, but she is a very persistent woman. She did make one interesting observation, though. Very often, she pointed out people who have anxiety attacks, such as mine, have only one recurring theme in their dreams— not several, as I have had. To be sure, she's had no training in psychology, but how do you explain this?"

"Karen makes a good point, but your case is obviously much more complex than most. Some persons whom we observe often exhibit symptoms caused by just one factor, such as fear of water, which may be traced back to a long forgotten frightening childhood experience. In your case, we have already identified two factors—water and choking in some form such as drowning. You've told me that you are not afraid of the water. Yet you are not a swimmer nor are you afraid that you are going to choke every time you eat a meal. My hunch is that there are more than two factors involved. Your anxiety attacks appear to be triggered by many things buried deep in your subconscious which are sometimes aroused by certain conscious visual stimulations."

She paused for a moment and looked directly at Al, who looked upset.

"Enough of this for the time being. How is your head? Are you still feeling dizzy? If you are still feeling any effects from your concussion, we cannot proceed today."

Al lied because he wanted to get on with the session.

"My head is much better, and I am not dizzy today. I want to find out as soon as we can what is causing these attacks. Let's get on with it. I'm ready."

That was good enough for Dr. Sawyer, who quickly hypnotized Al.

"Today, Al, I want you to go back in time to the seventeenth century—the 1600s. Are you living during this period?"

"Yes, I be."

"Revisit the circumstances of the day you died. What is the date?"

"Tiz fourtene Juin, one thoosand siex hundred ond fourty eighte."

"What is your name?"

"Mi nama es Peter Mitchell."

"How old are you, Peter?"

"I be thirty."

"What is your occupation or trade?"

"I be a historie professor at Cambridge Universite."

"Where is your home?"

"In Cambridge, England."

"Where are you now, Peter?"

"I be a prisonere in a dunjon in the Tower of London."

"Why are you there?"

"We hav civil war in England. I speke out against King Charles secundus ond trien to lead a revolte against the Crowne. Hiz army captured me ond imprisoned me."

"What is your sentence?"

"I wille be biheeded."

"When are you to be beheaded, Peter?"

"Thies morn. Thei wille come for me soone."

"How long have you been in prison?"

"About six months."

"How have you been treated in prison?"

"I be beten bi the garde. Thei puncheon me ond kikke me in mi head ond all over mi body. I be hungry. Thei onle give me bread ond som water twice a day. Tiz cold ond dampf in heyre. I ache all over."

"What's happening now?"

"I hear the garde come for me. I be very afreyd."

"What are they doing?"

"Thei be holden me doun. One of thaem es pulle doun mi trousers. *O mi Gode*, thei be pusshen a sword in mi ass. The pain es terribil. Blod es everywhar. Thei hitte me wit clubben ond kikke me on the head. I falle. Thei pulle me up ond throwe me doun the tower stepe. I be lyin in a pool of mi blod at the bottome of the stepe. Mi nekke es broken. I be dien. All es blak."

Once again, the doctor, sensing the horror that Al was experiencing, returned him to consciousness.

"Return to the year 2010, Al. You are in Buffalo. You're all right."

"Oh, Doctor Sawyer, it was awful—the worst yet. I was so afraid. The pain was excruciating. It was another horrible death for me."

"I'm trembling myself from your ordeal. This past life has revealed much to us. There was no water or choking. But there was a broken neck, a traumatic head injury, another falling incident, and a perverse act of sodomy. Remember you were raped in San Francisco? Were you aware that you were speaking in Middle English?"

"Yes, I was, but I could understand your questions in Modern English."

"That's a new aspect of this case."

"No, Doctor—it really isn't. In my first dream, the hanging aboard the pirate ship, the language was like today's session. You called it Middle English."

"I had some difficulty understanding all of the words. I must replay the tapes and use a Merriam-Webster Dictionary to translate from Middle English to Modern English. Let's review what we know so far."

"You were beaten about the head and hanged on a pirate ship in 1448. There was water, but it played no part in your choking death. Middle English was spoken in the dream. In Salisbury, 1564, you dreamt that you chocked on a piece of meat. No water was involved that we know of. You were not beaten about the head, but you did violently hit your head on a heavy table as you fell to the floor and died. In 1776, near Valley Forge, Pennsylvania, you were thrown over a bridge into icy way, hit your head on a log, and drowned."

"As a woman in San Francisco in 1825, you were raped, beaten about the head, choked and thrown from a window, falling three stories to your death. During a severe storm in 1912, off the coast of Maine, you were thrown from your rowboat into the ocean, was castrated, dashed your head against the rocks and drowned. And today, from what I could understand, in 1648 you were tortured in the Tower of London. I believe that you were kicked and beaten about the head with a club, sodomized, and thrown down the tower's steps, breaking your neck. I'll have to check the tape on this at home tonight."

"Are you close to getting answers?"

"Very close, I think, Al. Falling has occurred in four of the cases. Choking or a broken neck have occurred in five of the cases, which is very significant. Water has played a part in two instances and sex acts in two. This is an amazing story of incarnations. I realize that reliving this ordeal has taken a lot out of you today, Al. Go home and rest, and please don't tell Karen anything. Promise?"

"I promise that I won't, Doctor."

At exactly eleven o'clock, Karen watched Al's car drive up the driveway and into the garage. She met him as he entered the house.

"How did it go today, Dear? You look beat. What happened?"

Despite his promise to Dr. Sawyer, Al could not help himself.

"Today was the most horrifying experience I have ever had. I cannot give you any specifics, but my suffering was excruciating. Things are beginning to come together and I'm very encouraged. All that I can tell you is that I have lived many interesting lives and experienced some horrific deaths. But, I long for the day when all of this will be over."

"Thanks for sharing that much with me, Al. I won't pressure you for anything more. I do want to apologize to you for the reincarnation argument we had yesterday. Hundreds of millions, perhaps billions, of people around the world believe in it, so who am I to decide that it has no merit? When I get a chance, I'm going to get some books from the library on reincarnation."

"That's a good idea, Karen. I'll read them too. We should learn more about other religions and their beliefs. We Catholics have been too isolated and protected. Who is to say that Catholics are correct about everything and everyone else is wrong?"

"We must try to be more understanding of other beliefs. Your experiences are making us both more open minded. Perhaps, someday, our priests will be allowed to speak to us more openly about other religious beliefs and have discussions about them."

"Karen, I'm proud of you. I think that you are beginning to see the light."

"I'm trying, Al. And please tell Dr. Sawyer that I am sorry for interfering. She's the doctor; not I. And I do respect her and trust her."

"I'm sure she'll be happy to hear that."

"I hope so. It's important for me to be on her side."

Al was positively amazed by this sudden change in Karen's attitude. He was relieved and thankful for this apparent one hundred and eighty degree turn by her. But Karen was not yet totally sold on the concept of reincarnation. She still had doubts and wanted to read about the subject to ease her fears. She thought about them.

I cannot understand why Al is going through so much pain and suffering. If reincarnation is fairer than one life per person, where is the happiness? Where is the reward? And what does the Catholic Church really say about reincarnation? Is it a serious sin to believe in it? Maybe all of my questions will be answered once I begin reading.

CHAPTER 23

Time was quickly passing. The Bills had a bye week in their schedule, which gave Al another seven days to recover from his concussion. Since he continued to mull over in his mind the idea of retiring, he wondered about what he would do if he no longer played football. With a degree in political science from the University of Virginia, he could take the same path which former Buffalo Bill, Jack Kemp, took in politics. Or maybe he could coach. There were always vacancies, but there wasn't much security there. If he doesn't have a winning record, often-times the coach doesn't last through the season. Al did not want to uproot his family, settle in another city, stay a couple of years, and then, perhaps, move again. They all loved the Western New York area.

The kids have important friendships. They're active in school. It would be wrong to ask them to sacrifice so much for me. On the other hand, Karen is flexible and can adapt to any change, large or small, he thought.

It was already late-November; the weather was turn-ing colder, and before long, lake effect snowstorms would be in the local forecasts. Lake effect snow occurs when cold air moves across the warm water of Lake Erie. The warm moisture is drawn up, cooled, and deposited as snow, usually south of Buffalo. The children had heard that Kissing Bridge Ski Resort, just south of Orchard Park, had opened last weekend, since they made snow artificially. They kept pestering their parents to take them skiing until they finally agreed to go Saturday.

Friday evening, lake effect dumped two feet of snow on the southern tier, including Colden, where Kissing Bridge was located. The Chapmans were up and ready early. Karen packed their lunches, while Al loaded the ski equipment into the van. By eight o'clock, they were on their way to the slopes, and it was still snowing. The parking lots were almost full when they arrived, but Al managed to get a good spot near the first aid station. After buying their all-day ski tickets, which set Al back $200, they were ready to hit the slopes for the first time this year.

Karen and Al were still struggling intermediate skiers, but Melissa and Jonathan were becoming experts. The slopes were crowded, mostly with teenagers intent upon racing straight down the hills without traversing. To add to the mix, snowboarders were now invading the ski areas and were becoming another hazard to skiers. The conditions were ideal; two feet of new powder on eighteen inches of base. The four of them rode the quad chair together to the top of Mistletoe, an intermediate slope. After several exhilarating runs, Karen decided to go into the lodge to claim a table and   set out their lunches, while Al and the children made one more run. Jonathan sped down the slope; Melissa remained with Al and together they traversed across Mistletoe. Al was tiring and intended to ski directly to the lodge. Father and daughter were slowly moving across the slope when Melissa looked over at Al and yelled.

"Dad, look out! There's a kid coming at you, fast!"

Her warning came too late. Al was hit from behind by an out-of-control teenager schussing down the hill. Speed was all he was concentrating on, not the safety of other skiers in his path. As he fell, the boy's skis hit Al full force in the head. After getting himself up and putting his skis on again, he stood over

Al, who was lying limp on the snow. Looking directly at him, without attempting to help or get help for the unconscious man he shouted at him.

"Look what you did, mister. Why don't you learn how to ski? You old people shouldn't be allowed on the slopes."

After picking up his poles, the teenager continued down the slope without looking back. Melissa, who was downhill a bit from her father, climbed up to him and screamed for help.

"Ski patrol, help! Someone please come and help my father!"

Minutes later, two ski patrollers arrived with a toboggan. Kneeling next to Al, they removed his skis, which had not released when he fell, and placed them crosswise in the snow above him in order to warn other approaching skiers of an accident. One of the men brought some smelling salts near Al's nose.

"Mister, wake up! Can you hear me?" There was a weak response.

"Where am I? What happened? My head hurts badly. Where is Karen?"

"You've been injured in a skiing accident. Try to move your arms and legs. Do you hurt anywhere else?"

"I don't think so. I don't know. My head hurts awful."

"Dad, a kid ran into you and his skis hit your head."

"Did you see who hit him?" one of the patrollers asked as they tried to slide Al onto the toboggan and strap him in.

"It was a young kid, about twelve or thirteen. He was wearing a red jacket and blue jeans. He's probably hiding in a car in the parking lot by now."

"We're going to take you down to the first aid station now, sir. Try not to move your head. Remain perfectly still, if you can."

They began the slow descent to the bottom of the slope. Then they helped Al into the first aid station and onto a table. There, he was carefully examined to determine if there were other injuries. Having decided that there were none and that Al was not critically injured, they decided not to call for the emergency trauma helicopter. "Is there anyone here with you, besides your daughter, who can drive you to Mercy Hospital?" one of the attendants asked Al. Looking at Melissa, he said, "Your father may need x-rays of his head."

"My mom is in the lodge. I'll get her," Melissa responded.

Karen was in disbelief when Melissa reached her and told her what had happened to Al. They quickly packed up all of the food, which Karen had put out on the table, and skied over to the first aid station.

"Melissa, go and find Jonathan and get him over here."

"All right, Mom—I'll get him."

Karen rushed inside and looked at Al sitting in a wheel-chair. "Al, are you hurt badly?"

"Oh, my head is killing me. I can't stand the pain. Get me to the hospital fast."

"How bad is his injury?"

"We don't believe that it's life threatening, but we've called ahead to Mercy Hospital to expect you. We'll help you get him into your car. Can you drive in this weather? The roads are treacherous."

"Yes, I can. What about accident insurance? Aren't you going to take down any information about the accident?"

"There is no insurance coverage for skiers. Your ticket clearly states that you ski at your own risk. KB is not liable for any injuries. We're sorry, but that's the policy."

"So are we!" Karen answered sharply.

Melissa and Jonathan arrived just as Al was being helped into the front seat of the van. Jonathan loaded everything in the back, and after everyone was strapped into their seatbelts, Karen turned on the ignition.

"Drive very carefully and try not to hit any bumps or holes. The hospital knows that you're on your way. They'll be waiting at Emergency for you."

Anxious to get going, Karen thanked everybody and drove carefully out of the parking lot and onto Route 240. With every turn in the road, Al moaned and groaned.

"Can't you go any faster, Karen? The pain is excruciating."

"Al, the roads are very slippery. I don't want to crack up the van getting you to the hospital. I can't jostle your head. I'm doing the best I can."

Actually, the ride took thirty minutes. At the emergency entrance, two attendants, who were awaiting their arrival, hurriedly brought a wheelchair to the van and carefully slid Al into it. He was wheeled immediately to an examination cubicle while Karen provided the necessary medical information to the admissions' nurse. Melissa and Jonathan sat nervously in the waiting room which was full of people.

After about a forty-minute wait, the resident physician came to examine Al, who was lying on a gurney, moaning.

"Hello, Mr. Chapman. I'm Doctor Miller. I understand that you have a head injury from a skiing accident at Kissing Bridge. We've had a lot of broken legs and arms from there today. How bad is the pain?"

"It's the mother of all headaches, Doctor. Please, can't you give me something?"

"I'm going to send you for x-rays first. I can't give you anything until we know how bad the injury is, Mr. Chapman. We have to be careful of hemorrhaging. Do you hurt anyplace else?"

"No, it's just my head that hurts. Please, give me something for this pain."

"All right, I'll have the nurse get it for you."

The medication did little to relieve the pain. After another forty minutes, an orderly arrived and took Al down the corridor to the x-ray department. In the meantime, Karen had gone to the waiting room to check on the children.

"Kids, we're going to be here for some time. You both must be hungry. Melissa, here's twenty dollars. You and Jonathan go to the cafeteria and get something to eat. Have a balanced meal: vegetables, chicken, fruit. Melissa, you know what to pick out for the two of you. When you're finished, come back here and wait for me."

"How is Dad, Mom?"

"We'll know more after they read the x-ray pictures, Melissa."

Karen returned to the examination cubicle and waited for Al to come back from x-ray. It was five-thirty when he finally returned. His face was ashen, and he looked ghastly.

"How are you doing, Dear?"

"Not very well. I need a stronger pain killer."

"Dr. Miller should be here soon, I hope."

It was seven o'clock when Dr. Miller reappeared. A hand-some, distinguished-looking young man in his twenties; he spoke directly to Al.

"Mr. Chapman, we're going to have to admit you. The x-rays show that you have a hairline fracture of your skull, just above your right ear. I'll give you something stronger for the pain, but it will make you sleepy. Don't try to fight it. You must rest. We'll get you to a room as soon as one becomes available. Tomorrow, a neurosurgeon will examine you more thoroughly and decide on the course of treatment for you. I would guess that you'll be with us for a few days—just as a precaution."

"That's bad news, Doctor Miller."

"You need rest, Mr. Chapman. This injury was not just an ordinary bump on the head—it's quite serious. A little bit lower and you might be dead."

"I feel woozy."

"Good. I gave you morphine, and it's taking hold. Now close your eyes and sleep."

A few minutes later, Al was taken to Room 507, where an aide helped him undress and get into bed. Within minutes, he was sound asleep. Karen kissed him softly on his forehead and tiptoed out of the room. It was almost eight o'clock when she stopped at the nurses' station to talk to the head nurse who was reading a magazine. Her nametag identified her as Sara Albright. Seeing some movement in front of her, she looked up at Karen and spoke.

"Can I help you?"

"Yes, Mrs. Albright. I'm Mrs. Chapman. My husband was just admitted to Room 507. Would it be all right if I called you later to see how he is doing?"

"Of course, Mrs. Chapman. Call anytime. I'll leave a message for the resident neurosurgeon, Dr. Matthews, to see you in the morning after he has examined your husband. Come in around eleven o'clock."

"Thank you. Please call me if there is any problem."

"We will, Mrs. Chapman. Don't worry. Your husband will be fine. His skull will heal, although it will take time."

Satisfied, Karen returned to the emergency waiting room where the children were watching *Law and Order* on TV. They were tired and eager to get home.

"How's Dad, Mom? When can he come home?"

"He's sleeping now, Jonathan. It looks like he'll have to stay here a few days. He has a skull fracture and they want to keep him under observation."

"Will he be all right?"

"Yes, but I think he'll have to take it easy for a few weeks, Melissa."

It was almost ten o'clock when they arrived home. Karen called the hospital and was told that Al was resting comfortably. Jonathan unloaded the car and brought their nearly frozen lunches into the kitchen. Reheated in the microwave, they tasted pretty good to the weary family. In bed by eleven, Karen could not sleep.

"Poor Al. What else can happen to him? He's having such bad luck. This latest injury will surely make it impossible for him to play football again."

Sunday morning, they arose early for eight o'clock Mass at Saint Margaret's. After Mass, Karen took her children to the Towne Restaurant. Before they left home, Karen made sure that both children had their homework with them. It was just about eleven o'clock when they arrived at the hospital. Once again, the children went to the waiting room, while Karen went up to Al's room. As she entered, she could hear him talking to someone, but she saw nobody in the room. He apparently was hallucinating.

"Mary, I'm so sorry, so terribly sorry for what I did. I deserve every bit of punishment that I get. God knows my heart. I am truly sorry."

Astonished, Karen stood at the door and listened, while Al continued speaking to the empty room.

"Yes, I know that you have been watching me. My daughter, Melissa, sees you."

"Al, who are you speaking to?" Karen interrupted.

He seemed to be half asleep and did not answer. Then a tall, handsome, gray-haired man entered the room.

"Mrs. Chapman? I'm Doctor Matthews. I examined your husband earlier this morning. As you know, he has a skull fracture. Just to be on the side of caution, I want to keep him here under observation for a few days. It takes time for a fracture of this nature to knit. We must watch for swelling of the brain. What he needs most now is rest."

"Dr. Matthews, I think that Al has been hallucinating. When I arrived, he was speaking with someone in the room, but there wasn't anybody here. Is this to be expected?"

"That's quite common, Mrs. Chapman. Perhaps it's the medication. Don't worry about it. I understand that he has had prior concussions playing football. We must be careful dealing with any head injuries. You can call me if you have any concerns about his condition. So far, he's doing okay, the pressure in his skull is stable, and I'm pleased."

"Thank you, Dr. Matthews. Oh, I almost forgot to ask you. Is it all right if our children visit their father? They're anxious to see him."

"Of course. It's okay, but only for a few minutes for the first two days. Al must rest."

"I understand. They won't stay long."

Karen remained with Al for almost an hour and watched him sleep. So as not to awaken him, she kissed him lightly on the cheek and whispered in his ear.

"Sleep well, Dear. See you tomorrow."

In the waiting room, the children were busily working on their schoolwork, or so they wanted her to believe. She decided not to let them see their father yet.

"Come on, kids—we're going home. It's way past lunchtime. Your dad is still heavily sedated and asleep now. You both can visit him tomorrow after school but only for a few minutes. The doctor doesn't want us to tire him."

"Good. Then we'll see him tomorrow when he's awake."

At home again, Karen quickly prepared grilled cheese sandwiches. Afterward, Jonathan went to his room to work on his computer; Melissa remained in the kitchen to help her mother with the dishes, but she had something more serious to discuss with her.

"'Mom, guess who I saw on the slopes yesterday watching Dad after the accident?"

"Not that blonde kid again? Why am I not surprised? She's everywhere your father is lately. What was she doing this time?"

"You guessed it. She was standing there in the snow next to Dad, watching him and smiling, and counting on her fingers again."

"Are you sure?"

"Pretty sure. I think she wanted me to see her counting."

"Melissa, today, as I was entering your dad's room, I heard him talking to someone, but the room was empty. He was speaking to a 'Mary' and telling her how sorry he was for what he did. The doctor thinks he was hallucinating. I'm not so sure that he was."

"Mom, Dad could have been talking to the blonde girl. Maybe her name is Mary."

"I'm thinking the same thing. I wish I knew who she is and why she's hanging around your father. Is there anything more you can tell me about her?"

"I've told you everything I know about her, Mom."

"I believe you have, Honey. You've been a big help in all of this."

After the children had left for school, Karen decided to call Dr. Sawyer.

"Dr. Sawyer, it's Karen Chapman. I have more bad news about Al. He's in Mercy Hospital with a fractured skull which he got yesterday skiing at Kissing Bridge. Unfortunately, he'll be in the hospital for a few more days, and of course, will miss his appointment with you tomorrow. I was wondering if I could come in tomorrow instead of Al?"

"Another head injury? Of course, you may have Al's appointment, but could you come in Wednesday at nine instead of tomorrow? Is there a problem, Mrs. Chapman?"

"Wednesday will be fine. I can't say too much over the phone. It's about the little blonde English girl. I think Al saw her in the hospital and was talking to her."

"We'll discuss this when you come in Wednesday. However, I'd like to go and visit Al before then. Would that be all right? What room is he in?"

"It's okay for you to visit him, I'm sure. He's in Room 507."

"Room 507? That rings a bell for some reason. I'll try to see Al tomorrow morning before I make my rounds at the psychiatric center."

"I'm sure he will be happy to see you, Dr. Sawyer."

"Thanks for calling and letting me know about the accident. This will set our sessions back quite a bit, I'm afraid."

"Doctor, I almost forgot to mention it to you. Melissa saw the little girl on the slopes after Al's accident. She was watching him and smiling as usual and appeared to be counting on her fingers."

"Melissa certainly appears to be a very sensitive and psychic little girl. She has seen the girl around Al on several occasions, hasn't she?"

"Yes, she even saw her on TV at the football game in which Al sustained a concussion. She was standing near Al watching him after he was injured."

"Did she see her counting there also?"

"Yes, I believe she did. What do you make of this counting business?"

"I don't know, but I think Al knows and, sooner or later, we'll all know what it means. We'll talk about all of this Wednesday."

"Okay, I'll see you Wednesday at nine o'clock."

After hanging up the phone, Karen decided to prepare a tuna fish casserole for dinner so she could pop it in the oven when they returned home from the hospital.

It was exactly eleven o'clock when she entered Al's room. He was sitting up in his chair, looking a little grumpy, while Dr. Matthews was examining him.

"Good morning, Doctor. How is Al doing?"

"Mrs. Chapman, he's doing as well as can be expected, considering the seriousness of his injury. There will be some noticeable improvement each day. His headache seems to be better today. There is little swelling. I'll be able to take him off all medication soon."

"That's good to hear, isn't it, Al?"

"I guess so."

"I'd like you to sit up in your chair for a couple of hours every afternoon and evening if you can, Al," Dr. Matthews suggested.

After the Doctor left, Karen stayed with Al until one o'clock while he ate a light lunch. She noticed he was tiring, so she started for the door.

"The children want to see you today after school. We should be here about three-thirty."

"I'm anxious to see them too. It's boring sitting here all alone."

"Now close your eyes and rest for a couple of hours. We'll see you later. Love you."

"Love you too."

The children were happy to see their father, but they talked constantly. Al soon became exhausted from all of their chatter. Recognizing this, Karen abruptly ended their visit after just fifteen minutes.

"All right, kids, your Dad is tired. We've got to get home so you can work on your homework."

"Aw, gee, Mom, we just got here," Jonathan complained.

"You can come back to see me later in the week. I'll be able to talk more then."

"Okay, we'll be back. We miss you, Dad."

"Al, is there anything I can bring you from home?"

"Yes, could you bring me some of those books we were discussing the other day?"

"I'll go to the library tomorrow and bring them to the hospital when you're a little better and can see to read."

"Okay, boss."

"Oh, Al, have I been promoted?"

"Yes, but only until I get home."

"Easy come, easy go."

All three Chapmans kissed Al and waved goodbye as they left his room. He was already dozing off.

"Mom, will Dad ever be able to play football again?"

"I doubt it very much, Jonathan. He's had too many head injuries."

"I'm glad, Mom. I want him to be home with us more," Melissa commented.

"I do, too, Honey, but that's a decision that your father must make for himself."

"I know, Mom, but I worry about him getting hurt so often lately."

The three of them left the hospital and walked to the van. It didn't seem natural for Karen to be driving instead of Al.

"It's your turn to sit in the front, Jonathan. Fasten your seatbelts. Would you kids like to stop somewhere for supper? It's nearly five o'clock. I'm quite hungry."

"'Could we go to the Italian Gardens, Mom? They have a huge salad bowl there that I like. It doesn't have a lot of fat in it."

"And don't forget about the breadsticks, Melissa. Sounds good to me. How about you, Jonathan?"

"Sure. I like their lasagna."

Karen had completely forgotten about the casserole she had previously prepared.

"All right, it's going on five o'clock now. We can get there for the early bird specials. We should be home early enough for you to get at your homework."

"Mom, did Grandma harp about homework all the time when you were in school?"

"You bet she did, Jonathan. It paid off too. My good study habits and grades helped me get a college scholarship and saved my parents a lot of money."

As they pulled into the restaurant's parking lot, Karen could not help but be sad.

"It just doesn't seem right—the three of us going out to eat without your father. I don't like having to handle the check and figure out the tip for all of us."

CHAPTER 24

Although she didn't need one since she was one of Al's physicians and did have medical access, Dr. Sawyer picked up a visitor's pass at the information desk at Mercy Hospital. She did not want to be identified by others who might wonder why a wellknown football player was seeing a psychiatrist. She knocked before entering Room 507. Al awakened to the sound of her melodious voice. He looked at the clock on his bedside table, which indicated it was ten minutes to seven in the morning. The room was overflowing with flowers and well wishes from around the country and she could tell that he was loved and respected by many.

"Good morning, Al. How are you feeling? These head injuries are getting to be a habit with you. Judging from all of these flowers, the word has spread far and wide about your accident. What's going on?"

"I don't know. I guess I'm going through a bad luck period. It's beginning to get to me, so I've decided to retire from football—too many head injuries. I wanted you to know before it became public. I don't want to risk damaging my brain anymore. With my history of concussions, it's too much of a gamble. I have enough money to provide for me and my family and for the kids' educations and still be able to live comfortably."

"I think you've made a wise decision. You must consider the ramifications of being permanently disabled if you're injured again."

"How did you know about my accident?"

"'Karen called me, terribly upset, to cancel your appointment for today. In fact, she asked if she could have your time."

"Oh no. Why is she doing that? She knows that I don't want her interfering in my case. Why doesn't she listen to me?"

"Apparently, she wants to discuss that little girl, whom she is now calling 'Mary,' and how Melissa fits into all of this. Somehow, there is a link between Melissa and this girl. She is coming in to speak with me tomorrow morning."

"I'm angry with her about this, Doctor."

"I understand that you're upset but let me handle this. Right now, I have something else to discuss with you that Karen told me about. It seems that this little English girl appeared to you yesterday in your room and spoke with you. Karen said that you were delirious and speaking to someone she believes you called 'Mary.' Do you remember that conversation, Al?"

"I have a vague recollection of hearing Mary speak with me, but the actual details of the conversation are like a fading dream. I can't hold on to them. They're gone, and I can't recover them."

"Can you remember anything about Mary? Think. Who is she? What is her connection to you? Have you ever seen her before?"

"I cannot consciously remember anything about her."

"Apparently, she knows you and has been watching you for a long time—months, maybe years, maybe centuries. In fact, Al, when you're able, we can try to retrieve that conversation that I believe is vital to your case."

"It will be quite a while. Right now, all I want to do is sleep. My head feels like it's in a vice. I'm not sure if and when I'll ever be able to remember anything about Mary."

"Karen and Melissa have been discussing Mary, whom Melissa has seen near you for months."

"I'm aware of that."

"Karen and I will talk about this tomorrow. We really do need this input from Karen and Melissa, Al. They know more about Mary than anybody."

"I suppose you're right, but I still think that Karen should keep her nose out of what you and I are doing."

"I understand what you're saying, Al, but the genie is out of the bottle. It's too late now. Before I leave you to rest, I want to let you know that I have discovered another common link, which I found when I replayed all of your tapes."

"I can't imagine what it could be."

"It's head injuries. Let me quickly review them for you. In the pirate dream, you were beaten about your head before you were hanged. The guards in the Tower of London clubbed and kicked you repeatedly in the head. In Salisbury, England, you severely injured your head on a table corner as you fell to the floor. At Valley Forge, you hit your head on a log wedged in the frozen stream. The rapist in San Francisco punched you in the head. In Maine, you smashed your head against the rocks when your boat broke up. You sustained a concussion in the Jets game. Now, you just fractured your skull in a skiing accident."

"That's strange, Doctor. It never occurred to me that I had head injuries in all of these regressions and the pirate dream also. I was concentrating on water, falling, and neck injuries for the most part."

"You're beginning to sound like you're buying into the reincarnation theory. Are you?"

"I always try to keep an open mind about new concepts. In the beginning, I must admit I did think this stuff was just plain crazy. Now it makes a little more sense to me. Karen thinks it's nonsense and against the teachings of the Catholic Church, as you know."

"To tell you the truth, I must say that when I spoke with her, I got the impression that she was at the crossroads between accepting or rejecting the theory of reincarnation."

"That's a new twist. The reappearances of the little girl, Mary, may have her wondering. When do you think we can meet again? This accident has upset our schedule."

"Whenever your doctors release you from the hospital and let you know what you can and cannot do. And of course, when you yourself feel up to it. I won't rush you."

"I'll call you when I'm ready. Thanks for coming."

"Al, I'd like to apologize to you for going against your wishes regarding Karen. Trust me. I am not going to break our doctor-patient confidence."

"You know I trust you, Doctor. Just try to keep Karen in check. Can you do that?"

"Certainly, I'll do my best. I must go now. Your other doctors will be coming in shortly, I expect. I hope you can go home soon, Al."

"Me too. I'm already tired of this place."

After visiting Al for over an hour, Dr. Sawyer left to go to the psychiatric center to make her rounds. Since she was running late, she made a call to Rosie to let her know that she would not be home for dinner.

"Rosie, it's one of those days. I'll be home late tonight. I have to catch up on some paper work in the office tonight. Explain to the girls that I'll see them tomorrow morning before they go to school. Tuck them in bed and kiss them goodnight for me."

"I will, Dr. Elizabeth. Should I save your dinner?"

"No, I'll pick up something. Maybe I'll have tonight's dinner for my lunch in my office tomorrow. I'll warm it up in my microwave oven."

"Okay, Doctor, I'll pack it up for you and refrigerate it."

"Thanks, Rosie. I'll see you later."

As Elizabeth drove along the streets of Buffalo, Al's various punishments troubled her and she talked to herself.

"There were just three sex related punishments; one rape in San Francisco, an unnatural sodomy in the Tower of London, and a horrific castration on the coast of Maine. Were London and Maine meant to be more painful and memorable than all the others?

Often, upon awakening, we forget all or part of a dream. Maybe Al has not recalled everything, as I've been relying on his memory alone. Karen was with him and heard everything about the dreams firsthand. Indeed, Karen is becoming more essential in this complex case than Al or I had originally realized. Maybe she can recall more about the dreams than Al can."

It was nine-thirty and she was visibly shaken when she pulled into the parking lot of the red brick Buffalo Psychiatric Center on Forest Avenue, and parked her Camry in her assigned parking space. She was already tired, but still had about eleven more hours left in her day. Bill, the security guard, greeted her as she entered the building through the back entrance.

"How are you this morning, Dr. Sawyer?"

"Just fine, thank you Bill, but I'm a bit tired."

"When you're finished in here, I'll walk you to your car. I don't want you going to the parking lot alone. If I'm not here, just ring the bell and I'll come."

"Thank you for your concern, Bill."

The screams and cries of the mentally ill patients upset her as she made her way to the heavily guarded third floor where many of the most dangerous schizophrenic patients resided. The guard on duty unlocked the door to the ward and admitted Elizabeth. Inside, an orderly accompanied her on her rounds. The patients presented themselves differently. Some smiled and reached out to grab at her. Others sat silently in a catatonic position, staring blankly ahead. Some were restrained in their chairs to prevent them from harming themselves. Elizabeth could see the frustration, desperation and anger in their eyes.

I wish I could wave a magic wand and instantly bring these poor souls back to reality, but I cannot. Most of them are destined to spend the rest of their lives here.

CHAPTER 25

It was Wednesday, and Karen was anxious to speak with Dr. Sawyer. She hurried, made all of the green lights on Delaware Avenue, and arrived early for her appointment. It was eight forty-five when she hung up her coat, signed her name on the yellow sign-in sheet, and seated herself in a dark blue leather armchair in the waiting room. The doctor's secretary, Barb, informed Karen that the Doctor was caught in heavy crosstown traffic and would be a few minutes late. The pale blue walls were soothing to Karen's eyes, as were the four Monet prints of garden scenes which adorned the walls.

"Al never mentioned anything about this beautiful outer office."

At nine-thirty, Doctor Sawyer entered unseen through a rear door which all doctors seem to have. She spoke briefly to Barb. Then the doctor herself opened the door to her office and greeted Karen with a warm smile and a firm but friendly handshake.

"Come in, Mrs. Chapman. I'm sorry to be late, but the traffic was wild. It's nice to finally meet you in person. Phones are so impersonal, don't you agree? Please have a seat."

Karen sat directly opposite Dr. Sawyer. She looked around the office, hoping to see the infamous recliner, but the doctor diverted her attention.

"Did you know that I saw Al in the hospital yesterday? I guess I surprised him, but I was very worried about this latest accident. I questioned him about the little girl, Mary."

"That's one of the reasons I wanted to meet with you today. What did he have to say about her?"

"Not very much, I'm afraid. When I saw him, he was still very tired and had little recollection of the conversation you thought he was having with the little girl whom you apparently think is named Mary."

"I overheard some of what Al was saying to her. He was telling her how sorry he was for what he had done and was begging for her forgiveness. He called her Mary. What do you make of this?"

"It sounds to me like Al and this little fifteenth-century girl, Mary, knew one another. There is no telling what kind of relationship they might have had. We'll have to wait until he feels well enough to come in for another session. Maybe then we can retrieve the conversation. I don't want to draw any conclusions at this time, but I am forming a hypothesis."

"Can you tell me what it is?"

"No, I can't, Mrs. Chapman. Although Al is your husband, I am bound by doctor-patient confidences, and Al and I have to work through this together. I am sure that he will tell you everything when the time is right, once he understands what is causing his anxiety attacks. Whatever the cause, he must accept it and try to integrate it into his present life situation. When he can do this, he should be cured."

"Will his anxiety attacks disappear then?"

"That's the million-dollar question. It all depends upon Al. We still have a way to go before we will know if he can properly assimilate all of the data and reach closure. We might need two more sessions to get all of the pieces to the puzzle."

"I don't understand everything you've said, but is it possible that he may not be cured?"

"Yes, that's always a possibility, but we must keep a positive attitude. This is a difficult case which, hopefully, can be solved."

"Now I'm worried, Doctor. Please do everything you can to help him. I cannot bear to see him suffer anymore."

"I will do my best, but remember, we are sailing in uncharted waters. The subconscious mind is unpredictable."

"Dr. Sawyer, please don't misunderstand what I'm about to say to you, but I'm terribly bothered by all of this reincarnation talk. I'm afraid that Al is beginning to believe it. We are Catholics, and reincarnation is not one of the Church's teachings. You are treading on dangerous ground with Al. I do not want him to give up his religion."

"Oh, Mrs. Chapman, don't ever think that I'm trying to turn Al against Catholicism. If reviewing so-called past lives helps him to understand why he has those anxiety attacks, then you'll have to resign yourself to it for the time being. You do not have to believe in reincarnation. Just let your husband deal with this as he sees fit, and I am sure that he will still be a good Catholic when this is all over."

Embarrassed by Dr. Sawyer's terse response, Karen quickly changed the subject.

"I was wondering about our daughter, Melissa. She says that she has seen the girl, Mary, around Al for months. She believes that Mary knows her and sometimes acts like she would like to speak to her but doesn't. Melissa is often frightened. Do you think Mary is a ghost?"

"I'm not sure, but it sounds like she could be. If your research on the clothing that Mary wears is correct, we're dealing with a fifteenth-century ghost. How is Melissa coping with all of this?"

"She seems to be handling it all right. Her schoolwork hasn't been affected that I can tell. She is still an A student. She is a very precocious ten-year-old."

"It certainly sounds like she is. Mrs. Chapman, do you recall what Al told you about the Salisbury dream? Did he say anything about hitting his head?"

"I don't believe he did. All I remember is that he said I woke him up as he was dying on the floor. I'm sorry I can't be more helpful. Now it's time for me to go to the hospital to see my husband. Thank you for seeing me today."

"Give my best to Al. Tell him to rest and stay upbeat. Keep in touch."

Karen left the office, unsure if she had learned anything at all from the meeting. She was both encouraged and discouraged by Dr. Sawyer's words. When she reached the hospital, she found Al in poor spirits and in great emotional distress.

"I want to go home, Karen, but Dr. Matthews said that I have to stay for at least one week. I'm bored here with nothing to do. The TV programs are terrible."

"A fractured skull doesn't heal instantly, Al—it takes time. Be patient. It will heal."

"Karen, have you been to the library yet to get the books I asked you to get on reincarnation? Or have you forgotten?"

"No, I haven't forgotten. I'll go tomorrow morning, I promise."

"Get me a couple of introductory ones. I want to learn about the religions that teach it, evidence for it, case studies—whatever you can find that will be simple enough for me to understand. I'm at the point now, where I must accept it or reject it. And if I reject it, I will end the sessions with Dr. Sawyer. Karen, I hate myself. I think God is punishing me with head injuries and I don't know why."

"I saw Dr. Sawyer this morning, Al. You've got to be more patient. I know that she's going to help you. Reincarnation is a dilemma for both of us because of our Catholic faith, but let's keep open minds. Don't do anything that will upset you. Rest."

"Okay, if you say so."

"I say so."

Karen left Al after only a short visit. She changed her mind and decided to go directly to the Orchard Park Library instead of waiting until tomorrow. Unsure of the subject matter, she asked the librarian, Emma Dillon, for help.

"Miss Dillon, I'd like to get a couple of basic books on reincarnation—just introductory ones. Would you have any at this branch library?"

"I believe so. There has been a lot of interest in the subject lately. Let me check the computer to see what we have here."

In a few minutes, she returned with two books.

"I've read both of these books and found them quite easy to read. It gives the reader a glimpse of what this fast-growing belief is all about."

"What do you mean fast-growing?"

"Well, I understand that almost one-third of Americans now believe in reincarnation. Of course, most of the far eastern world accepts it as gospel truth. By the way, you might also want to familiarize yourself with the idea of karma. It's also discussed in these two books and seems to tie in with reincarnation."

"I think these will be fine, Miss Dillon. Now could you also find me something on regression therapy and psycho-hypnosis?"

"I'll get you one I know about."

She returned with one large volume.

"This is about the science of psychotherapy. It is a good beginning."

After thanking her for her help and glancing at her watch, Karen left the library in a rush.

"The children will be home from school soon. It's almost three," she said aloud.

The big yellow bus was just coming down their street as she pulled into the driveway. Karen met the children at the door and then went to the kitchen to prepare dinner. Afterward, while Melissa and Jonathan worked on their homework in their rooms, she curled up on the couch in the den and began reading the textbook on psychotherapy.

She learned that the hypnotized person must be able to focus on a voice or an object. The stronger the concentration, the better the results. Also, the more intelligent the person, the more likely that person is to be hypnotized. A subject will cooperate more readily if he trusts and has confidence in the therapist.

"So far, this process fits Al to a T.'"

She further learned that regression therapy is used to help people who have recurring dreams, inexplicable phobias, and déjà vu experiences. As these often past-life traumas are examined during regression therapy, the clients often resolve their emotional problems, and the traumas cease.

"Dr. Sawyer is doing this with Al," she acknowledged and continued reading.

The therapist helps the patient integrate the often-painful past life events into their present lives. After dinner, and the children were in bed, Karen read through most of the night and began to understand what Dr. Sawyer was attempting to do for Al.

"I guess she's on the right track after all."

Her eyes were getting tired. She reluctantly closed the book and went upstairs to bed. As the night wore on, she could not sleep. Curiosity got the better of her, and she picked up one of the books on reincarnation, which she had brought upstairs with her. Fascinated, she read until dawn.

I'm finally beginning to make some sense out of this. Reincarnation really isn't anti-Catholic, as I had thought. Nevertheless, there is still much for me to resolve in my own mind. To be sure, I cannot let Al or Dr. Sawyer ever know that I've read a book on reincarnation, after all I've preached against it. And, I find this concept of karma equally intriguing. Maybe I was a Hindu in a past life. Watch it, Karen! Don't let yourself be drawn into this trap.

Soon, it was seven o'clock and thoughts raced through her mind.

"Time to get the children up for school, prepare breakfast, and get ready to visit Al in the hospital. I hope I can stay awake. What should I tell him? I'll just hand him the two books on reincarnation without telling him that I glanced through them. There is no need to even mention the book on psychotherapy. He doesn't have to know everything."

When Karen arrived at the hospital at eleven o'clock, she could tell that Al was feeling a lot better. His pain had subsided a great deal and his color was much better.

"Did you bring me the books?"

"Yes, I brought you these two which the librarian recommended. They should keep you busy for a few days, anyway."

"Thanks, Karen. I really appreciate your getting them for me."

"You're feeling better today, aren't you? You look a lot better."

"Yes, I believe I'm over the hump. Maybe I can be home by the weekend."

"I hope so. We miss you. The repair jobs are piling up and the checkbook is a mess."

Karen sensed that Al was anxious to start reading. She made an excuse for leaving so soon.

"Al, I hope you don't mind, but I have to go shopping for food. We're low on everything, and I think the kids are getting tired of grilled cheese sandwiches."

"'Not at all. I'll just sit here in my chair and read all day."

"Don't tire your eyes too much. I'll be back tomorrow. Love you."

"Love you too. Thanks again for all you are doing."

"No problem, Al. That's what our marriage vows are all about."

Al started reading immediately, and like Karen, he couldn't put the books down. He read about the Bible and reincarnation, case studies of people who remembered past lives, and karma. The words stimulated his thought processes.

I didn't know that some passages in the Bible imply that Jesus believed in reincarnation. In Matthew 11:13–14, Christ seems to be saying that John the Baptist was the reincarnation of Elijah. According to Dr. Sawyer, the Jews of Christ's time believed in reincarnation. And in Revelation 13:10, it says, 'If anyone slays with the sword, with the sword must he be slain.' This passage frightens me for some reason.

As he read far into the night, he became more understanding of what Dr. Sawyer was trying to explain to him.

The doctor hasn't lied to me about any of this. I must remember to question her about where she learned so much about reincarnation. I want to ask her about karma, which I find to be intriguing. In Galatians 6:7, it states, 'A person reaps what he sows.' I wonder if that's what I've been doing through my lifetimes.

His doubts about reincarnation were disappearing, leading him to make a firm decision to continue with Dr. Sawyer. Now, he was more anxious than ever to get on with the regressions.

Things are beginning to come together in my mind and are making more sense. This karma concept seems to explain my case, if I understand its meaning correctly. I'm suffering and dying through the centuries because of something I did—some sin I committed. Whatever it was, it must have been a dilly.

CHAPTER 26

Recovery from his fractured skull was a slow process and one week after his accident, Al was discharged from the hospital. Dr. Matthews had left instructions for Al to rest for three more weeks. There was to be no strenuous exercise; no football, no car driving, and no stress. Monday morning, he called Dr. Sawyer to let her know what his situation was. It was eight forty-five, and the doctor was already in her office and answered the phone herself.

"Hello, Dr. Sawyer—it's Al. I'm home from the hospital and according to Doctor Matthew's orders, I won't be able to see you for at least three weeks; I'm grounded. I have to avoid any strenuous activity or stress."

"Obviously, our sessions are very stressful for you, but I really expected you to be out of circulation for a longer time. This interruption really won't put us too far behind."

"You'd be proud of me, Doctor. In the past week, I have been reading about reincarnation and am trying to educate myself on the subject. I asked Karen to bring me some books from the library, and whenever I had some pain-free moments, I read. My mind is swimming with the ideas l was introduced to in the books. Someday, when you have time, I'd like to discuss them with you because you seem to be quite an expert on the subject. I have a few questions I'd like to ask you."

"I have some time now. We'll consider this a non-professional call. Fire away."

"To begin with, I've read that reincarnation was removed from Catholic teachings in 553 AD because it was considered to be too much of an Eastern influence. Is this true?"

"The Church denies it. When you asked me about this before, I didn't think that you were ready for the answer, so I didn't tell you the whole story. The Catholic Church at that time may have wanted more power over the minds of its people. The belief in hell and damnation in one lifetime strengthened the Church's control over its flock. This teaching had been simple and effective for many centuries, but many people today are challenging this view because it seems unfair and illogical."

"I understand that reincarnation appears to represent the continuity of life. When we fail to accomplish our desires and goals in one lifetime, they spill over into future incarnations. We accumulate different experiences and memories from the past and express them in the present. How do we do this, Dr. Sawyer?"

"Some of these expressions are done consciously, and others are done subconsciously. By means of our past behavior, we manifest ideas, knowledge, and beliefs. We affect and are affected by our own ideas and those of others who become a part of our present lives. Ultimately, we all benefit from one another's past experiences. Reincarnation is the vehicle which brings us together in order that certain events can occur in our lives. Every happening in our lives has a purpose. Our souls learn and grow through all kinds of experiences no matter how insignificant they may appear. It is a maturation process for the soul.

Now, Al, I'm going to introduce you to something that will really boggle your mind. You may not run across this theory in your readings. I am sure that you know that DNA contains the record of all of our biological traits as manifested in the nuclei of every one of our cells. This information is passed from parents to offspring. Some now theorize that there is also a spiritual DNA which stores the record of all of our deeds and misdeeds for all of our lifetimes. Every action, no matter how unimportant it may seem at the time, may result in a reaction, which affects another soul as well as our own. We are responsible not only for the effect of our actions upon ourselves but also upon others. In the blink of an eye, something we may say or do, good or evil, may have a great impact upon the physical or emotional life and soul of another."

"I'm beginning to understand, but why do I suffer such violent deaths in every incarnation? I must have an evil soul."

"I'm certain that is untrue, Al. By identifying similarities in your past and present experiences, we may be able to find out why you're suffering. We don't want these violent incidents to reoccur in another incarnation, but that may not be within our power to control. If you rid yourself of all fears, your anxiety symptoms should disappear."

"Are you saying that I am the cause of my suffering?"

"In a way, I am saying just that. Are you familiar with the quote from *Invictus* by William Henley? 'I am the master of my fate, I am the captain of my soul.' Al, do you know what karma is? I think it's time to introduce you to this concept."

"I've seen the word in connection with reincarnation, but I don't quite grasp its meaning. It has something to do with cause and effect, doesn't it?"

"Sort of. Karma is a word which is derived from the root, *kri*, which means 'to do.' Hinduism teaches that a soul has the power to do things or make decisions which can influence its destiny. It's a form of justice administered by the soul—that which is due it but what is fair and acceptable to the soul. Karma both rewards and punishes. There are rewards for acts of kindness, but there are also punishments initiated by evil acts."

"Are you saying that the soul determines its own fate?"

"Yes, I am. Karma is like having a personal accountant or a built-in computer. It keeps a record of all of our good and evil acts. Personally, I believe that the good that we do may to some extent balance any punishment due us for our sins. For example, if a person lays down his life unselfishly for another, that may help to balance somewhat the punishment due that person for some horrible sin he has committed. One's karma can be very severe if the soul so decides."

"Do you think that my soul is punishing me for a sin I've committed in the past?"

"It looks that way, if you accept karma. On the flip side of the coin, rewards can be great. In *The Summa Theologica* of Saint Thomas Aquinas, he speaks of a 'hundredfold reward' due for works of perfection, such as martyrdom. Part of a Baha'i prayer includes the statement, 'He who cometh with one Godly deed, will receive a tenfold reward.' This certainly is very positive."

"But what about the punishment? Is there anything in the Bible about the extent of the punishment assigned to the soul?"

"Well, there are a few passages in the Bible, which are worth noting. In Genesis 4:23–24, after Cain murdered his brother Abel, God punished him severely, but Cain was fearful that someone would kill him too. The Lord said that whoever killed Cain would be punished sevenfold. Again, in Genesis 4:23–24, Lamech speaks of a seventy times sevenfold punishment for himself for killing a man who wounded him, and a youth for bruising him. In Leviticus 26:18–28, God warns the Israelites of the punishment that will be levied against them if they repeatedly disobey His Commandments. He threatens a sevenfold times sevenfold times sevenfold times sevenfold punishment for persistence in disobeying Him. That amounts to over two thousand times the original punishment for an offense. The punishment for committing one grievous sin is repeatedly multiplied each time the sin is recommitted. That is severe."

"I think I understand. I am being punished because of my karma, and I have made a decision to accept my punishment as a way of atoning for my past sins."

"That's basically the idea, Al."

"But what initiated this decision on my part to suffer this way?"

"We're still searching for the cause, Al. In our next session, I want to take you back to the fifteenth century when Mary may have lived. I believe that Mary is the key, both in your past and present lives. She could provide us with information we need to clear up this mystery about your sufferings."

"I hope I'll be able to survive that session."

"You'll be all right as long as you keep in mind that fear is your enemy. Don't fear the present or the future because of the past. Fear can be destroyed by love. You must understand the memories of the past, and love all of your soul's decisions to punish or reward."

"This is a lot for me to assimilate. Whatever my sin was must have been horrible. Am I being punished sevenfold as the Bible suggests? Oh, I have one more question for you, Doctor."

"What is it, Al?"

"I was wondering, while we've been talking about the soul, just where is the soul housed in the body?"

"'Nobody knows for sure—in the heart, the brain, or in the cells. We just do not know."

"I'm afraid I've taken up too much of your time today. I'll make an appointment with your secretary for three weeks hence, when I should be cleared by my neurosurgeon. Then we can examine my life and death in the fifteenth century. I can't say that I'm eager. The suffering I have endured has been so real that I'm more frightened before each regression."

"Remember what I just told you about fear, Al. Let go of it. We're going to determine the causes of your anxiety attacks,

I promise you. By the way, your wife, came in to see me last Wednesday."

"I know. She told me. What did the two of you discuss?"

"We had a nice visit. We talked about the little girl, Mary, and her connection with you and Melissa—nothing you and I haven't already discussed. Mainly we discussed her feelings about reincarnation and her concern that you are going to lose your religion because of it. I tried to assure her that your faith is strong and this would not happen."

"She didn't have any objections to my request for books about reincarnation."

"I'm glad to hear that. The last thing I want is for the two of you to doubt Catholicism. Reincarnation is just one long-neglected belief of Catholicism, Al."

"We'll work it out. Don't worry."

"I'm sure we will. Now, I'll put Barb on the phone. She'll set up an appointment for you in three weeks. Have a nice Thanksgiving. Here's Barb."

"Mr. Chapman, how is December eleventh at nine o'clock?"

"That sounds all right. For the time being, I'm free as a bird."

"It's almost Christmas. Where did the year go?"

Al finished his conversation and hung up the phone as Karen entered the room.

"Who were you talking to Al?"

"Doctor Sawyer's secretary. I made an appointment for December eleventh. Dr. Matthews thinks I should be okay by then."

"That's after Thanksgiving. You'll have time to enjoy the holiday and prepare for Christmas. We'll have more time together too."

"And three weeks to be apprehensive about my next session. I wish I could get it over with now. I hate this waiting."

"You're home for three weeks, so you can take it easy and rest. Your orders are to do absolutely nothing. I'll take care of everything around here while you get your strength back."

"Okay, I'll do what you say."

"Al, I was eavesdropping on your conversation with Dr. Sawyer just now, and I heard you mention the word karma. What was that all about?"

"Oh Karen, what am I going to do with you? You never quit. Anyhow, I can tell you that karma means that the soul decides how one is to be punished for past misdeeds. My soul may have decided that I should be punished."

"Al, that's terrible. I don't like that idea."

"It seems awfully harsh to me too, but the soul apparently wants to grow in grace and goodness. It knows what is best for it—reward or punishment."

"It's sort of like earning brownie points, isn't it?"

"That's a great way to put it, Mrs. Snoop."

That remark didn't sit too well with Karen. She turned and went into the kitchen to prepare lunch for them, mumbling to herself.

"I must have been a spy in my last life—maybe during World War I," she joked. "Probably the British against the Germans."

But it demonstrated that reincarnation was working its way into her way of thinking a little bit at a time. She was becoming less resistant to the concept.

CHAPTER 27

Over the next three weeks, Al began feeling more comfortable with himself. Because of their readings, he and Karen discussed regression hypnosis, reincarnation, and karma. Both were reading voraciously about these topics, and at times, their discussions became quite cerebral and argumentative, but they were discussing.

"Al, are you beginning to doubt Catholicism? How can you accept reincarnation and karma and still call yourself a Catholic? What's happening to you? I'm worried about you."

"I'm not giving up my religion. I'm just opening up my mind to new concepts and blending them with some of the old teachings of the Church. One life for a soul just doesn't make sense to me. How can a newborn child who died at birth be judged when it hasn't lived long enough to sin or do good works? Surely, it must take many lives for a soul to work on correcting faults and striving for perfection. For my own part, I struggle just trying to be patient with people who don't share my beliefs."

"Al, what happens to the belief in resurrection in all of this? This is a basic Catholic teaching. At the Last Judgment, the body is reunited with the soul."

"I'm not sure, but I've read that the soul grows in purity as lessons are learned, regardless of the body. Imperfections are refined and the soul rises to a higher level as the goals it sets for itself are met. Maybe at the resurrection, all of the bodies unite with their one soul, and at the Last Judgment, a soul's rewards and punishments are defined."

"How does a soul decide what goals to set for itself?"

"Perhaps each incarnation is completed, there is a review of one's life and former lives to assess progress or lack of it. The soul and its guides scrutinize every aspect of the soul's lives. Together, they decide what has already been accomplished and what the soul needs to work on. They make decisions about every aspect of the next incarnation such as place of birth, parents, gender, marital status, education, vocation or profession, punishment for sins, and the kind of death the person will experience."

"Are you telling me that we pick how we are going to die? I don't want to do that. In my opinion, no one would. There would be too much fear associated with knowing."

"The soul does not fear death. It is the consciousness that is sometimes paralyzed by a fear of death. A belief in reincarnation negates that fear. The soul is filled with love and understands that love can dispel fear."

"Do we reap what we sow? Is the karma concept an eye for an eye, a tooth for a tooth, tit for tat, what goes around comes around?"

"I'm not sure about that. It seems to me that the soul decides what punishment is just. Then it might decide that it could be two eyes for one. Or a whole set of teeth for one tooth. Ultimately, I believe that we do reap what we sow. This can also mean rewards as well as punishments."

"According to what you're telling me, the soul decides everything before we're born. Does that mean that you decided that you would be a professional football player?"

"I guess I did, based upon my goals and lessons to be learned, whatever they are, but I'm puzzled as to why anyone would choose to be a hotel housekeeper and have to clean toilets and dirty rooms instead of being the owner of the hotel."

"I think I can answer that one. That soul is learning about humility and serving others. Remember how Jesus washed the feet of his Apostles on Holy Thursday before his crucifixion? That was humility."

"You're really good at this, Karen—I'm proud of you. You've learned so much."

"I've tried, Al. It hasn't been easy for me, as you know. I still have problems dealing with the Catholic church's teaching on purgatory but, we'll leave that discussion for another day. I've also been doing some reading on regression hypnosis because I wanted to understand what you've been going through. I read that suggestions made by the therapist can influence what the person may recall from his subconscious. Does Dr. Sawyer ask leading questions that could influence your responses? This could put into question the reliability of your answers."

"As far as I know, during our sessions, she asks no leading questions. Her questions are short and to the point and usually require simple, clear-cut answers. She is very professional and definitely goes by the book. That is why her reputation as a hypnotherapist is rapidly growing."

"I wish she would let me sit in on your next session, but she has made it clear to me that I cannot because of doctor-patient confidence. Would you object to my presence, Al? Wouldn't you like someone cheering for you?"

"I would be embarrassed to have you present. In good time, I will share everything with you, but presently, I'm just not ready. As it is, I'm baring my soul to Dr. Sawyer, and that's very private. These regression sessions are extremely painful for me. I don't want to expose you to that. Anyhow, there are no cheering sections there."

"Alright, Al, I'll respect your wishes. Maybe in a few more weeks, you'll have all of the answers to this mystery which is making me so nervous."

"Relax, Karen. I am confident that we are getting close—very close."

That discussion being over, they both picked up their respective books and continued reading. Then Karen looked at Al and continued the debate.

"Al, please don't get the impression that the concepts of reincarnation and karma are totally unacceptable to me. It's just that I can't suddenly undo thirty plus years of Catholic teachings. They can't all be wrong."

"It's the same for me too. I still accept most of the teachings, but growth and change are happening all around us. Remember when Catholics were told that they would go to hell if they ate meat on Friday? Well, do you really believe that all of those poor people that did so are burning in hell right now? And is there really a hell? Pope John Paul wrote in *Crossing the Threshold of Hope* that there was no eternal hell. Few people, if any, will remain there. He implies that God will save everyone and hell will be empty."

"I think the Pope may have been misinterpreted on that one, Al."

"Perhaps, but he is the Pope, and is infallible, and shouldn't err in his teachings. Now, Karen, let's get back to reincarnation. This book I'm reading documents cases of children who remember people, houses, and neighborhoods they once lived in during another lifetime. Apparently, if an incarnation takes place shortly after death, usually between ages two and five, the child often remembers his previous life."

"I'd like to read about that, Al."

"My eyes are tired. Here, take my book and read chapter ten. But remember to keep an open mind about all of this."

Karen accepted the book and read while Al relaxed in his chair.

"Listen to this, Al. I can't believe it. A two-year-old child living in Cleveland was riding in the backseat of her mother's car. Suddenly, she broke into song and began singing all of the lyrics of 'Chattanooga Choo Choo,' which was the favorite song of the forties of her recently deceased grandmother. The child never heard nor was she taught the lyrics. She just began singing it without any prompting."

"That is amazing, isn't it? I thought you would be spellbound by these cases. Read another one for me."

"Here's a good one. An Indian girl named Swirnlata, at age three, remembered a town she had lived in prior to her present incarnation. She gave a detailed description of the house she lived in and described the area around it. She said her name was Sonya Rashid and claimed that she had two sons. When her father took her to this town, she met her former husband and one son whom she recognized. She also noted changes that had been made to their home since she died of a lung malady. Afterward, she continued to revisit her former family, who accepted her as 'reborn.' This is unbelievable, Al."

"These cases are all documented, and there are thousands more, which have been researched by scientists and medical doctors from different religions around the world."

"Why do so many of these cases occur in India?"

"I don't know. Perhaps it's because they believe in reincarnation there and they are more likely to recognize it if it occurs."

Al was very happy that Karen had taken such a strong interest in reincarnation. At ten o'clock, her eyes became heavy, and she reluctantly placed the book on the coffee table, open to the last page she was reading. Then she changed the subject.

"My parents have invited us for Thanksgiving dinner, but I declined because you need time to fully recover from your head injury. My mother suggested that we all go to Russell's Restaurant for a quiet evening instead."

"That's okay with me, as long as I feel up to it."

"Well, you know how much my mother loves to cook and entertain, so she also invited us for Christmas dinner, and I accepted for us. The kids will be happy too. Jonathan likes to play with my father's trains in the basement, and Melissa loves to help Mom make her pumpkin and mince pies, which of course, I enjoy eating."

"There you go again—the dessert queen with the sweet tooth. You know, Karen, I'm going to miss getting that turkey every year when I retire."

"What did you say, Al? You're retiring?"

"Yes, I've made up my mind. I'm not returning to football this year. I'm retiring. Frequent injuries were getting to be life threatening."

"I'm glad, Al. I was always worried about you in every game."

CHAPTER 28

The next three weeks of Al's recovery were uneventful and boring. He still had some soreness in his head, but the severe pain was long since gone. Dr. Matthews gave the okay for Al to resume light activity; walking and short drives, and he could play catch football with Jonathan. But there was to be no strenuous physical activity, and of course, no football. However, he could resume his sessions with Dr. Sawyer. He was happy about that because he had missed her more than he wanted to admit to himself.

When the day of his appointment finally arrived, he and Dr. Sawyer were both early for the nine o'clock session. Ordinarily, Al failed to take notice of what the doctor was wearing, but on this day, he was extraordinarily focused on her appearance. He could not help but notice how lovely she looked. She was stunning in an electric blue suit and a tailored navy-blue blouse. Her light blue suede shoes and blue stockings were a perfect complement to her suit. A pearl necklace and small pearl earrings completed the ensemble. He noted and was pleased that she wore no rings on her fingers.

"You must have a big date today, Doctor."

"What makes you think that, Al?"

"Well, you look absolutely gorgeous today, but you do every day, of course."

Blushing, she fibbed a bit, because she wanted to look especially attractive for AI.

"Thank you for the compliment, Al. No date. I wanted to give my spirits a lift. I have the winter blahs from all of this cold and snow. It seems to be never ending this year. I can't wait until spring arrives, so I can go jogging. I love Buffalo, mind you, but I'm not big on winter sports like you are, although my daughters love to go sledding at Chestnut Ridge Park. My favorite seasons are summer and fall."

"It's all a matter of personal interests. So you jog? I never would have guessed it."

"Yes. At least I pretend. I peter out after about a half a mile. These irregular hours don't permit me to have a normal schedule. Okay, Al, enough about me. How are you feeling; physically and mentally? Are you ready and able to take the next step today? We've lost quite a lot of time."

"I'm feeling much better, thank you. I'm eager to begin. And if you believe that, I have a London bridge in the Arizona desert I'd like to sell you. Actually, I do want to get this session over with quickly though."

"Then, let's proceed to the task at hand."

Al focused on a shiny gold button on Elizabeth's suit instead of the usual swinging pendulum. The doctor was aware of this and began counting. Her face was flushed.

"Five, four, three…"

"Al, I want you to go back in time to the fifteenth century; the early 1400s. Are you living then?"

"Yea, I be."

"Where are you living?"

"I libba in London, England."

"What part of London do you live in?"

"The south street districtus."

"What is the year?"

"Tiz fourteen hundred ond ten."

"What is your name?"

"Mi name es James Avery."

"How old are you James?"

"I be twenty-eighte yeren auld."

"Do you have a trade or occupation?"

"I be a gardiner."

"Are you married?"

"Yea."

"Is your wife with you?"

"No, we hav a big argumente. I leve the hous in anger."

"Why did you argue with your wife?"

"I drinke ond gamble mi monie away."

"What are you doing now, James?"

"I be walke acros the Waterloo Bridge to mi ale hous."

"What month is it?"

"Tiz Novembre."

"What is the weather like?"

"Tiz cauld ond dampf. Thore be a thikke fog movin in."

"What is the time?"

"Tis goen on eighte houre."

"Are you alone on the Bridge?"

"No, someone be comen."

"Who is coming?"

"Thore be a wiman wit a yonge lass."

"Are the woman and girl talking?"

"Yea."

"What are they saying?"

"The wiman telle the lass to move over ond let him passe."

"Are they frightened of someone?"

"Yea, I thinke thei be afrayd of me."

"What happens next?"

"I walke into the wiman."

"Why did you walk into her?"

"I be angry wit hir."

"Why are you angry with her?"

"She calle me a dum mon."

"Do you say anything to her for calling you a dumb man?"

"I wille showe ye who be dum. Ye be no laedy."

"Does anything else happen, James?"

"Yea. I grabe hir ond throwe hir down. I jumpe an hir."

"What does she do?"

"She screme ond fighte ond kikke."

"What do you do next?"

"I be tearen hir clothin off hir ond rapen hir. I be choken ond punchen hir in hir head."

"What is the little girl doing while you are raping her mother?"

"She be shouten ond trien to pulle me off hir mither."

"Does the woman say anything to her?"

"'Yea, she yelle, 'Run, Mary. Run. Get halp.'"

"What happens next?"

"The wiman be very stille. I thinke she be dead. I be afrayd. I dragge hir to the side of the Bridge ond throwe hir into the River Thames below."

"What does Mary do when you throw her mother over the Bridge into the river?"

"She be standen on the bridge, scremen hir head off."

"What is Mary saying?"

"She yelle, 'Mum. Mum. Someone halp. Mi Mum es in the river.'"

"Can you describe Mary?"

"She be small. She be about nyne or ten yeren auld."

"Can you describe Mary's clothing?"

"She be weren a lang dres, dark in colour. She wear high-buttoned shoes."

"What color is her hair?"

"Tiz blonde."

"What are you doing now, James?"

"I be walken to the lass to finische hir off. I hear peple shouten. I be afrayd ond run away. I disepir in the fog."

"Did you hurt Mary before you ran away?"

"No, I did not. Many peple comen befor I coulde hurt hir."

"Do you know what happened to Mary?"

"I do not know. I run ond hid."

At this point, the Doctor becomes concerned about Al's emotional state. He was perspiring and breathing heavily, and the color was draining from his face.

"All right, Al. One, two, three four… You're back in Buffalo. It's 2010, Al. Everything is fine now."

"Oh, Doctor Sawyer, that was awful. I'm a horrible murderer and rapist."

"This is a real shocker. I wasn't expecting this. But we have answers now."

"Doctor, we finally learned that the little blonde girl is named Mary, and she probably is the daughter of the woman I murdered in London in 1410. Now I know why I am afraid of bridges, heights, and water. But, why is the ghost of Mary, if that's what she is, stalking me?"

"I don't know, Al. We'll have to probe further at a later date. But, all of the common threads are present in this incident—a head injury, choking, rape, falling, and water. A rape occurred only once before in San Francisco, but there was sodomy in the Tower of London incident. So there is a painful sexual link."

"This session explains the anxiety attack I experienced on the River Thames cruise when I saw the Waterloo Bridge from the Silver Bonito. Doctor, I am so ashamed and so sorry. How could I have committed such a monstrous crime? I killed Mary's mother. That poor little girl was left alone without her mother."

"It's not for me to judge you, Al. Our souls are ever evolving. We learn from our mistakes, and you certainly are a good person in this life. This has been a very traumatic experience for you this morning and you must be exhausted. Go home now and try to relax. Don't try to figure anything out by yourself, and please refrain from discussing any of today's session about James Avery with anyone, especially Karen. We still need to find out more about him."

"I'm not certain I want to know any more about that beast. Maybe the police caught him and sent him to the gallows. This all began with a hanging. It would be a fit punishment if he died by hanging."

"Let's not presuppose his fate. We'll try to determine what happened to him next week. I'm curious to know too."

"I'll try to prepare for what awaits me in the next session. Today's revelation can never be forgotten."

"Good. Remember, Al—fear is your enemy."

"I'll try to remember, but before I leave, I have a question to ask you."

"What is it?" she asked, hoping for something personal.

"Karen and I have been doing a lot of reading together about reincarnation during the last three weeks. We've read case studies of children, mainly from the eastern countries such as India, who recall their previous lives. Why do children, and not adults, remember their former lives?"

"I'm not totally certain. I guess that it's probably because they are reincarnated very soon after their deaths. Their previous lives haven't yet faded into their subconscious. Also, they may have been brought up to believe in reincarnation. What we refer to as déjà vu, they call memories."

"That's a reasonable explanation for that question, but I imagine that I will have more questions later as I read more. Thanks, Doctor. I'll see you next week."

Al left the her office in a solemn mood. His acceptance of the concept of reincarnation was totally shaken. If he accepted it as truth, he was a murderer; if he rejected it, he would be back on square one with no answers.

I don't believe I killed that woman. This is not the real me. I'm not a killer nor a rapist. I would never do such evil things.

Instead of driving straight home, Al decided to swing by Wilson Stadium to talk to Coach Schultz. John was in his office working on next week's game plan for the New England Patriots.

"Al, my buddy. How ya doin'? We've all missed you around here and we can't win without you. When are you coming back to work?"

"That's what I wanted to talk with you about, John. I'm retiring and won't be back anymore this year or next. I cannot risk any more head injuries because they're becoming life threatening for me."

"I'm sorry to hear that, Al. I won't try to talk you out of it. You know what is best for you and your family. Football is a dangerous sport. The money is good, but the career is short. What will you do for the rest of your life?"

"I've been thinking about coaching. What do you think, John?"

"You would be an outstanding coach. The guys need someone like you around them to look up to. I would want you on my staff if an opening arises."

"That's good to hear, but I'm not so sure I'd be a good role model for the young guys. Remember what I did to Ron Jefferson?"

"That was a mistake—we all make them. But, that wasn't you that day. You are one of the finest men I have ever known, and don't you forget it."

"Thanks, John. I appreciate your kind words."

"Keep in touch, Al. Take care of yourself. Let me know what you decide to do."

"I will. Now get back to work. I've used up enough of your game planning time. Get those Pats Sunday."

"No problem. I'm about finished. Take care, buddy. Oh, by the way Al, I'm sorry you didn't get your Thanksgiving turkey, but you can still pick up a ham for Christmas at the Bill's office."

Feeling much better about himself, Al then picked up his ham and left the stadium, perhaps for the last time, got into his Jeep, and drove onto One Bills Drive.

Back in her office, Elizabeth sat at her desk, admitting to herself that she was indeed very attracted to Al. She wondered how such a warm and gentle man could ever have killed anyone.

If Al killed that woman in a past life and is suffering horribly for that sin now, what sins might I have committed that could come back to haunt me some day? Am I curious to know about my past lives? Not at this moment. 'Ignorance is bliss.' Surely, it was a Christian who coined that phrase.

She continued mulling this thought over in her mind.

On the other hand, I'm curious to know if Al and I knew one another in a previous lifetime. Were we once married to one another? Was I his child or his mother or father? Whatever the association, it is clear to me that there is a bond between us now. That's as far as I will allow my fantasizing to take me. He is happily married to another woman now, and I'm not going to upset that union because of a school girl crush.

Having settled that dilemma in her mind, Elizabeth put on her coat, left her office, and drove home to her children and continued with her present life.

"I wonder what Rosie has prepared for dinner tonight? I'm famished."

CHAPTER 29

As usual, Karen greeted Al at the door when he returned home from his session with Dr. Sawyer. He appeared down.

"How did it go today, Dear? Did you learn anything new?"

"I don't want to talk about it. I'm beat and I'm going upstairs to rest. No lunch for me. Call me when it's time for dinner."

Karen respected Al's need for privacy and didn't pursue the topic any further over the next week. She knew that he would confide in her when he was ready to do so.

Al was very apprehensive about his impending appointment with Dr. Sawyer. He could not bring himself to believe that he was a horrible killer and rapist and that he had murdered Mary's mother. Doubts about the concept of reincarnation continued to occupy his thoughts. They were relentless. He was emotionally drained.

Would another murderous monster emerge from my subconscious in the next session? I am not a murderer. I can't kill anything—not even a bug. If there is proof that I was James Avery in the fifteenth century, perhaps we could look up old death records in London if they were not destroyed during World War II.

Nevertheless, he forced himself to keep his Tuesday appointment. Without the usual preliminary happy talk, Dr. Sawyer soon guided Al into his subconscious.

"Al, you are James Avery, who has been living in London in the fifteenth century. I want you to revisit the day of your death. Are you in London now?"

"Yea, I be in Mead's Ale Hous in London."

"What year is it?"

"It be fourteen hundred thrittene."

"It is fourteen hundred and thirteen. How old are you now, James?"

"I be thirty-three yeren auld."

"Are you married?"

"No, mi wyfe leve me."

"Why did your wife leave you?"

"I be a drunkard."

"What are you doing in the ale house today?"

"I be playen a tabel game calle Nard ond drinken ale."

"Are you alone?"

"No, thore be three ither men at mi table."

"What are you and the three men talking about?"

"We be arguen. I be winnen all of the monie. Thei thinke I be cheten. Thei be very angry wit me."

"What do they say to you about your cheating at Nard?"

"'Keepe your cheten hande on the table, Jim, so we kan see wat ye be doen. We be onto you, Jim', one of the mon calle Jake telle me."

"Are you cheating James?"

"Yea, but I be drunk ond lie to thaem."

"What do you tell them?"

"I be no chete, Jake. Take back thaem worte."

"What does Jake say to you when you tell him to take back his words?"

"'I wille not. If ye be looken for a feight, I be your mon. I wille beat hel out of ye.'"

"Are you fighting with Jake?"

"Yea. Jake punche me in the head. I be losen the feight. 'Jake, do not cutte me.'"

"What is Jake doing?"

"He be comen at me wit a broken tankard. Two mon be holden mi hande. O God. Jake be cutten mi throte from ear to ear. I be bleedin to death on the flor. Thei be laughin at me ond talken to me."

"What do they say to you as you bleed to death on the floor from your cut throat?"

"'Too bad, Jim. Ye chete once too often. Ye got wat was comen to ye.'"

"Are you dead, James?"

"Yea, I be dead on the ale hous flor."

"How do you know that you are dead, James?"

"I be rushen out of mi body."

"Are you going to the golden Light?"

"No, but I be in a butifel gardin. Thore be flowers all around ond birds singen like a melodie. Thore be luv all around me. I niver want to leve hyre."

"Are you alone in the beautiful garden?"

"No, thore be three persone in white gowns wit me. Thei directe me to sitte wit thaem on a marbel bench."

"Who are these persons you are sitting with?"

"Thei be mi guides."

"What do they say to you?"

"Thei be tellen me thaet I be dead ond be in another dimension away from Earth. I be dead, but all of mi aches ond pains are gone. Mi cutte throte es healed too."

"You are dead but are healed. Are you afraid anyway?"

"No, tiz very peaceful heyre in the gardin. I be very happe to be heyre in thies butifel place."

"Are you in heaven?"

"I thinke I be, but I do not understande how a bloke lik me coulde be in heven. Thore es suppose to be another place for mi kinde."

"Are you able to see the beautiful Light I've heard about that dying people see?"

"No, I be not gude enough."

"Tell me everything that's going on."

"We're sitting together on the bench reviewing my last life as James Avery and my previous incarnations, which go back thousands of years, as Simian, my soul's name. I remember all of my past lives. It's like watching a movie—all of my lives are whizzing by. Everything I ever thought or did is recorded on my eternal file for me to review."

"Movies haven't been invented yet, James. It's only 1413 in Earth time. How do you know about movies which were invented in the twentieth century?"

"I do not know how I know of things in the future—I just know them. There is no sense of time here. Centuries are like seconds. Time is not important."

"What has happened to your Middle English dialect?"

"I am Simian, the name God gave my soul when He created me. I have no dialect, nationality, race, or creed. I can speak to you in your own language. The guides are focusing on my last life as James Avery. My soul is carrying a heavy burden from that life. James Avery horribly murdered a woman; Jenny Murray, the mother of a ten-year-old girl named Mary. Now, with counseling from my guides, I must decide what my punishment is to be for this sin and thus cleanse my soul. Amos, my chief guide, is telling me what is expected of me."

'Simian, as you know, you have sinned grievously. Your soul is heavy with guilt and sorrow because of this evil deed. We hope that you will agree to a punishment, which will purify your soul and ultimately return it to a more Godlike state.'"

"What punishment are they suggesting to you?"

"I must agree to suffer, tenfold, the pain and indignities which I caused Jenny, the victim, to endure. Everything I did to Jenny, I will have to experience in future incarnations. Only, my sufferings will be greater than Jenny experienced at my hands. And there will be ten separate incidents which will occur over the centuries."

"Where is Jenny now?"

"She is standing at the side of our group, watching our meeting. She is referred to as a victim observer and is not allowed to speak at the meeting."

"What sufferings are you to endure, James?"

"Everything I did to Jenny—rape, choking, head trauma, falling from heights, drowning, and death, only more painful."

"Why is drowning included as a punishment?"

"Jenny was still alive when I threw her over the Waterloo Bridge into the River Thames. She did not know how to swim. I must experience this too."

"Must you accept this punishment which seems terribly severe? What will happen to you if you refuse?"

"It is my choice to accept the punishment or to do nothing. In the latter case, I would continue my next incarnation without recompense or spiritual growth. Or I could remain here, at a lower spiritual level, with little chance for my soul to rise to a higher level. My soul would always yearn for the Light until it accepts the punishment due it. Being without the Light is hell for the soul."

"Does that mean that you could murder again in another incarnation?"

"Yes, that is a possibility if my soul is not cleansed of the sin of murder."

"What is your decision, Simian?"

"I will accept their counsel and the punishments. I wish to be with the Light."

"When will your punishments begin?"

"Immediately. I am to be reborn in England again, and upon reaching adulthood, I will become a sailor on a pirate ship in the English Channel."

"Will you return to the Light between incarnations?

"No, I am not to return to the Light again until my tenfold sentence has been completed. That is when my soul will have been cleansed from the sin of murder."

"What is Jenny doing now?"

"She is smiling lovingly at me. I instinctively know that she has forgiven me because she wants my soul to advance in purity."

"What has happened to Mary, Jenny's daughter?"

"Mary died of pneumonia in an orphanage, two years after her mother's murder. She has been awaiting my soul's return and has agreed to spend her heaven monitoring my progress in my future incarnations on Earth. Mary will witness each of the ten events. She will be cheering me on."

"Is this revenge on Mary's part?"

"No, there is only love here. Mary wants my soul to succeed. This is part of her karma. She suffered greatly in the orphanage after I deprived her of her mother's love. This is another debt I must repay in another incarnation."

"Explain again what 'tenfold' means."

"My punishment will take place in ten separate incidents. Each will be more painful, and my suffering will be much greater than that which I forced Jenny to endure. Most of these ten events will result in my own death."

"Does your last death, as James Avery, count as one of the ten?"

"Yes, because James Avery's suffering was intense, the event was counted as the first of the ten. However, Jake's soul must eventually deal with Jim's murder if it is to advance in purity."

"How often will your soul reincarnate?"

"At least once a century."

"Will you be judged after each of your deaths?"

"No. As I said before, I will not return to the garden and my guides until my soul's goal has been attained. Then I will again meet with my guides to evaluate my lives."

"Is God present with you now that you have accepted the punishment?"

"I feel the Light's loving presence everywhere, but I am yet not worthy to spend eternity with it. I am at a lower level than Jenny, Mary, or my guides. My soul is eager to return to Earth until the 'tenfold' debt is paid. It is difficult to leave this loving place, but I must."

Feeling that the session should be terminated at this point because it had lasted longer than the others, Dr. Sawyer brought Al out of the hypnotic state.

"One, two, three… Al, you're back in Buffalo. It is 2010. Are you okay? That was unbelievable, wasn't it? And beautiful at the same time. We now have answers to many of our questions."

"What a glorious experience that was. I didn't want to leave that beautiful place, and I long to see the Light. But it is a relief to finally know the reasons for what has been taking place in this life."

"Everything makes perfect sense now, Al—even Mary's counting. Now we know that she was tabulating each of your punishments. She and Jenny have truly forgiven you."

"And she was happy after I had successfully completed each incident. She was expressing an amazing amount of love. What a lovely soul she is, showing us so many exemplary qualities—love, forgiveness, sacrifice, and consideration for others.

Although she's a ghost, I love her. I'm still going to miss her even though I never actually saw her here. Now that her work is finished with me, she can enjoy the Light. She certainly has earned that reward. I really believe that I am going to be all right now.

"I am inclined to agree with you. For the moment, our business here is finished. I'm going to end our sessions at this point and release you. I don't expect you to have any more anxiety attacks or punishments, but if you do, call me at once. Of course, I'd like to know how you're doing anyway, Al."

"I want to thank you for everything you've done for me, Doctor. You've helped me discover so much about myself and the meaning of life. I've learned not to let fear rule my life. Love will take its place now."

"That's the key, Al. Now that we know the cause of your symptoms and fears, you should be able to handle everything from here on. Always remember what your purpose in life is."

"I surely will. Now I'm going to go home and tell Karen the good news and the whole story. Goodbye, Doctor Sawyer. You are one super doctor and a beautiful lady. I will never forget you."

"Goodbye, Al. I will miss you. May your future lives be happy. Please call me."

"I certainly will, Elizabeth."

Their eyes met, and at that moment, they both knew what they could never have dared to say to each another. Elizabeth saw Al to the door and watched as his car disappeared down Delaware Avenue. Tears welled up in her eyes because she knew she would probably not see him again in this lifetime.

"Undoubtedly, it's for the best. My romantic feelings toward him were bordering on the unethical and could have hurt my professional career and his marriage."

But she could not stop thinking about the punishments to which Simian had sentenced himself. Tenfold was a very severe sentence for a soul, she thought to herself. Then her thoughts turned to Mary, and she began counting.

First, the regression to the beating death of James Avery in a barroom brawl in London. Second, the anxiety attacks on the Maid of the Mist and Skylon in Niagara Falls, Canada. Third, the dream about a hanging death of a sailor on a pirate ship. Fourth, a regression of sodomy, a fall and broken neck in the Tower of London. Fifth, a regression in Salisbury where Al choked on food, hitting his head as he fell to the floor. Sixth, a regression to the drowning and head injuries in a Valley Forge creek. Seventh, a regression to the rape and fall to her death of a maid in a San Francisco hotel. Eighth, a regression to the drowning, castration and head injuries off the coast of Main. Ninth, the fractured skull and fall on a ski slope at Kissing Bridge.

"That's only nine. What did I miss? Where is the tenth? I did not include the two Bills-Jets games on the list as I believe that the first game was more an example of Jefferson's karma being more dominant than Al's karma. The second game was strictly a revenge activity and does not warrant including it on the tenfold list. Al's mild anxiety attack on the River Thames cruise ship also is not on the list. It is merely a precursor of punishments to come after Jenny's murder. Oh god, what is the tenth? I've got to call Al to warn him—Simian's ordeal is not yet over."

Elizabeth knew that Al didn't have a cell phone in his car, and he wouldn't be home for at least thirty minutes. There was nothing she could do but pray and wait until he reached home.

"I don't want to worry Karen. I'll call him this evening from home."

The office door suddenly opened, and Barb showed in the next patient, Dorothy Evans. She immediately seated herself in the recliner which Al had sat in moments before. She felt a small object on the chair's seat cushion, reached down, picked it up, and looked at it.

"Dr. Sawyer, someone must have lost this in this chair. Isn't it a Saint Christopher medal? I haven't seen one of these in many years—not since before the Catholic Church rescinded his sainthood."

Elizabeth's face turned ashen as Mrs. Evans handed her the medal. She tightly grasped the medal, which she knew Al always carried with him, and placed it in her suit jacket pocket. Although she wasn't superstitious, the look of worry on her face told another story. It was too soon to call Al, who was hurrying home, unaware of his uncertain future. Her mind went into overdrive.

Should I call Karen? No, I won't. There is nothing she could do. Al should be home in about twenty minutes. Please drive carefully, my darling Al. Why did you have to lose your Saint Christopher medal? That's nonsense. Christopher never existed, so how can he protect Al if he never was?

Returning to the conscious world, she realized that she had forgotten about her patient, who was sitting in the recliner with a bewildered look on her face.

"Dr. Sawyer, are you all right? You look like you've seen a ghost."

"I just may have, Mrs. Evans."

Then whispering to herself, Elizabeth said a silent prayer. "God help you get home safely, Simian."

CHAPTER 30

Wanting to share the good news with Karen, Al sped along the streets of Buffalo. His mind was racing, trying to assimilate all he had learned in today's session. Traveling well beyond the speed limit, he raced onto the Skyview Bridge, an elevated span which rose high above one of the busiest parts of Buffalo and a small piece of Lake Erie. Gone were any doubts he had about reincarnation. Finally, everything was crystal clear to him. He was cured and he was happy. It was starting to snow, and he wasn't paying attention to his driving. His speed was in excess of seventy-five miles per hour when his Jeep hit a sheet of ice and skidded into, up and over the guardrail of the bridge. The car dropped into the water, about one hundred and fifty feet below. Just before impact, Al caught sight of a smiling Mary, standing along the shore. She was holding up all ten fingers for him to see, followed by the thumbs up sign. At that moment, Al experienced no fear; only peace and love as he left his body and sped toward the Light which beckoned him.

The car entered the still-unfrozen but cold water and sank immediately, trapping him. He had neglected to strap on his seat belt. The vehicle landed upside down, with all doors locked and all of the windows tightly closed. There was no escape. A driver in the car behind Al on the bridge saw the accident and called 911 on his cell phone. The Coast Guard was dispatched to the area, where it was believed the car entered the water, but it was one hour before divers could get to the scene. By then, it was too late to save him. Another hour passed before the car was raised and Al's body removed and taken by ambulance to Mercy Hospital. Al was identified through his driver's license, which was found in his wallet in his jacket pocket.

Karen was home alone, feeling down and listless for no apparent reason. Her mind wandered to thoughts of Al and how the session with Dr. Sawyer had gone. She was concerned that he was late in getting home. It was two o'clock when the doorbell rang. Thinking that Al had forgotten his key, she rose from her chair in the den, walked slowly to the door and opened it. Two uniformed Orchard Park policemen stood before her.

"Mrs. Chapman?"

"Yes, what is it, officers?"

"There has been a bad accident involving your husband, Mrs. Chapman. Could we come in to speak with you?"

"Oh my God. Is he all right?"

"No, ma'am. His car skidded off the Skyview Bridge and into the water below. We'd like you to go to Mercy Hospital with us. Is there anyone whom you want to call?"

"Dead? No, no, no—not my Al. I want to call my parents. What should I do about my children who are in school?"

"Can someone pick them up at the school?"

"Yes, my parents can get them. Give me a minute to call them."

"Take all of the time you need, Mrs. Chapman."

With shaking hands and tears streaming down her cheeks, Karen dialed her parents' number to tell them the terrible news. Joe answered the phone.

"Dad, oh, Dad, Al has been killed in an accident on the Skyview Bridge. The police are here now to take me to Mercy Hospital."

"Oh my god. No, Karen. Al is dead? How awful. What can we do?"

"I don't know the details, just that he skidded off the bridge into the water. Please call Saint Margaret's and pick the kids up at school now. Don't tell them anything, but bring them to Mercy Hospital. I'll tell them myself. Oh, and call Al's parents in Florida. Mom has their number. I have to go now, Dad."

"Wait, your mother wants to talk to you."

"Karen, Dear, I heard what happened. I'm so sorry. Al was such a wonderful man. Do you want us to be with you at the hospital?"

"First, pick up the kids at school and then meet me at the hospital."

"We love you, Karen. We are so terribly sorry. We'll see you at the hospital soon."

"I love you too, Mom. I don't know what I'll do without Al. He was my husband and my best friend."

"You'll carry on the best you can for the sake of the children. You must be strong, Karen. It will take time, Honey—one day at a time. And don't worry about Al's parents; I'll notify them and invite them to stay with us. This is horrible for them too."

"Thanks, Mom. I saw Al alive just six hours ago—I just can't believe he's gone. Bring the children to the hospital as soon as you can. I'll wait for you there."

The police and Karen arrived at the emergency entrance to the hospital in twenty minutes. A waiting nurse immediately took Karen to a small room where, soon thereafter, a tall young resident doctor appeared to speak to Karen.

"Mrs. Chapman, I'm Dr. Louis Cooper. I'm so terribly sorry for your loss. Can I get you anything; coffee, tea?"

"No thanks, Doctor. Just take me to see my husband."

"I'll take you to see him shortly, but first let me prepare you. His injuries are severe. He apparently drowned, but he has massive head injuries which he received when the car hit the water. Unfortunately, he was not wearing his seatbelt, and his neck was broken when the airbag deployed."

"Did he suffer, Doctor?"

"We can't be sure. There was still air in the car, and he was alive for some time after impact. I doubt that he was conscious, considering the severe nature of his head injury."

"Oh god, my poor Dear Al. Why did this have to happen to him? Can I see him now, Dr. Cooper?"

"Of course. Come with me, Mrs. Chapman."

Karen entered the examination room where Al lay covered with a sheet. When the doctor carefully uncovered his face, she was unprepared for what she saw.

"He's smiling. He's been killed in a terrible accident. Why is he smiling?"

"I don't know, Mrs. Chapman. Sometimes, that is a reflex reaction."

"Oh, Al, why did you leave me? I need you. We all need you. I love you so."

Dr. Cooper left Karen alone with Al. After a few minutes of silent prayer, she kissed his already cold lips and squeezed his hand. A social worker entered the room and offered to help Karen make the necessary arrangements for the removal of the body to a funeral home. When that difficult business was completed, a nurse took her to a private waiting room where Evelyn, Joe, and the children were sitting. Karen's face was wet from crying.

"Mom, where's Dad? Has something happened to him? Nobody will tell us anything," Melissa demanded.

"Children, give me your hands. I have some very bad news to tell you. Your father was killed in a horrible accident on the Skyview Bridge. He's in heaven with God now."

Melissa and Jonathan began sobbing immediately in Karen's arms. Joe and Evelyn joined in the tear fest. Devastated by their loss, they went to the car and drove home with Joe and Evelyn insisting on staying overnight. No one was hungry, but Joe had a pizza delivered anyway. They ate, perhaps out of habit, and stared into space without speaking. Jonathan broke the silence.

"I wish I had told Dad that I wanted to be a football player. I disappointed him. He wanted me to be a linebacker," Jonathan sobbed.

"Your father wanted you to be whatever would make you happy, Jonathan," Karen added, putting her arm around his shoulder. "You never disappointed your father."

"I wonder if Mary was in the car with Dad when it crashed," Melissa commented.

"Who is Mary?" Evelyn asked.

"It's a long story, Mom. I'll explain it to you some day when all of this is over, and we have lots of time. Did you get in touch with the Chapmans?"

"Yes, but they're in Africa, on safari. The travel agency will have them call you."

"Were there any witnesses to the accident, Karen?"

"There probably were, Dad. I suppose I'll get the complete police report after the investigation is complete."

"That bridge is too dangerous. It's closed half of the winter because it is too slippery," Joe groused.

"I wish it had been closed today, Dad."

The news of Al's death spread quickly throughout Western New York and across the nation. All of the television and radio stations made it their lead story on the six o'clock news. Soon thereafter, the phone began ringing nonstop. After the first ten calls, Joe turned on the answering machine and let it take over. Al's parents did call Karen; they would not be able to attend Al's funeral but were wiring flowers and would call Karen upon their return from Africa. This response from them upset her.

"I guess Africa is more important to them than their son."

They all sat up most of the night, sharing memories of Al and the good times they had together and how much he was loved.

Wednesday morning, Karen met with Andrew Long, a representative of the Siegfried Funeral Home, and completed all the preparations, including choosing Al's clothing for burial. Finally, the additional blue socks he wore under the Bills' regulation red socks were put in the bag. The wake was to be Thursday and Friday from two to four and seven to nine. The private funeral would be Saturday at nine o'clock at Saint Margaret's; family and invited friends only.

Thursday, at one-thirty, Joe and Evelyn drove Karen and the children to the funeral home. Upon seeing Al in the casket, Karen sobbed uncontrollably.

"Karen, you've got to be strong. You can get through this, Honey. When it's all over, let the tears flow. We'll help one another."

"I'll try, Mom."

Thousands of fans and mourners queued up outside to pay their respects. They came early and continued filing past Al's casket long after viewing hours had ended. Karen graciously greeted everyone, accepted his or her warm expressions of sympathy, and put up a brave appearance. The last person left at eleven o'clock.

Exhausted, Karen knelt at the casket and whispered, "I know you're watching over us, Al. I need your strength for the hours, days, and years ahead. Please help me take your place as head of our family. Save a place in heaven for me. I long to see you again, Dear."

Saturday morning, Saint Margaret's Church was filled to capacity, despite the request that the funeral be private. The overflow of people spilled onto the front sidewalk in front of the church. The day was sunny, but there was a cold brisk northwest December wind. Father Howard Wright celebrated the beautiful high Mass, making his homily short but inspirational. Then Coach Schultz gave the eulogy. Karen listened, but only heard a few words.

"Al Chapman not only was a gifted football player but was my close friend. I never met a kinder, gentler human being. Everyone loved him. We will miss him terribly, but our loss is heaven's gain. Farewell, old buddy."

One after another, Al's friends rose to exalt his fine character and to tell what a great role model he had been to them. Karen heard very little of the accolades accorded her husband, as she was immersed in her own thoughts, remembering all of the good times she and Al shared together through twelve years of marriage and before.

The graveside service at Holy Cross Cemetery was conducted by Father Wright and was mercifully brief. After the final blessing and goodbyes, the grieving family walked toward the waiting black limousine. Before stepping into the car, Karen looked back over her shoulder and caught sight of the sunlight reflecting off the silver casket.

"Goodbye, my darling Al. I will love you forever. Watch over us. We need your help," she whispered into the cold wind.

The funeral breakfast was held at the Orchard Park Country Club, where Al had been a member. Karen moved slowly from table to table, greeting everyone and thanking him or her for their prayers and kind offers of help. She wished that her ordeal was over and she could just go home and cry.

Sitting at the last table she stopped at was Dr. Sawyer. When she saw Karen, she quickly rose from her chair and extended her hand in sympathy. Unable to speak to Karen at the wake because of the crowds, she offered her apologies and condolences.

"Karen, I'm so sorry. I'm in shock. I can't believe what has happened. I saw Al just before the accident. He was jubilant when he left my office to hurry home to you. When you are ready, please call me. I have much to share with you that I'm sure will make you feel better."

"I will do that, Doctor, as soon as I have recovered somewhat."

It was almost three o'clock when Karen and the children arrived home after the funeral and breakfast. Joe and Evelyn went to their own home, knowing that Karen wanted to be alone with her children.

Karen spent the next three weeks writing thank-you notes and taking care of business—insurance policies, social security, annuities. Al's parents never called her. She was learning how to cope without him. It was difficult making all of the decisions alone.

One morning, sitting alone in the kitchen after the children had gone to school, she remembered that she was supposed to call Dr. Sawyer when she felt up to it. Her life was beginning to have some sense of normalcy again, so she dialed Dr. Sawyer's number. The doctor herself answered the phone.

"Hello, Dr. Sawyer—it's Karen Chapman. I finally found the time to call you. Can we get together and talk?"

"Karen, I've thought of you often. How are you doing?"

"I'm surviving. I don't know how though. I miss Al terribly. It's so hard doing everything without him. I'm trying to do things he always took care of."

"I understand what you are going through. It is a huge loss for you, but I think I can now share some information that Al and I uncovered in the last two sessions. You will be surprised and, I hope, happy for him when you know everything. Can you come into my office tomorrow at ten? I'll cancel all of my other appointments for the day so we'll have plenty of time to talk. I have much to tell you. And I'll play the tapes of all of Al's sessions so you can better understand what he went through."

"I can be there at ten. That's very nice of you. I'm very curious, because Al wouldn't tell me too much near the end of your sessions."

"Well, you're going to hear everything now. Prepare to hear an often unbelievable but beautiful story. I'll be waiting for you tomorrow, Karen."

"I'm looking forward to it, Doctor."

Karen hung up the phone and began to guess at what Dr. Sawyer was going to tell her that was so beautiful. Surely, from what she knew of the regression sessions, they were anything but beautiful. Al would always say, "Karen, all I do is suffer and die every week."

She wondered if she should even mention the word reincarnation.

"What were Al's final words before he left the doctor's office for the last time? Was there any message for me? Should I just sit there and listen, or should I ask questions?"

Her mind raced with memories of Al and how much he wanted to learn the causes of his anxiety attacks. Al wouldn't let her help him, no matter how much she tried. He would just look at her and say, "It's my life; butt out."

He could have said, "They're my lives," she thought.

Karen couldn't believe what she was thinking. Suddenly, she had accepted the premise that Al had lived many lives before she met him.

Was it possible that she had been a part of his earlier lives? *Could I have been his wife or his daughter in a past life? Or husband?*

That thought brought a big smile to her face. "Ridiculous."

She realized that she had come a long way in her beliefs to even entertain such thoughts. The dilemma with Catholicism was now a thing of the past.

Would Al be surprised that I'm thinking these thoughts about reincarnation? Maybe he's putting these ideas in my head. I wouldn't put it past him.

Now she was eagerly looking forward to Wednesday's meeting with Dr. Sawyer, and wondered how she should act.

How will we get along? Will she be cold toward me after all of the awful things I said about her? I hope I don't say anything stupid that might derail the meeting. I need her so I can find out everything that took place at those sessions. I hope I have all of the answers soon. I suppose I'll never know if she had personal designs on Al. Now neither one of us has him. Stop it, Karen. There is no room in your life for jealousy. Al would be shocked about your thoughts.

She looked at her watch. It was almost three o'clock.

"The children will be home from school in a few minutes and they'll be hungry. I'm glad I baked raisin oatmeal cookies this morning. What can I make for dinner? I'm out of ideas. I guess we'll go to Chicken Chalet. The kids love their barbecued chicken, and so do I. They can have the cookies for dessert when they get home after dinner. Here they come. Put on your best 'everything is fine' mother's smile, Karen."

CHAPTER 31

It was exactly ten o'clock on Wednesday when Karen arrived at Dr. Sawyer's office. Elizabeth was waiting for her and welcomed her. Karen seated herself in the recliner, which she knew Al had sat in so many times during his regressions. It seemed strange for her to be there, since it was not easy for her to control her emotions. She envisioned Al sitting there week after week suffering and dying. Tears welled up in her eyes and began streaming down her cheeks. She took a tissue from her purse and dabbed at her eyes.

"I'm sorry, Doctor. I guess I'll never get over this. It's different if you lose an elderly parent who is expected to die before you. It comes as no surprise, but the grief is still strong. But Al was in the prime of his life. He wasn't supposed to die. I thought he was immortal. Do you want to know something, Doctor? There is no such thing as closure—you never get over the loss of a loved one, believe me."

"I can only imagine the magnitude of the horror you've been through these past weeks, but I am hopeful that after our meeting today, you will feel much better. You will be happy for Al, not sad. Words can never do justice to the complexities of this story."

"Al had tremendous respect for you as a doctor and a human being. I knew very little about what went on here in the hypnotic regressions, but I was there with him during all of his dreams and anxiety attacks. Yet he shared very little of these sessions with me. However, he did tell me that I would know everything in due time. That time is now, isn't it?"

"Yes, it is, Karen. When Al left my office after our last session on that fateful day, I was positive that he was rushing home to tell you the whole story. He was so happy. We felt that we finally had all of the answers, and he was cured. His last words were, 'I'm going home to Karen and will tell her everything.'"

"It's reassuring to know that Al was thinking of me in those final minutes."

"That is why I am now going to share the tapes of the sessions with you. I am certain that his wish was to convey this information to you, and I have no reservations about breaking the doctor-patient confidence. What you are about to hear is both upsetting and soothing, ugly and beautiful. Much will be left open to your own interpretation."

Dr. Sawyer began by playing the tape of the first session, in which Al related the hanging, chokingand head injury experienced in the pirate and Salisbury dreams. He also told of his anxiety attacks on the Maid of the Mist, at the Skylon Restaurant, and on the Silver Bonito cruise.

"I witnessed all of those attacks except the Silver Bonito one. I was unaware of that attack, Dr Sawyer."

"Al didn't want you to know about it. He didn't want to ruin the River Thames cruise for you. He knew you would be upset, and you would have insisted upon taking him to see a doctor or to a hospital in London."

"He was right about that. I would have made him see a doctor in London."

The tape of Al's first regression revealed his drowning death off the coast of Maine, in which Al told about his severe head injury, bleeding and the horrible castration. There was also a brief heated discussion about reincarnation and Catholicism.

"This tape unnerved Al. Old beliefs die hard. He was unsure of what to believe. Regression to a former life was a new concept for him, Karen."

The second regression uncovered the rape, beating, and falling to her death of Jane Dawson in San Francisco. This upset Karen noticeably, and at this point, Dr. Sawyer interrupted the tape.

"Are you all right, Karen? Do you want to stop?"

"I'm okay. I never knew that Al was once a woman. That must have been very difficult for him to swallow. Please go on."

"Yes. It was very troubling for him. We do not always reincarnate as the same sex as lived before."

The tape continued with Al speaking about the little blonde girl whom Myra Johnson saw near them at Stonehenge, and again at the Bills' game. Karen smiled broadly when Al talked about feeling no pain at the moment of his death; all went black before the onset of pain. Al received a concussion after this tape in a Bills - Jets game. The little girl made another appearance at that game.

"That's when Melissa and I determined from her clothing, that she was a fifteenth century English girl."

"That's right, Karen. That research was very useful to the case. It helped us focus on the origin of Al's problems."

The next session was about the drowning death of John Mason at Valley Forge. "That death was very much like Al's own death, wasn't it?"

"Yes, they were quite similar, except for the horse."

The next tape dealt with the torture, sodomy, and death of Peter Mitchell in the Tower of London. Karen wept throughout Al's unbelievable suffering and death there.

"That was horrible. No wonder he refused to speak to me about what he was going through. I never should have pressured him. I feel so guilty now."

"I didn't want Al to tell anyone about these experiences. It would have been doubly painful for him if he had said anything. Once was enough for him."

"I understand that now, but I didn't before."

Because Al fractured his skull on the ski slopes, there was a gap of several weeks between sessions. However, the little English girl appeared to Al in the hospital, and from that point on, she was identified as Mary. Al could not recall the conversation with Mary.

"It was during Al's recovery period that we began reading about reincarnation and karma. He was really into it. We had some heated discussions during that time. I'm afraid I muddied the waters, but I was learning."

The second last tape dealt with James Avery and the rape, beating, and murder of Jenny Murray on the Waterloo Bridge. Mary, her daughter, witnessed the crime. This revelation was traumatic for Al and Karen as well.

"This tape is awful. I cannot believe that my Al ever could have committed such a monstrous crime. Al was a kind and gentle man whom everyone liked."

"He wasn't Al Chapman then—he was James Avery. It is not for us to judge him. Remember, Karen, do not lose your focus on the whole picture by dwelling on just one life. Our souls evolve over the centuries. The next tape will blow your mind."

"I'll try to control my emotions the best I can. Anyhow, we finally found out who the little girl Mary was."

"Yes. The biggest part of the mystery was solved at this point, but this knowledge nearly destroyed Al. I was very worried about his emotional well-being after this session. He was deeply affected by it, and I was fearful that he would quit at that point."

"I can see why. How could he witness such evil without cracking?"

"Without a doubt, Al was one of the strongest men I have ever met. Experiencing this murder was unbearable for him."

"That's the day he came home and went right upstairs without speaking to me."

Finally, Dr. Sawyer played the last tape, which depicted the death of James Avery and his after-death experience in the garden with his guides and the Light. Karen began to cry again as Al's soul accepted the "tenfold" punishment recommended for the murder of Jenny Murray. The voluntary presence of Mary at all ten events pleased Karen.

"I am comforted by the love that is evident in this last tape, especially that shown by Jenny and Mary. Do you believe that Mary was with Al when he died?"

"That wouldn't surprise me. I have counted all of the "tenfold" events, and now there are indeed ten, if we include James Avery's death. That was the only time that Simian's soul went to the Light. Earlier tapes all tell a tale of darkness. In many of those cases, reincarnation occurred shortly after death. The first incarnation after James Avery's death took place in a few years, which is instantly in 'heaven' time. Undoubtedly, his soul was anxious to begin his first preordained punishment."

"Do you think that Al went to the Light this time?"

"I am sure that he did, and if we can believe everything on the tapes, his soul has been cleansed of the murder, and he undoubtedly has risen to a higher level in heaven."

"Will he be reincarnated again?"

"Of course, but probably not for hundreds of years. I would guess that he's resting now and enjoying his 'afterlife.' He certainly earned it."

"Will I ever see him again? I want to so much."

"I have no doubt that you will, Karen—many times. You had such a loving union this time that you may both want to continue in the same circle again and again, but not necessarily as husband and wife."

"Doctor Sawyer. I don't know how to ask you this."

"What is it, Karen. Don't hesitate to ask me anything."

"Well, could you hypnotize me? I'd like to find out if I knew Al in one of his incarnations that you discovered—perhaps the fifteenth century."

"We could try now, if you wish. Are you familiar with the process?"

"Yes. I've been reading about hypnosis, and I think I'm prepared to try it."

"You know that you will be aware of everything that is said, don't you?"

"Yes. I know that."

"Then let's begin. Concentrate on this swinging pendulum that I'm holding, and count backwards from five."

"Five. Four. Three..."

Karen was quickly in a hypnotic state and heard the Doctor speak to her.

"Karen, I want you to go back in time to the early part of the fifteenth century. Are you living then?"

"Yea. I be."

"What is your name?"

"Mi name es Lionel Hawkins."

"How old are you, Lionel?"

"I be thritty-five yeren auld."

"What is today's date?"

"Tiz eighte Novembre 1410."

"What do you do for a living?"

"I be a techer at the Chaucer Scole For Ladde."

"Where do you live?"

"I libba on Exton Street in London."

"Are you married?"

"No. I be a bachelor. I libba by misef."

"Do you do your own cooking and cleaning?"

"No. I hav a houskeepe."

"What is your housekeeper's name?"

"Hir name es Jenny Murray."

"Is Jenny married?"

"No. Hir husbande abandoune hir ond hir little daughter. I trie to halpa theim all I kan."

"What is Jenny's daughter's name?"

"Tiz Mary."

"How old is Mary?"

"She be ten yere auld."

"Are Jenny and Mary with you now?"

"No. Thei be goen to Bible studie at Sanctus Augustine's Catholicus Chirche."

"Where is the church located?"

"The chirche es acros the Waterloo Bridge an the ither sid fram heyre."

"What time is it?"

"Tiz seven forty-five in the evning."

"What is the weather like?"

"Tiz cauld ond dampf ond a fog es movin in."

"'Lionel, because of the fog, did you accompany Jenny and Mary across the Bridge?"

"No. Jenny telle me, 'no thanke ye. We wille be fin.'"

"Did they cross the Bridge safely?"

"I do not know."

"Lionel. It is six o'clock the following evening. Are Jenny and Mary there with you?"

"No. Thei aren not heyre."

"Where are they?"

"Jenny was murdere an the Waterloo Bridge last nigt."

"How do you know that she was murdered on the Bridge last night?"

"Mi neighbour es a nigt watchmon. He coma ond telle me. Jenny was throwen in the river ond droune."

"Did they catch the murderer, who threw her in the River?"

"No. He escapene."

"Did he hurt Mary before he escaped?"

"No. He did not."

"What happened to Mary?"

"Thei putte hir in Sanctus Luke's Orphanage."

"Why didn't you take Mary in, instead of letting her be put in an orphanage?"

"I wante to, butta it wolde not be propre; a bachelor ond a yonge lass."

"How do you feel about what happened to Jenny?"

"I be devastare. I sitte heyre ond crie by the houre. I blame misef for not accompanien thaem acros the Bridge."

"Did you love Jenny?"

"Yea. I luv hir, butta she did not know of mi luv."

At this point, Dr. Sawyer thought that they had learned enough about Karen's past life as Lionel Hawkins and returned her to the conscious state.

"One. Two. Three… You're back in Buffalo, Karen. It's 2011. That was quite a surprise, wasn't it?"

"Doctor Sawyer. I'm in shock. Did you hear who I was? I was Jenny's employer, Lionel Hawkins in 1410. And I was in love with Jenny, whom Al murdered."

"I heard everything, Karen, in Middle English. You did have a connection with Al in 1410, although an indirect one. The circle of life finds us playing many different roles. I never expected you to be a part of this case, but there you are!"

"Do you realize who I am? I am the wife of the man who murdered Jenny, who was loved by me when I was Lionel Hawkins. Are you confused?"

"Somewhat, but it does make a lot of sense now. There are many relationships in this case—past and present."

"How does Ron Jefferson fit into all of this?"

"I'm puzzled by that too. The only explanation I can think of is that it was part of Jefferson's karma. Ron used Al's moment of human weakness to cleanse his own soul."

"And what was Myra Johnson's role in this scenario? Do you think she was a ghost?"

"I think she could see spirits—nothing more. She did make us aware of the presence of Mary around Al. That was important. Karen, how do you feel about Al's tragic death now?"

"I feel much better and I'm happy for Al, because his soul has paid its debt. But I'm sorry for myself because I won't see him again. I'm having trouble adjusting to that."

"You will feel Al's presence around you often. He hasn't left you spiritually—only physically. When you are desperate and in need of help, you might sense that he is with you and assisting you like a guardian angel. Never be sad. Rejoice in the completion of a very good life."

"I'll try to remember that when I feel lonely."

"Oh, Karen. I almost forgot. I found Al's Saint Christopher medal in the recliner after he left that. It must have fallen out of his pocket."

"It didn't protect him that day, did it?"

"How could it, Karen? It was here in the recliner."

With the medal in her hand, Karen left Dr. Sawyer, convinced that Al's love surrounded her. As she headed home to begin the rest of her life, she drove onto the Skyview Bridge and glanced in her rearview mirror. For an instant, she thought she caught a glimpse of Al and Mary walking arm in arm and waving to her.

"Maybe it was just wishful thinking, but I'll take it," she told herself.

The rest of her day she kept busy, cleaning out drawers, reading more about reincarnation and karma, and waiting for the children to come home from school. As usual, she was at the door to greet them.

"How was school today, kids?"

"Great, Mom. Sister Joseph has started to pick on her pet, Jim, and she's off my back. I have a ton of homework, and I'm going to get at it right now."

"Good, Jonathan. Your dad would be proud of you. How was your day, Melissa?"

"Pretty good, Mom, but I couldn't wait to come home to tell you about the weird dream I had last night. I didn't have time this morning."

"Let's go into the kitchen, Honey. I have some hot chocolate ready. You look like you're going to burst if you don't tell me about the dream."

Karen poured the hot chocolate while Melissa began describing the strange dream she had the night before.

"Mom, I dreamt about Dad. I saw him sitting in a beautiful garden, just as clearly as if he was still here with us. He looked so happy and so handsome. There were flowers in bloom everywhere and birds were singing. You could feel love all around."

"What a beautiful dream, Melissa."

"That's not all. Here's the weird part. The little British girl, Mary, was there."

"You saw Mary with Dad?"

"Yes, and she knew me. She looked right at me and called me 'Mum.' Isn't that British for Mom?"

"Yes, it is. That is strange. Did your father speak to you?"

"He looked straight at me and said, 'I be verray sory, Jenny. Plese forgiv me.' I don't understand any of this, Mom, do you?"

"My God. This is unbelievable. I can see the whole picture now. It's so beautiful."

"What picture, Mom?"

"I'll tell you someday, Melissa, when it's time. Right now, you may be a little young to comprehend the entire story. We'll discuss it in a few years, Honey. By the way, Melissa, I found this beautiful blue ribbon in my dresser drawer today. I was saving it for gift wrapping, but I thought it would look lovely in your hair."

Melissa took the ribbon and fashioned it into a bow for her hair.

"Thank you, Mom. I love it. I'll wear it to school tomorrow."

"It looks lovely, Melissa."

Karen was surprised that Melissa didn't raise any more questions about the dream. She didn't know how long it would be before the topic was revisited, and wasn't sure that she was ready to get into the reincarnation argument again. Suddenly, she had the urge to call Dr. Sawyer, who was still in her office, reviewing the day's cases.

"Dr. Sawyer. I'm sorry to disturb you. I'm getting to be a pest, I know. You're always so busy, but something remarkable has happened, and I just had to tell you about it."

"You're not a pest, Karen. What happened?"

"Melissa had a strange dream about Al last night. She saw him with Mary, apparently in heaven."

"How wonderful. He must be trying to communicate with you. How did he look?"

"He looked handsome. Evidently, there were no visible signs of injuries from the accident."

"I've read that all of the blemishes, scars, defects, and sicknesses do not go with us when we pass into the next dimension. Physically, Al is now perfect."

"I'm glad to know that. Al was pretty banged up. But wait until you hear about the rest of the dream. Al called Melissa 'Jenny,' and Mary called her, 'Mum.'"

"That's incredible, Karen. This continues to be an amazing tale that has a life of its own that keeps on revealing more hidden facts."

"It certainly is remarkable. Can you believe that Melissa was Mary's mother, Jenny? That explains why Melissa could see Mary, and Al and I couldn't. Melissa did not remember Mary as her daughter, but Mary knew Melissa as her mother. How do you explain that?"

"We usually do not consciously remember our previous lives. Mary remained with Simian after her mother's murder through all of his incarnations. Melissa's dream is another indication that Mary was with Simian in any incarnation, but we cannot be certain that they were not together in the other incarnations. They probably were."

"I don't know if I want to believe what Melissa's dream is telling us. I've been giving a lot of thought to the idea of punishment due to sin since Al's death. He paid for his sin tenfold, so his soul could rise to a higher level in heaven. But, what happens to the Hitlers and Stalins of the world? Where do their souls go?"

"Karen, that's a mind-boggling question. Let's use Al's case as a model. Simian, as his soul was called, wanted to rise to a higher level and accepted the tenfold punishment. Imagine what punishment Hitler would have to accept for the murder of six million Jews. Let's guess that Hitler's soul would never repent because it did not love God and would not accept severe punishments, which could last eons. His soul loved evil. But just to be fair, suppose that Hitler, at the moment of his death, repented. That might indicate that his soul would accept the punishment due it in order to escape the lowest level, which we on earth call 'hell.' Most souls hunger for God and the Light—evil souls such as Hitler's do not strive for perfection and reunion with God."

"Do they reincarnate ever?"

"They may choose to reincarnate just to continue their evil ways on earth. It is not to be expected that they would ever repent, because they do not love God. In John 14:2, Jesus said, 'My Father's house has many mansions.' Every soul has merit and a free will. It's a lovely concept that teaches us that we have choices; from the basement to penthouse, depending upon our sins or good deeds. Whether it is a tenfold or a million-fold punishment for our sins, or a hundredfold reward for our good deeds, we reap what we sow. That's karma."

"This whole experience makes me want to start my life over as a better person. It makes you wonder what the punishment for stealing or lying would be?"

"I don't know, Karen. We can't all be Mother Teresa, but we can strive to climb up the ladder, one rung at a time. Because Al graced both of our lives, we are better for it now, I am certain. His remarkable life is a model for all of us to emulate."

"We can all change for the better if we try. Well, Doctor Sawyer, I think the story is complete. Thank you for helping me to understand my life better."

"You are welcome, and please keep in touch. Let me know how you and your children are doing. Goodbye for now, Karen."

After the conversation had ended, Elizabeth sat at her desk trying to pull all of the pieces of the puzzle together into one giant mosaic. She pulled Al's folder from the active file and added her latest notes on Karen/Hawkins, Melissa/Jenny, and

Melissa/Mary. She quietly reviewed her own history and its' impact on this case.

"In all of the months and sessions with Al and Karen, neither ever asked me how I became such a staunch believer in reincarnation and karma. Perhaps they would have been more receptive if they had known about my upbringing. I could have told them that I was born in Dublin, Ireland in 1972, of Catholic parents—Patricia and Timothy Sawyer. My parents were killed in a tragic train accident in New Delhi, India, when I was only eight years old. By prior agreement, I was adopted by my parents' best friends, Jane and Uday Kareishi, since my parents had no close relatives. The Kareishis had been my godparents and loved me dearly. Although I was baptized a Roman Catholic, Uday insisted upon bringing me up versed in Hinduism. Privately, however, Jane Kareishi, who was a Catholic, instructed me in the beliefs of Catholicism. I would often sit and listen to Uday tell me stories about his and other family members' recollections of past lives in India. The concepts of reincarnation and karma fascinated me, and at a very young age, I was aware of the contradictions between Catholicism and Hinduism. There were also similarities which kept me attracted to both religions. Although my formal education took place in London, I attended Harvard and Georgetown University Medical School in the USA. The Kareishis eventually moved to Sarasota, Florida, where they still reside. They often visit me and the girls here in Buffalo."

Elizabeth continued to think about Al as though he was nearby, reading her thoughts. *We could have argued for hours if he had only known about my religious upbringing. I probably wouldn't have told him too much anyway, even if he asked. It could have prejudiced the case, and all of our work would have been lost.*

Elizabeth stood before the filing cabinet a moment longer, holding Al's folder tightly to her breast. Then she carefully placed it in the "closed" file.

ABOUT THE AUTHOR

Tenfold author, Marilyn Fiegel, is a retired high school chemistry teacher and science curriculum coordinator of the West Seneca Central School District in New York State. She earned a BA degree in chemistry from the University of Buffalo and EdM and EdD degrees in science education from the State University of New York at Buffalo. Her thirty-five years of teaching experience included one year in Germany teaching dependents of U.S. military personnel.

Since retiring, Dr. Fiegel has authored several high school science text books. Interests which aided Dr. Fiegel in the writing of *Tenfold* are TV viewing of National Football League games, international cuisine, travel, history, skiing, and astronomy. Her Catholic faith also played a major role in developing the *Tenfold* story.

CPSIA information can be obtained
at www.ICGtesting.com
Printed in the USA
FFHW020410140819
54306735-59984FF